Storming Virtue's Walls

Katherine had used her fiercest voice to tell the handsome stranger that she was the noble widow of the heroic Lord Duncan MacLean—and that the stranger should instantly leave her castle home.

The stranger only smiled—a hard, harsh smile.

"Have you not heard of the pact with the devil that the MacLeans have—to come back from the dead?" he asked. "Indeed, they are cursed with the nine lives of a cat. On the brighter side, however, their taste in women has always been the finest."

With that, he brought his lips down on hers. It was a kiss meant to frighten, as he crushed her to him, storming her as if she were a castle under siege. It was nothing like Kate had ever experienced, this wild and demanding assault. She could barely catch her breath before the bombardment be⸺ ⸻is hands tangled in her hair, ke⸺

But that was not th⸺ not even the sensati⸺ row. The shock was ⸺ der. . . .

The
Devil's Due

Rita Boucher

A SIGNET BOOK

SIGNET
Published by the Penguin Group
Penguin Books USA Inc., 375 Hudson Street,
New York, New York 10014, U.S.A.
Penguin Books Ltd, 27 Wrights Lane,
London W8 5TZ, England
Penguin Books Australia Ltd, Ringwood,
Victoria, Australia
Penguin Books Canada Ltd, 10 Alcorn Avenue,
Toronto, Ontario, Canada M4V 3B2
Penguin Books (N.Z.) Ltd, 182–190 Wairau Road,
Auckland 10, New Zealand

Penguin Books, Ltd, Registered Offices:
Harmondsworth, Middlesex, England

First published by Signet, an imprint of Dutton Signet,
a division of Penguin Books USA Inc.

First Printing, April, 1996
10 9 8 7 6 5 4 3 2 1

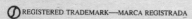

Chapter One

Ian Dewey thought longingly of the silver flask in his middle desk drawer. However, the solicitor knew full well that it would require far more than a dram or two to ease the fear churning in his belly. Making a pretense of rummaging through the documents in his hands, Dewey surreptitiously eyed the man lounging in the leather chair. There was no need to see the name upon the papers, for they were absolutely unnecessary to confirm the stranger's identity. Just one look at that forbidding visage was sufficient.

"You will find them all in order," Duncan MacLean said, his voice harsh with impatience. As a former army officer, his experience at penetrating procrastination was vast. He had not come all the way to Edinburgh to watch a nervous solicitor twiddle his thumbs. "My mother thought that I might have need of those marriage lines someday, for she was quite sure that my father would have attempted to deny me if he could beget another heir. Her fears were needless it seems; you say that I am Bertram MacLean's only child."

"Aye, that you are, my laird" Dewey said, his voice climbing to a high-pitched squeak as that uncanny one-eyed gaze focused cuttingly upon him. Hard as tempered steel, that grey eye was, and cold as a dirk on the throat. "Ye have the look of him, sair." The waving hair, dark as a moonless midnight, framed a face that seemed chiseled from granite, weathered and timeless as the mountains themselves, a countenance that was handsome still, despite scars. Aye, it could be none other than "Beelzebub" MacLean's spawn, for his son had the identical look. Young MacLean had that selfsame scowl that could turn a man to stone and if the line bred true, that come-hither smile that turned women into flighty fools. "It gave me a start to see ye, if I might say."

"You and many others," Duncan said, giving a bark of humorless laughter. "Resurrections are usually reserved for the saints among us. Still, I would venture to say that two years was a sufficient sojourn in hell, even for a MacLean. Now, what is the disposition of my property?"

"Well, my laird . . ." Dewey began tugging at his neck linen as if it had abruptly become too tight. MacLean's caustic smile made the scar on his left cheek seem like a macabre extension of his mouth. Aye, Beelzebub's get looked fit to out-devil his sire. "Ye had already been given up for daid when your father passed on. We made evera effort to find an heir, but nae mon came forward. Mr. Cheatham and Mr. Howe, my partners, even went so far as to write to your comrades in arms to see if ye had made mention of any mair distant kin, but we could find nary a one. As far as we can determine, ye are the last of the MacLeans of Eilean Kirk."

"Or the last one willing to admit to the name," Duncan said cynically. "I confess myself scarcely surprised, Dewey. We MacLeans have always tended to destroy ourselves when we cannot wreck havoc on others. So tell me then, if there was no claimant to the MacLean mantle, what has become of my affairs?"

Dewey hesitated, clearing his throat several times. "Well, my laird," he continued timorously, "yer personal effects were distributed, just as ye had specified in that will ye made—"

"The bequest consisting of my ring and the collection of Blake's work?" Duncan asked anxiously. "What became of that?"

"Aye, it was sent to his lordship as ye had wished," the solicitor said. "The book of poetry and the MacLean signet, although I must be saying, that it was a laing time before we could puzzle yer will out. A hastily scrawled document it was—"

"I wrote it just prior to the battle," Duncan explained.

Dewey nodded, although his look was disapproving. "Aye, irregularly done, but legal for all that. Witnessed right and tight."

Had it been a premonition that had prompted him to re-

make his last testament on that day? Duncan wondered as the lawyer droned on. *In the past, some of his people had been gifted with the Sight.* His spirits lifted slightly, then fell as he realized that Adam would likely have gone to Wellington and demanded a court-martial if he had understood the meaning of those notes in the margins and those carefully underlined Blake passages.

Although Adam had always been something of a boor, his integrity was absolute. Even though Vesey was Adam's brother by marriage, Duncan had little doubt that Adam would not have hesitated to lay charges. Unfortunately, that volume of *Songs of Innocence* contained the only concrete proof of Vesey's crimes. If Adam still possessed that book, then Vesey would hang. However, without it, Duncan would be hard pressed to prove his accusations.

"Write to his lordship," Duncan commanded. "Or better yet, I shall proceed to Portugal. I have some business that I must discuss with Lord Steele, and Adam is most likely there with Wellington. Until then I intend to open up the town house on Belvedere Square—"

"You canna, my laird," Dewey croaked like a bullfrog in distress. "It's been sold."

"What!" Duncan roared, the timeworn chair giving an eldritch creak as he leapt up and lunged over Dewey's desk as if to take him by the collar.

"Aye," Dewey said, cowering in his seat. " 'Tis wha I hae been trying to tell ye, sir. All but one of the properties have been sold. Ye canna blame us. The Home Office confirmed that ye were daid, and in the absence of an heir, all reverts tae the Crown."

"And in the meantime, I am virtually penniless," Duncan said, seething. Bad enough that the precious book of proof was out of his hands, but this turn of events would make matters even more difficult. Duncan had hoped to get started at once, but during his clandestine stay in London, Duncan had determined that his enemy had grown more powerful. There was a peerage in the offing, it seemed, and Vesey's highly-placed friends would likely protect his back. Once he had a full artillery of damning evidence, the task would be simpler, but Duncan had no illusions that the battle would be won solely on his proof. Despite his war record, his reputation as the "Mad MacLean" was none too savory. Certainly his credibility could not fail to be improved by the weight of wealth behind him. "So it seems the Crown decided to take my fortune."

"Nae, nae, my laird, not permanently," Dewey said, his Scots burr rasping heavily in growing uneasiness. He opened his desk drawer and searched frantically, finally pulling out a small ledger, speaking rapidly all the while. "It shouldna be too difficult to recover nearly evera penny under the circumstances, but it may take some time. I can arrange credit for ye easily enough. The auld laird left a substantial estate as ye can see from his accounts, and we can borrow upon your expectations."

Duncan considered that possibility. He could begin the skirmish immediately, but that might be somewhat risky. If Vesey were to get wind of what was in the offing, he would likely find ways to throw obstacles in Duncan's path. Until his fortune was secure and the evidence firmly in hand, it was best to remain in relative obscurity.

"Ye should nae have any problems securing whatever you wish. He was a canny man, your sire. If ye would but look at the last page." He extended the book with shaking hands.

"Aye, canny indeed," Duncan remarked as he accepted the inexpensively bound volume, leafing through it gingerly for the cheap paper was flaking away at the edges. Every farthing of expenditure was accounted for in a handwriting so crabbed it was almost impossible to discern. "Not many men have the wisdom to consistently wed elderly heiresses on the verge of death," Duncan commented, giving a long low whistle as he came to the final figures.

"Surely, my laird, you canna think . . . your ain father . . . " Dewey sputtered. "To speak so of the daid . . . 'tis blasphemous."

"Mr. Dewey, you forget that I am a MacLean. In our family our only faith is that we hold nothing sacred," Duncan said, his voice deceptively soft as he sat down once again. "Certainly no profanity would suffice to describe my father; he was a greedy, selfish man who stole land and livelihood from his crofters. He drove my mother to her death in despair, and I suspect that those unlucky females that he married found that they had gotten an unsavory Scots bargain."

Dewey regarded the young MacLean in uncomfortable silence, for nothing that had been said could be denied. At last he took a key from his pocket and opened the middle drawer, staring longingly at the flask before picking up the small pouch beside it. "Ye shall be needing some funds, I suppose," he said, setting the clinking purse before his client. " 'Tis but a hundred pounds, but at the least t'will get you decent lodging and clothes. I will draw you more on account once the banks open on Monday."

"I have no intention of being here come Monday," Duncan said, making a sudden decision as he weighed the bundle of coins in his hand. What would be the use of staying in Edinburgh without the financing to proceed with his plans? Word might travel, and it would be best to play least in sight. "How long do you think it will require to put things to rights?"

"I canna say, my laird. We have ne'er had such a thing happen before," Dewey replied raising his hand and beginning to count off items on his fingers. "We mun write every heir named in your will, few though they were, recover your assets, rescind the sales of the property, deal with the Crown. Och! It may take months."

Duncan clenched his fists, trying to contain his anger and impatience. Months! But he had learned at great cost the dangers of proceeding rashly. He would be a fool to pursue the matter without sufficient resources lest Vesey escape the net. At least the scoundrel had sold his commission and would no longer be in a position to endanger innocent men. Vengeance had waited for two years. Duncan could afford to bide yet a bit longer.

The cowering figure of the solicitor behind the desk convinced Duncan of the wisdom of his choice. Certainly he had no wish to endure the repeat of the experiences that had driven him hastily from London. The ill-concealed disgust in the eyes of everyone who saw his scarred face had made him wince. But worst of all were the reactions of women . . . his former mistress had fallen into a dead faint at the mere sight of him. "You mentioned that one property has not yet been sold," Duncan remarked with a scowl. "I suppose that I shall live there until this mess has been undone."

"Ye canna, my laird," Dewey protested. "For 'tis the Castle upon Eilean Kirk and we couldna find a buyer. I even inquired from Laird Steele himself if he knew of anyone who might find it desirable, for ye ken tha' many an English fool wants his ain draughty Gothic keep these days. But even Walter Scott himself couldna sell th' auld edifice. The place is naught but a pile of rubble."

"It always was," Duncan commented. "Even while my father lived, they say 'tis part of the curse."

"It has become mair so," Dewey said, stirring uneasily at the mention of Prince Charles's legendary bane. "We couldna find a mon willing to live on the place, so ramshackle it was. Not a pennypiece did the old laird put into the upkeep. For yer father, rest his soul—"

"My father's soul, if he had one, Mr. Dewey, is doubtless roasting in hell," Duncan commented, his eye narrowing in anger. "I will not abide any pious pretense, for we both know what manner of man he was. I have little doubt that the few crofters who remain dance on his grave, if any troubled themselves to give him a Christian burial."

"He was a hard mon," Mr. Dewey murmured in understatement, recalling the older MacLean. If even half of the stories told were true, even Hades was too temperate for that reprobate's soul. "They say he haunts the castle. That was yet another reason that we couldna find a caretaker."

"So that is why you wish his soul rest," Duncan said with a chill laugh. "I doubt that my father's spirit is clanking about the place, Dewey. As I do, he abhorred crowds. If the legends are true, there are veritable hordes of ethereal MacLeans that neither heaven nor hell would claim, haunting Eilean Kirk. However, if, by chance, I do meet up with my sire's ghost, there are a few choice comments that I had always planned to make. T'was his good fortune that the French deprived me of the opportunity to attend his deathbed."

"But surely ye willna wish to stay in that auld pile of stanes," Dewey said, chins quivering as he shook his head.

"My man, Fred, and I are quite adept at making do," Duncan remarked, half to himself. "I daresay that Eilean Kirk Castle will seem like Carlton House after the accommodations in the place they called La Purgatoire."

Dewey looked at MacLean with pity. "Ye can stay in my

ain house, my laird," he offered in a rush of generosity. " 'Tis nae fitting for a hero to be staying in a place no better than a cow's byre. Yer exploits at Talavera were the talk of Edinburgh!"

"Aye," Duncan admitted mockingly. "A MacLean in the dispatches. Beyond belief, is it not? But then, the MacLeans of Eilean Kirk have always been the talk of Edinburgh."

"They say that ye near won the battle by yersel'," Dewey said, ignoring the earl's sarcasm. "A brave thing, sair, a verra brave thing. 'Tis a miracle that you escaped that Frenchy prison."

"There are no miracles, Dewey," MacLean said, his jaw setting in a hard line. "And bravery is but a label given to those who have faced terror after the fact. Eight men left La Purgatoire with me; six of them had families, wives and children waiting in England. If miracles truly existed, those with something to live for would have come safely home. As it was, only myself and my batman, Fred, endured, two men who could have perished with none to shed a tear."

"Will ye come with me then for the night? We can find a place for yer man," Dewey said, wondering how to make his wife see the good business sense of providing MacLean with accommodations. Once his funds were recovered, the laird would be one of the richest men in Scotland.

"Thank you for the offer, but I cannot accept," he said, forcing himself to be civil in the face of the solicitor's obvious pity. Duncan found the sudden sympathy far more difficult to bear than the man's pomposity. The solicitor's chamber was closing in on him, stifling him. Blast those newspaper accounts of Talavera! He had wished nothing more than to be left alone, but the Home Office had insisted upon making a hero of him. "I am not anyone of note, despite what the papers may say. I merely survived. A cow's byre will do quite nicely, provided the cow has no objections. Notify me at Eilean Kirk when my affairs are in order," he said, rising to leave.

"Aye, my laird," Dewey agreed, almost weak with relief at the rapidly dawning realization that Mrs. Dewey would likely have cut him to bits with the sharp side of her tongue had he insisted upon dragging the earl home with him. Despite young MacLean's heroism, he was still a man with a powerful curse upon him. Ian Dewey was a firm believer in miracles and as such put his faith in curses as well. The MacLean family's damnation was a matter of creed.

All of Scotland knew of the MacLeans of Eilean Kirk, how The MacLean Robert and his sons had turned their coats at Culloden. For English gold and the Hanover George, Robert had betrayed comrades and True King by giving his family's allegiance to the bloody Butcher. It was well known that the Bonny Prince himself had put his malediction upon the MacLeans' heads.

Of course, like most such condemnations, Charlie's curse had held out one tantalizing hope of deliverance, as much to frustrate the MacLeans as to offer salvation, the legend told. For the breaking of MacLeans' bane entailed sacrifices that no MacLean had ever been willing to make, Dewey reflected as the last of the traitor's line walked out the door. Perhaps the English Crown would not get the Culloden blood money back now, but it would soon enough, for young MacLean looked like a man with Death dogging his footsteps. The earl's tall frame was gaunt, with flesh of an unhealthy grey-tinged pallor hugging far too tightly to the bone. The lack of food might be remedied, but the curse?

Duncan paused at the foot of the stairs, looking at his companion thoughtfully before taking up the silently offered reins.

"What news, Major?" Alfred Best asked at last, unable to read his master's brooding countenance.

"It seems that we have come to the parting of the ways, Sergeant," Duncan said with a rueful grimace.

Alfred Best looked at him reproachfully. " 'Tis th' third time today, sir, an' it ain't but eleven o' th' morning. Thought that we agreed that yer can't fire me but three times a day. T'ain't like yer ter break yer word an' that means th' whole rest of th' afternoon without yer threatnin' ter turn me orf. T'will like be more'n yer can bear."

"No, Fred," Duncan said, putting a hand on the small man's shoulder. "It seems that the Crown has gotten hold of my inheritance, and it will take some time to wrest my family's gold from the Treasury's greedy fingers. So it is not to be the soft life that I promised you, my friend. The only thing left to me is an ancestral heap of stones that is more of a hovel than any decent crofter's cottage." He opened the purse that Dewey had given him and began to count out half the coins.

Tears began to form in Fred's rheumy eyes. "Just like that. Do yer think a few days in Lunnon 'ave made me go soft, sir? Just g'bye, been fine knowin' yer—"

"I did not say that it had been fine, Fred," Duncan said, his expression taking the sting from his words. "In fact, you are the most insubordinate, loutish excuse for a batman that I have ever known. I swear you nearly cut my throat every time you shave me. Sometimes I think that it was your razor that put this scar on my phiz and you merely placed the blame on some innocent French guardsman."

"Yer face is like a ruddy mountain, sir. Any other man with less of a steady hand would 'a kilt yer long ago," Fred said, falling into the familiar banter.

"Why I ever agreed to take you on as my valet, heaven alone knows," Duncan grumbled.

"Punishment for yer sins," Fred said.

"You are a good man, Fred," Duncan said, counting out the fiftieth coin and putting the rest into his own purse.

Fred's mouth flew open. "Ain't what yer supposed t'say, Major."

"I am afraid that I must deviate from our usual script," Duncan said, proffering Dewey's pouch. "Your half of this hundred pounds should be enough to help you get a decent start. As soon as I get my hands on the rest of my money, you will have enough for that tavern you have always been talking about. You deserve a good bed, Sergeant, preferably one with a woman to soften it."

"Yer think I'd leave yer for a skirt an' a down tickin'? Are yer ter let in th' loft, sir?" Fred ventured, eying the pouch as one would a serpent on the verge of striking. "I'm goin' where yer go, Major. An' if yer sleepin' on a stone bed, I'm for th' rocks as well."

" 'And thy people shall by my people,' " Duncan quoted, his eye rolling upward. "A Cockney Ruth the Moabite, heaven help us all."

"Aye, a bite might do us both some good," Fred said cheerfully, tightening the girth on his saddle. "Just show us th' way ter this Cockney Ruth's place, and we'll get a bit o' tucker. Allus feel better after summat ter eat, I says. Yer could use a bit o' fattenin', Major, or should I be callin' yer 'milord' now?"

"Call me 'milord' once, Fred, and you *are* fired," Duncan said emphatically as he mounted his horse. "Are you sure you want to come with me?" The thought of losing his long-time companion was causing surprising discomfort.

"Aye," Fred said. "Someone 'as ter keep yer out o' trouble, milord."

"Fred, you are fired!" Duncan said.

"That's four!" Fred crowed, his rubbery face stretching into a huge grin. "That's another five shillin's yer owin' me, Major, a total of seven pounds. Add to what I won from yer at cards an' wages, comes ter more'n hunnert pounds all told, so's yer can't fire me now, ye can't afford ter!"

"Devil take you!" Duncan called, his sight blurring slightly as he turned his horse's head northward.

"Question is *where* he be takin' me," the little man mumbled, hastily mounting his horse and galloping after his master.

Kate woke to the sound of distant thunder echoing in the mountains of Wester Ross. From the window of her bedchamber, she could see the silver waters of Loch Maree ruffling white with the rising wind. Clouds, grey and heavy with the promise of violent fury, gathered over the distant summit of Beinn Airidh Charr. With a cry of dismay she ran down the back stairs, bare soles slapping on the worn stone. For all that it was midsummer, the kitchen garden had nearly been obliterated by a pelting hail in the previous thunderstorm. They could ill-afford to lose what little produce remained.

"Daisy," she called into the bowels of the antiquated kitchen. "How could you have let me sleep so long? I intended to rest for only a few minutes, yet you have allowed me to dream most of the afternoon away."

" 'Tis exhausted you were, milady," Daisy Wilkes said, turning from the hearth to wag a wooden spoon at her mistress in a gesture of rebuke. "As it is, I can't for the life of me think how I let you climb up on that roof. A wonder it is that you didn't fall and break your neck, I swear. What his lordship would have said, I can't imagine."

"My husband would have been shocked to his blue-blooded marrow, I venture. No doubt Lord Steele would have preferred that we had drowned in our beds. He always did claim that I lacked the dignity for the lofty position of his lady," Kate said, biting her lip in worry as she hastily tied an apron over her worn round gown. "I only pray that the patches I fashioned will hold, else we will wish that we had fins and gills tonight. There is rain aplenty on the way. I am going out to the garden to salvage what vegetables I can."

" 'Tisn't right," Daisy said, shaking her head, "you, a lady, grubbing in the dirt. If only . . . "

"It is no use to wonder," Kate said, frowning as she searched for a basket. "And 'tis lucky indeed that I was raised an army brat, else we would not have gotten this far. If you recall, Daisy, it was you who transformed me from Colonel Braxton's brat into a lady."

"Now don't you go saying such things," Daisy rebuked. "Your blood was as blue as your husband's, for all that your ma chose to follow the drum."

"Yes, I come from good blood, and so, for that matter, does black pudding. A great deal of good my illustrious ancestry did me," Kate commented caustically as she rummaged through the cupboard. "My bloodliness and three shillings would admit me to Vauxhall, and at present I do not have the coins to spare. There it is!" She waved the rush basket in triumph.

"You *always* was a lady," Daisy said as she crossed the room and took a bonnet from the peg by the kitchen door, holding it out pointedly. "Made you look like one, was all I did, and I swear that I'll try to keep it that way, for your dear pa's sake. So proud, he was, when you wed a lord."

"Yes, it did make Papa very happy," Kate said with a wistful smile. "He had always thought that he had done Mama a great wrong by asking her to live the life of a soldier's wife." She shook her head as if to banish the bittersweet thoughts and took the bonnet from the maid's hands, replacing it on its peg. "No, Daisy, I was not born to be a lady, and if you fear for my complexion, my friend, it is far too late. I am as dark as a nut from working out of doors."

"But milady, the sun's still strong, but for the few clouds . . . " Daisy began to protest, her brown eyes mournful as a calf's.

"I thought we had agreed, Daisy, that you would stop addressing me as 'milady.' 'Tis just 'Kate' and 'Daisy' betwixt us now." Kate opened the door and stared at the darkening sky, trying to gauge how long it would be before the first drops fell.

"It don't seem right," Daisy said, pulling the bonnet down once more and thrusting into Kate's hand. "You a lord's widow an' all."

"The title is of no use any longer. In fact, if we find ourselves on the run once again, it could definitely present a danger. It was only a matter of luck that no one heard you 'milady' me on the journey," Kate said, tying the frilly confection on her head in surrender and slinging the basket over her arm. Certainly it was ludicrous to scrabble about in the garden, wearing a bonnet that had cost more than the cow that they had purchased. In fact, she fully intended to take off the ridiculous bit of muslin as soon as she was out of sight, but for the present, it might placate Daisy.

"Who'll hear me call you 'milady' in this forsaken place?" Daisy complained with a wave of her hand. "The sheep? The children from the village who run from this place as if the devil himself lived here? 'Tis haunted they think this place! And then there's that fool curse."

"The curse is something of a blessing, from my way of thinking. I would much rather people believe this place inhabited by spirits, for that will keep them from asking questions," Kate said, touching the older woman on the shoulder. The maid's dejected look stirred feelings of guilt as Kate recalled Daisy's gregarious ways. "Oh, my dear, I am so sorry that I involved you in all this. You could easily be in London right now, I am sure. Half the ladies in the *ton* were trying to lure you away from me, and I know for a fact that Lady Jersey herself offered to double your salary if you would leave my employ. It was selfish of me to bring you here, I know."

"As if I would have done otherwise," Daisy said, her broad nose rising with an insulted sniff. "Needed me, you did, you and the little one. After what your papa and mama done for me, you think I wouldn't stick by you, milady?"

Kate dropped the basket and embraced the woman fiercely. "It is 'Kate,' " she whispered. "Even if by some miracle we are ever able to go back, you must always call me 'Kate.' "

"If that day comes, I shall call you 'milady' and be glad of it," Daisy said prosaically, holding the young woman at arm's length and reaching up automatically to tuck a wisp of copper hair into the bonnet. "Like a little girl you are with your hair always a mess . . . Kate."

Kate beamed at her in approval. After half a lifetime spent in service, it was extremely difficult for Daisy to reverse the force of habit, treating her former mistress as an equal. "Now I can be *le dernier cri* for the goats," Kate said, an impish smile on her pixie face as she stooped to retrieve the fallen basket. "Is Anne outside?" she asked, pausing at the door to slip her feet into wooden pattens.

"She were heading toward the orchard," Daisy informed her, a smile transforming her moon face, "with that no-good dog wagging along behind her. The two of them are sticking their noses everywhere. Caught her in the pasture this morning, I did, pulling at the cow's teats and squirting milk into that hound's mouth, as if we don't need every drop for ourselves. She giggled when I scolded her. *Giggled*, milady. A good sign, I'd say."

Kate felt her throat tightening. "That is a very good sign indeed," she said, a trifle hoarse with emotion. "How I wish that I had been there, for it has been so long since I have heard my daughter laugh. I believe that her progress can be deemed excellent, when just four months ago she would shriek if we strayed from her sight."

"Milady do you think . . . ?" The maid's hopeful eyes finished the question.

"I do not know, Daisy," Kate replied softly, brushing back a tear. "I do not know if Anne will ever speak again. She has come so far . . . I suppose that all we can do is hope and try as best we can to make her respond, day by day, bit by bit."

"Runnin' about like a wild thing," Daisy said dubiously.

"Poor child must resemble her mother," Kate said with a smile.

If the older woman saw the pain in her eyes and heard the regret in Kate's voice, she did not mention it. Daisy watched with a sigh as Kate disappeared from sight, looking for all the world like a village girl, clog-shod and ragged, but for the bonnet. Only a discerning eye could see the natural grace, the confidence of carriage that neither clothes nor the other trappings of poverty could conceal. Perhaps some-day . . . Daisy shook her head. Someday was a foolish dream, and she was not one to indulge in fancies. Here and now was far too difficult, and tomorrow might be worse, she thought as she started down the overgrown path to the or-chard. For now, there was the problem of finding Anne and bringing her home before the storm.

Kate tugged the bonnet free as she stepped carefully among the rows, hands automatically stripping the stalks and vines of anything that looked remotely ripe. She knew full well that the small cucumbers would barely be of use for pickling, but she refused to sacrifice so much as a single bean to the coming storm. Coventry, the cow, was already in the byre, lowing mournfully as she awaited the afternoon milking, and William, the goat, and his harem joined with her in a chorus of bleating sympathy.

She could only hope that the crumbling stone pen would hold through the coming tempest. A distant cackle reminded Kate of the sorry state of the chicken coop. It had nearly blown away in the last rain, and given the threatening look of the thunderheads, it would not survive the approaching bout of foul weather.

There is so much to be done, Kate thought in desperation as she looked across the courtyard at the gaping maw where the rotten remains of a beamed oak door creaked on a rusty brass hinge. The ancient crenellated towers of the bailey rose above her like clawed fingers against the sky, their crumbling ruins dark and forbidding. Even though the east wing of Eilean Kirk Castle had reputedly been erected after Culloden, it was almost as much of a shambles as the time-worn main building. Pigeons flew through the broken win-dows, seeking shelter from the rising wind, and tendrils of overgrown vines on the stone gargoyles writhed like Medusa's hair. Charlie's curse, according to the local lore:

The structure built with bloody gold would fall as surely as the family that constructed it. Considering the castle's macabre appearance and the unsavory MacLean legend, it was little wonder that the native inhabitants thought the place haunted. Certainly, years of neglect had rendered it almost unfit for human habitation.

Kate looked regretfully at the developing ears of corn and set the last pepper in her basket before hurrying back to the kitchen to set the vegetables on the table. Then it was outside again, but there was so much to be done that she scarcely knew which task to turn to next. The air was thick and heavy, weighing her down with weariness that went far beyond mere physical fatigue. A sense of futility overwhelmed her. In the time since her husband's death, life had become a battlefield, with every day composed of a series of skirmishes in a fight for survival.

"She isn't to be found, milady!" Daisy came up the path, her brow furrowed with worry. "Called and called, I did. Could she have gone into the older part of the castle, do you think? Rotted and dangerous, those wood floors are. Near went through one when first we came here, I did."

"She fears the dark, Daisy," Kate reminded her, trying to reassure herself as much as the maid. "I doubt that she would play there."

"Annie! Annie," Daisy shouted frantically, raising her voice against the wind.

"She cannot answer you," Kate said, attempting to remain calm. "Did you try calling for the dog?"

Daisy shook her head. "Cur!" she cried. "Come here, you mangy Cur!" But the rumble of thunder swallowed her words.

Kate put her fingers to her lips and blew a piercing whistle, which was instantly rewarded with an answering yap. "Hardly ladylike, but it works," she said in answer to Daisy's look of disapproval.

Within minutes Anne topped the hill, her little legs pumping as she ran through the heather, herded toward the two women by the determined collie.

"Thinks the lass is a lamb, it does, the mangy cur," Daisy said, sweeping the child into her ample arms, pulling her apron over the girl's blond curls to shield her from the first raindrops.

"Thank heavens for those misguided instincts," Kate murmured, bending to pat the old dog on the head. "There will be a soup bone for you, tonight, laddie, and that is a promise."

Cur barked, as if in understanding, his tail wagging as he followed the women and his two-legged charge into the kitchen.

Chapter Two

Duncan clambered up the sheer rock face, childhood memories supplying hand and footholds where an adult eye could discern none.

"Not agin! I ain't comin' arter yer this time. Yer gonna get yerself kilt, Major!" Fred wailed from the base of the cliff. "And where will that leave me, I arsk ye?"

"Your concern for my person is most touching, Fred." Duncan called. With a grunt of satisfaction he heaved himself up over the edge; then he lay panting for a moment, his cheek pillowed on the cold stone. Despite the fact that his strength had been steadily improving, the climb had been far more difficult than he had anticipated. Nonetheless, when he rose to his feet, he was glad that he had made the effort. Beinn Airidh Charr rose to the west, its summit obscured by gathering thunderheads. Where the sun still held sway, Loch Maree sparkled in jewel-bright splendor, its placid waters lapping at the rocky shore. Slowly, Duncan's gaze was drawn eastward, but the sight that he sought was shrouded in mist.

The wind whistled like a mourner, rising in keening echoes as it whipped through his hair. Eilean Kirk . . . a peculiar mixture of fear and longing filled him. Like a fever in the blood it was. For the past twenty years he had thought himself cured. After all, he had been a mere stripling of fourteen when his mother had taken him from the crumbling ruin of her marriage. But now the call of that pile of cursed stones pulsed within him with almost overwhelming force. This was his birthplace, and although it had never been a true home, it was pulling him back like a flame-crazed moth.

He had never intended to come back. Even now, every shred of sensibility screamed that he ought to climb down, get on his horse, and ride southward as fast as the nag could carry him, leaving behind those bitter memories that were suddenly surmounting long-built barriers. But Eilean Kirk was a sickness in the blood, as addictive as the poppy or the bottle. There was no place to run to anymore, no place to hide from the boy that he had been, the man he had become . . . or was there?

Duncan looked over the edge of the sheer precipice into the dizzying depth. A peregrine wheeled lazily, riding the currents. As a child, he had often dreamed of flight, soaring with the falcons. It would be so easy to step off the edge, to have one winged moment before oblivion. No bleak past to haunt him . . . no empty future to fear. A rock crumbled beneath his feet, sending a shower of rubble into the water far below.

"Major! Major!" the whisper came on the wind.

. . . *"What shall we do, Major?"* Blevins's voice was asking, the whites of his eyes wide with terror in his powder black face. *"They have us surrounded, sir."* Duncan could see the silent accusation on their faces, hear the French soldiers demanding surrender. A dozen anxious expressions demanded his answer . . . It was his fault . . . all his fault.

The stiff breeze billowed his shirtsleeves, puffing them to the proportions of great white wings. Who would care? A second of flight; an end to pain. Duncan stared sightlessly into the fog-shrouded distance.

"Major? Maaajor!" Fred's voice echoed forlornly from below. "Where are yer?"

Retreating thunder rumbled, and the haze lifted suddenly to reveal Eilean Kirk, suspended like an emerald amidst the storm-grey waters of the loch. The arches of the stone causeway glittered like the fine filigree of a pendant. Duncan suddenly realized that he had been anticipating this moment. Through those endless days of confinement, this was the vision that had kept him sane, the knowledge that beyond those prison walls, Eilean Kirk Castle had stood defiantly against the sky, awaiting his return.

Duncan's hatred of that place and the miserly man who had inhabited it had kept him alive as much as his desire for vengeance. But the final reckoning with his parent that he had rehearsed so many times in his mind would never take place. Now, ironically, that moldering wreck was his. If his father had sought to plan retribution, the late earl's twisted brain could not have conceived a better one. The notorious heritage of the MacLeans was upon Duncan's shoulders now. *You can cheat the old man yet,* came the soft, insinuating inner voice.

"Maaajor! Are yer all right?"

Reluctantly, Duncan stepped back from the brink. Shaking his head like a sleeper waking, he began to turn away when a stray wisp over the castle caught the corner of his eye. The unbroken wavering band certainly did not have the appearance of mist. Pulling out a small spyglass from his pocket, he peered through the lense intently, sweeping the magnified landscape several times before returning to the rim of the plateau. Fred's anxious face stared up at him from below, and Duncan waved reassuringly, a sinking feeling in the depths of his stomach. There could be no peace, not yet. Despite his father's death, there were still scores to be settled. Once the MacLean fortune was in his hands, he would bring Vesey to justice. Then the ghosts of his men would leave him in peace, and he would be free to seek his own repose.

"As I said, 'tis an easy climb. Care to come up and see the view?" Although his tones were teasing, Duncan found himself breathing deeply, trying to ease the pounding of his heart. Was this part of Charlie's curse then, these moments of darkness that brought him to the verge? Even in the depths of La Purgatoire he had never come so close to stepping over the edge. Would melancholy accomplish what French bullets had not?

"Think I'm a bloody mountain goat, do yer?" Fred grumbled, heaving a silent sigh of relief. "I'm waitin' on yer down on solid ground, I am, and don't be lookin' ter me ter scrape yer guts from the gravel if yer decide ter come down too quick."

"I shall not," Duncan said, beginning his descent, "since I fully expect that you will cushion my fall."

Fred cursed under his breath, muttering an entire litany of blasphemy until his master reached the ground. "Yer daft,

Major. These old bones o' mine ain't fit ter spend another
soakin' night in the open, and there yer went wastin' more'n
an 'our up on that rock."

Duncan was startled. An hour? It had scarcely seemed
more than a few minutes. "You chose to throw your lot in
with me, Sergeant. You are more than welcome to turn back
if you wish," he said harshly.

Fred's answer was an indignant harumph.

"We should be at Eilean Kirk just past nightfall," Duncan
said, automatically checking his saddle girths before putting
his boot in the stirrup. "And you of all people ought to know
that time spent in reconnaissance is rarely wasted."

Fred's bushy eyebrows rose in question.

"There is smoke coming from one of the chimneys," Duncan said, mounting his horse. "It appears that we have
company."

"The coop is utterly destroyed, Daisy," Kate said, surveying the splintered wood in despair.

Daisy held up the mangled body of a bird. "Might as well
have this 'un for dinner," she said philosophically.

"And she was one of our best laying hens," Kate moaned.

"Ain't lost none o' the geese, at least," Daisy said. "A
sight more sense than the hens, they had. Drowned in the
puddle, three o' them. I'll hang them up to season."

"And four more out in the woods somewhere," Kate said,
shooing a goose with her skirts.

"Supper for the foxes most likely," Daisy said, putting a
hand on the broken gate of the goat pen. "Won't find 'em
now, not with night coming on."

There was a series of sharp barks followed by protesting
cackles. The two women looked up to see Cur herding a
quartet of chickens, expertly evading their pecking beaks as
he drove them forward.

"Why, I have never seen the like," Kate exclaimed in astonishment, putting her hands on her hips.

"Me either," Daisy said, rushing forward to shoo the
chickens into the corner of the courtyard where Anne quietly
scattered handfuls of corn. "Well, now, that's mostly the lot
of them. T'weren't near as bad as we feared."

"We cannot leave the animals out here," Kate said with a

frown. "The cow byre did not sustain much damage, but there is not enough room for the goats there as well. There is no repairing the coop, I fear."

"But where'll we doss the creatures down for the night?" the older woman asked.

Kate gazed thoughtfully at the kitchen door.

"Oh, no," Daisy said, following the direction of her mistress's stare. "You'll not be putting that lot in my kitchen, you won't."

"I was thinking of the servants' hall, Daisy," Kate said.

" 'Tis the only decent room in the place," Daisy protested.

"Other than the bedroom," Kate conceded, "but unfortunately, it might be a trifle difficult to drive the goats up the stairs."

"Aye, I suppose you're right," Daisy said with a sigh. "Bring the barnyard in, then."

Anne smiled in delight as the two women began driving the poultry in through the kitchen door, but she clapped her hands in glee when they tried to lead the goats, bleating and resisting into the servants' hall. Kate was beginning to think that it would be impossible to move the stubborn beasts when Cur yapped at their heels. With the skill of a four-legged matador, the collie evaded William's horns and shepherded the animals through the door in a matter of seconds.

"Good dog," Kate said, bending to pat Cur on the head.

Anne put her hands round the dog's neck, burying her face in the tawny fur.

"And what about me?" Daisy grumbled. "Don't I get a hug, too?" Anne ran over immediately and threw her arms around the woman's legs, nearly sending her over backward. Mollified, Daisy sat down wearily in a nearby chair. She jumped up abruptly at the cackle of protest and eyed the occupying chicken with disgust. "Came near to being a soup, you did, stupid feather-ball."

Anne pointed and laughed, a loud gurgling noise that shook her small body. Kate looked at Daisy in wonder, sharing the miracle of her daughter's laughter before joining in the infectious sound. Soon the three of them were erupting in torrents of giggles punctuated by barnyard noises, which only urged them into further mirth. Anne sat in the chair watching them get the animals settled. By the time all was done, her eyes were closed, thumb firmly placed in the center of her mouth.

"You see, Daisy, nothing is without purpose. Even this," Kate said as she lit a candle and put her sleeping daughter on her shoulder. She gestured at the menagerie roosting and milling about her. "Anne laughed and now she is going to sleep smiling."

"Aye, it was worth it, at that," Daisy admitted, brushing a stray lock from the child's head. "And if we could but get her to speak again, I'd live in the Tower with the royal lions, I would."

"Perhaps . . . they say that time heals all things. Perhaps if we give her time," Kate said, praying that it would be so.

" 'Tis, a lucky thing that yer recalled the tunnel," Fred said in a hushed voice, raising his candle. "Pity we got 'ere well after dark. Now we don't know 'ow many of 'em there is 'ere. Leastways, we was able ter get round th' dog. T'would 'ave been a near thing, puttin' it down afore it barked warnin'."

"The courtyard should be almost directly above us," Duncan said, his palms cold and sweaty as he counted out the paces. Twenty . . . . thirty . . . soon they would be inside the castle. The air was stale, noxious; the walls sheened with the slimy sweat of damp, far too reminiscent of the dungeons of La Purgatoire for his comfort. "The tunnel to the dungeons should be just ahead. We must stay to the right or we could find ourselves wandering for hours. This castle is riddled with secret exits, some that I likely dinna even know of."

Fred nodded at the wisdom of this. "Always a good idea to 'ave a back door, I'd say."

"Shh!" At the top of the stairs, Duncan put a finger to his lips and silently counted ten paces. He felt for the lever in the wall, trembling inside when he could not find it. *Think man . . . think . . .* he told himself as his heart began to beat a panicked thrum. A boy's stride . . . he stepped back, stifling a sigh as he felt the bar of pitted iron. The release clicked faintly, and he hastily blew out the candle. The panel swung open slowly, the rusty hinges screeching like a hoarse banshee. Duncan cursed under his breath. Now it seemed that all their stealth was for naught. They might as well have arrived with trumpets blaring. For a few heart-stopping minutes the two men waited in the corridor, but there was no sound, no sign that they had been detected. Finally, with a nod of his head, Duncan directed Fred toward the kitchen stairs.

Like a shadow Duncan slipped through the darkness down the empty hallway. The dank chill of the stone floors pierced the worn soles of his boots as he paused at each open room, scanning the shrouded furniture for signs of occupancy. Clearly, things had been recently disturbed. There were footprints in the layers of dust, blocks of space marking the places of pieces of furniture that had been moved. As he left the old wing, Duncan found further evidence of intruders. The moist, moldy smell was diminishing as was the thickness of the dust. It seemed that his uninvited guests had a penchant for cleanliness, Duncan thought with a grim smile.

The soft glow of candlelight spilled from beneath the doorsill like a guiding beacon. Slowly, Duncan cracked the door, glaring at the hinges as if daring them to make a sound. Hefting his knife, he slid into the room, edging around the pool of moonlight that flowed between the tattered remnants of the draperies. All the while he kept his eye on the mound in the center of the bed, trying to detect any change in the rhythmic rise and fall of the heap of blankets. When he reached the headboard, he doused the guttering candle before pulling the covers aside with a swift motion.

The sudden shock of cold night air was like a slap, bringing Kate to instant wakefulness. Her startled scream froze in her throat as a hand clamped over her mouth and cold steel pressed against her throat. She lay still, barely able to see the edges of an outline limned against the moonlight.

"Dinna cry out," the apparition warned softly.

Kate shook her head in an infinitesimal movement signaling submission. Mindful of her sleeping daughter huddled beneath the covers, she prayed heaven that he would not notice Anne and that the child would stay in slumber.

With deliberate care the intruder eased his grip, but the knife remained steady at her neck. "I will not scream," Kate whispered, trying desperately to think of some way to dis-

tract him. "Money . . . " she said. "If it is money you want,
I shall lead you to what we have, but first you must let me
get up." When the knife was withdrawn in seeming acquies-
cence, Kate pushed the blankets aside, lumping them into a
heap to mask Anne's presence.

Duncan watched as she rose in a fluid movement, the folds
of her flannel nightrail falling around the briefly revealed
curves of calf and ankle. As cool as moonlight, she was,
with a sangfroid that startled him almost as much as her
beauty. The beams of light played on her hair, coloring the
rich red with silver tints. Green cat's-eyes glittered in
the darkness, fear in their depths, yet her expression did not
otherwise betray her. Her carriage was ramrod stiff as she
turned to face him. He stepped into the moonlight, revealing
his face, and waited for her reaction, the horror, the shrink-
ing that was inevitable when members of the frail sex first
beheld his scarred countenance, but she did not recoil.

"Follow me," Kate said quietly, searching the stranger's
marred face for some sign of his intent. That single icy grey
eye was empty of any clue. The lack of visible emotion was
far more disturbing to her than the marks on his skin or the
hideous black patch. For a brief moment terror held her in
thrall, but she quickly passed the outer boundaries of that
initial fear. A minute movement from beneath the covers
caught her eye, but the intruder apparently had not seen it
because of his blindness on one side. With a cold sense of
purpose, she knew what she must do and quickly. Another
few seconds and he might notice that she had not been alone
in the bed.

It was a dangerous game, one that she would likely lose,
but it was her only chance. Kate turned her back to the intruder, moving to the door with calculated provocation,
swaying her hips in a manner that needed no interpretation,
even masked beneath a thick layer of flannel. She glanced
over her shoulder, giving the intruder a smoldering look
half-veiled beneath a curtain of thick lashes.

For a moment Duncan was startled. It had been a long
time since any woman had looked at him that way, not unless she had been paid well for her glances at any rate. Surprise quickly gave way to cynicism as he followed the
temptress in brushed cotton. He moved warily, expecting

some trap to spring momentarily. There was not long to
wait. They had reached a turn in the hallway when the
woman bolted abruptly. She sprinted rapidly out of arm's
reach, her hair flying behind her like a fox's tail before the
hound's nose. Duncan gave a grin of satisfaction as she disappeared down the kitchen stairs. Trapped between himself
and Fred, there was little chance of her escaping. He ran
down the staircase, fully expecting to find his manservant
holding her at the bottom, but he reached the final step just
in time to see her disappear through a door. *The servants'
hall*, he recalled, as he followed, *a room with no exits save
the tower. She would not evade him again.*

Kate glanced at her unstrung bow and the quiver beside it.
There would be no time to string it, much less nock an
arrow, and the door to the tower was kept locked, so there
would be no gaining time by hiding up there. She pulled a
chair to the wall, standing upon the unstable furnishing as
she attempted to pry the ancient blunderbuss from its place
above the mantel. Just as she had hoped, he ran in after her
without heeding his feet. He trod on one of the geese, and it
rose to peck at his legs, a hissing, angry bundle of feathers
protesting its disturbed rest. As he backed away, he slipped
on some goat droppings, falling into the nesting hens. They
began to cackle in an agitated chorus, waking the rooster to
protest for his brood, and he began to crow. William, the
goat, roused from his sleep, bleated irritably. Focusing on
the source of the disturbance, the billy goat lowered his
horns to charge the intruder. The stranger scuttled out of the
way just in time, placing a chair between himself and the
rampaging animal.

William wheeled and began yet another attack. The intruder raised the legs of the chair, and for a moment Kate
dared to hope that he would retreat. He edged toward the
kitchen door, brandishing the chair as a shield. William gave
a bleating battle cry and dashed toward his opponent, but at
the last moment the man slipped out of the way. William
was into the kitchen and the man slammed the door shut behind the animal.

Kate pulled the weapon from its mounting with a cry of
triumph, scrambling down from her perch upon the chair as
the intruder started toward her, a murderous expression on

his face. "Do not move," she warned, raising the heavy weapon with effort. The nanny goats bleated nervously as they heard William's frustrated cries from beyond the closed door.

"Madame," Duncan said, his lip curling in a mocking grin. "That weapon has not been fired since a Stuart was upon the throne of England and will likely not discharge again until the Jacobites are restored. I stand more chance of being pecked to death than being wounded by that anti-quated piece. Now, who are you and what are you doing here?"

All at once, there was a burst of curses from beyond the door, followed by a retreating bleat. "Roast yer on a spit, I will," Fred roared as he burst into the room, decidedly worse for wear, pushing before him a frazzled-looking Daisy, her hands bound behind her. "Damned goat tried ter turn me into a bleedin' soprano. Found th' woman sleepin' in th' pantry. Damme if she didn't pop me on me noggin with a skillet. A reg'lar tiger this un is."

"A lucky thing your head is so thick," Duncan com-mented in amusement.

"Don't look ter me like yer was doin' so well either," Fred said, taking in his master's bedraggled appearance. "Cor!" He looked around him wide-eyed. "It's Noah's ark, it is."

"Let her go, or I will shoot your compatriot!" Kate threat-ened in frustration. Was the man mad? For he seemed about to burst out laughing.

Fred looked at Duncan in puzzlement.

"'Compatriot,' as in companion, Fred. She says that she will shoot me unless you let the woman go."

Fred hesitated, but Duncan shook his head with a chuckle. "There is no need to release your captive. Any hope that she has of firing that antique is merely an exercise in wishful thinking," Duncan said, stepping directly in front of the muzzle. "For even if there is shot in that old blunderbuss, 'tis extremely unlikely that the powder is dry. And even if the powder is dry, I suspect 'tis as likely to blow up in the female's face as into mine. But then, any rearrangement of my visage is bound to be an improvement. However, I would mourn any damage to yours, lovely one.

"Let her go," Kate demanded hoarsely, but neither the

stranger nor his cohort made a move. She looked into the intruder's eye, pleading with him. "I *will* pull this trigger," she whispered, trying to convince herself as much as him. "Do not make me kill you."

"Why not, inasmuch as it might be saving the world from villains like myself?" Duncan asked, regarding her steadily as he walked toward her, wondering if she would indeed pull the trigger. He felt a stab of admiration; she had courage aplenty this wee Amazon, for she stood barely to his shoulder. Still, he doubted that her strength of spirit was sufficient to enable her to kill a man. *Who was she? And what was she doing in this hell hole?*

He wants to die. The thought struck her with all the strength of a physical blow as she stared at her advancing nemesis. *Now,* she told herself, as he stood at the mouth of the gun, the rod of metal the only barrier between the two of them. There was something in that grey depth that held her in thrall. Somehow, she could not pull the trigger back. She felt the weight of the gun leaving her hands and felt herself sagging. She was a fool. Now they were defenseless because of her cowardice. His arm came around her, supporting her, keeping her from falling down in utter despair.

"It would not have fired anyway," Duncan said, feeling a strange need to comfort her. She seemed so utterly bereft. Tears were slipping silently down her cheeks. He rested the stock against a nearby chair. It slipped, discharging as it fell with a roar and a flash. As the dust settled, Duncan eyed the blackened hole at his feet with curious detachment. "Then again, I have been known to be occasionally wrong," he said, coughing at the sulphurous smoke.

"I am sorry, Daisy," Kate apologized, looking at the other woman in anguish. "I have failed you."

"Never, milady," Daisy declared stoutly, her eyes glistening.

"Milady?" Duncan asked, his eyebrow arching sardonically.

"I am the late earl's wife," Kate said, seizing upon Daisy's slip of the tongue. "My husband, The MacLean, was killed at Badajoz."

Fred made a strangled sound, and Duncan eyed his manservant, warning him to be silent. "He left you in rather dire circumstances, it seems," he said, looking around the moonlit room at the gobbling, bleating, crowing circus of feathers and fur. "Or are you merely aping the latest fashion? I have heard that the Duchess of Oldenberg lives with a zoological menage."

"T'was the storm what knocked down the henhouse, y'see," Daisy began to explain, bristling at the implied disparagement of her housekeeping abilities. "And the goat's pen was near a wreck . . . " but her voice trailed off beneath the one-eyed man's quelling look.

Her captor's silent gaze sparked Kate's flagging resolution. Time was passing, and Anne might wake to find herself alone in the dark. The child would likely come looking for her. "We have not much," she said rapidly. "But I will give you the little money that we have if you will leave us in peace."

"Money?" Duncan said, feeling strangely distracted. He could feel her heart pounding a drumming tattoo, belying her courageous facade. But it was her eyes that betrayed her. Unlike most women, she was a poor liar. "Ah yes, money . . . But a trifle compared to the other riches that I have found." He raised his free hand to brush Kate's cheek. "MacLean's wife, you say?"

Kate quivered at his touch. "Take the money and go," she said, her voice hoarse as his fingers traced the arch of her throat. "I warn you, sir, the magistrate will deal harshly with a man who trifles with a lord's wife."

"Even a dead lord?" Duncan asked in amusement, pulling her closer to him.

"Especially a dead lord," Kate said, gasping as he brought her up against the hard length of him. There was no softness, only lean sinew, taut beneath his dark clothing. "My husband was a war hero."

"Oh, he was a war hero?" Duncan gave Fred a slow wink. The Cockney grinned.

"Duncan saved his regiment in the battle of Talavera," Kate spoke quickly, fighting against his grip, but it was like a vise holding her fast."

"They decorated him for valor."

That much was true; the wench's story was getting more interesting by the minute, Duncan thought, enjoying the sensation as she struggled against him. He tightened his grasp, bringing her close and circling her with his arms.

"He was killed while trying to overcome a French artillery position in Badajoz" she said, trying to recall all that she could about her late husband's fallen comrade. "He was blown to pieces, so mangled that there was nearly nothing left for burial."

"Is *that* the story they told?" Duncan asked. "Surely, they could have done far better than that? MacLean was far too intelligent for such foolish heroics, I hear. There was no better man when it came to protecting his hide."

"Not always," Fred said sourly, his comment punctuated by a plaintive bleat from the goats in the corner.

"Aye, true enough," Duncan said, his eye flinty as he recalled his failure. "Every man has his flaws."

"You ought not to not mock, sir," Kate said, conscious of his fingers splayed against the small of her back. She could feel them burning like a brand even through the thick stuff of her nightgown. "My husband was The MacLean of Eilean Kirk. Harm me, sir and I swear his ghost will haunt you."

"A MacLean of Eilean Kirk!" Duncan said, drawing back in a mock display of dismay. "Then it is true what they say of MacLeans?"

"Aye," Daisy pronounced darkly. " 'Tis a pact with the devil they have. The MacLeans come back from the dead, they do, to deal with their enemies."

"How very tiresome," Duncan said, cupping Kate's chin with his hand. He could feel her tremble and felt a twinge of regret, but she deserved all that she got for her ridiculous pretense and more. He might have let her go had she chosen to tell him the truth, but the affront of an outright lie deserved punishment. "Nonetheless, I *have* heard that the MacLeans are cursed with the nine lives of a cat. I have also been told that their taste in women has always been the finest." He brought his lips down upon hers, tasting the sweetness of that lying mouth.

It was a kiss meant to frighten. Duncan crushed her to him, ravaging with calculated lust, storming her as if she were a castle under siege, demanding nothing less than total surrender. But somewhere in the midst of the attack, he lost all constraint. Premeditated passion was replaced by a strange longing to lose himself in her softness; to pretend for a brief interval that this woman truly desired him, to dispel the utter loneliness that had dogged him ever since his face had become a mockery.

It was like nothing Kate had ever experienced, this harsh and demanding assault. She could barely breathe before the bombardment began anew. His hands tangled in her hair, keeping her captive. It was shocking to find that a part of her was responding to his caresses, almost eager to explore these new sensations that shook her to the very marrow. There had only been one man in her life, and her late husband's kisses had been few and perfunctory. Then the intruder's tongue began to plunder, consuming her like a fire raging out of control, and every last trace of curiosity was banished. She was being disloyal, wanton, an empty-headed fool. Terror welled up within her, but she knew that she could not give way to her fear. *Anne*, she reminded herself. *Think of Anne.*

Duncan felt her stiffen, begin to struggle against him, and he knew that he had achieved his aim. Slowly, reluctantly, he released her, expecting to see utter horror in those emerald depths. Instead, there was glittering anger, so strong and feral that he half expected her to hiss.

"Are you quite finished?" Kate asked, wiping her hand across her lips as if to clean them.

"Leave her be, you dirty scum!" Daisy shouted, lunging at Duncan, but Fred held her back.

"Canna a man even steal a simple kiss?" Duncan asked, feeling a touch of grudging admiration. Pluck to the backbone this one; it seemed that stronger measures might be required to force the truth from her. Gathering up a moonlit handful of her hair, Duncan rubbed it against his cheek. "A damned poor homecoming it seems to me, for a man given up for dead when he cannot even get a kiss. But then why settle for a kiss?" He scooped her up in his arms like a rag doll, setting the chickens to squawking as he started for the door.

"Let me go," Kate screamed, beating her fists ineffectually against his chest. If he brought her upstairs, he would surely discover Anne. "They will hang you, I swear they will, and if not, I shall kill you with my own hands, but not before I cut off your—"

"Tsk, tsk!" Duncan said, shaking with suppressed laughter. "I must admit that it is no wonder that I have forgotten marrying you, my lady wife, for you seem something of a shrew. Is that why I went off to war, do you think, Fred? Many a man has found the battlefield a more peaceable place than the marriage bed."

"Aye, 'tis true enough, Major," Fred said, trying in vain to stifle a guffaw. "A real spitfire that 'un. Don't look ter be a female that a man 'ud forget real easy though."

"True enough," Duncan said softly, watching the moonlight cast its alabaster glow on her flawless skin and trace the swollen line of her lips.

"It cannot be," Kate whispered, ceasing her struggles and looking at Duncan in dismay as the meaning of his words finally penetrated.

"Ah, but it is," Duncan said, his smile sardonic and chilling. "Duncan MacLean, at your service, madame. Now who in bloody hell are you?"

Chapter Three

Kate went limp, her eyes rolling, lids fluttering closed. A breathy sigh escaped her lips as she fell into a sham faint. She needed a moment to think, to concoct some kind of story that might satisfy her husband's former comrade in arms.

Their unwilling host would, in all probability, pack the lot of them back to London—or would he? Duncan MacLean had certainly not been typical of Adam's acquaintances. There had been more than a hint of envy in her husband's letters as he had described the "Mad MacLean." Fast horses, faster women, fortunes won on the turn of a card, were everything that Adam claimed to loathe. Yet, he had admired Duncan MacLean, and obviously that friendship had been reciprocated. Although Adam was long dead when MacLean's legacy was finally distributed, the well-thumbed copy of Blake's poems and the MacLean family signet were evidence that the regard was mutual. Indeed, it was the letter from MacLean's solicitor seeking a buyer for the deserted ruin of the Castle Eilean Kirk that had led her to seek shelter here.

His heartbeat thudded beneath her ear with a disturbing rhythm. Kate had always been good at thinking on her feet, but unfortunately, the connection between herself and terra firma had been temporarily severed. Trying to formulate a plan while nestled against a man's chest was deucedly difficult. Her lips could still feel the memory of that insistent pressure. The mingled scents of horse and man trifled with her senses, banishing all coherent thought.

"You brute!" Daisy shrieked. "Frightened the poor dear to death, you have."

"Best not try the stage," Duncan whispered softly in Kate's ear. "Siddons has naught to fear madame, especially not when the audience holds you in the palm of his hand. You are far too tense to be truly unconscious."

Kate gave no response, hanging as a deadweight, although the tickle of his breath on her lobe sent cold fingers up her spine. No, she could not tell Duncan MacLean the truth. Rakehell though MacLean might be, he likely had an arrow-straight sense of honor, seeing only from fletching to tip without the slightest allowance for any bends in the shaft. It was unlikely that MacLean would credit her if she spoke with candor, for at times she found the truth difficult to believe herself.

"Women have swooned at the sight of me, but you are a trifle late for using horror as an excuse," Duncan murmured, his lips lightly brushing her hair. "Perhaps I am a ghost, come to haunt you, a demon come to claim your lying soul, *Lady* MacLean."

She could not help but tense at his touch and knew that the pretense was over. It was not fair, truly. She had not wished him dead or wounded, but the deserted castle had been like a raft to a drowning man. Now, for Anne's sake, she had to salvage what she could. They would have to go overseas. Where would they be able to lose themselves? He would be looking for them.

"On the count of three, I am going to drop you," Duncan said. "I suggest that you recover yourself swiftly unless you wish to fall end first in a heap of goat offal. One . . . two . . ."

At three he released her, keeping hold of her arms as she landed upright. "Now, milady what have you to say to your hideous shade of a husband?"

The bitterness beneath his banter touched her. But despite the pangs of sympathy and conscience, Kate decided to take the offensive. With the truth barred, there was no reasonable defense that she could offer. "You are *supposed* to be dead," Kate said, regarding him in consternation. "And even if you are not, it is a poor excuse for rousing us from our beds and scaring us half out of our wits."

"*My* beds, *my* house," Duncan pointed out coldly. "As for your wits, madame, I shudder to think what a dance you might have led me if you were fully in possession of your faculties. As it is, you damned near killed me with that blunderbuss," Duncan said, watching the play of emotion in those emerald eyes. "Then as a MacLean, it would be my ghostly duty to come haunting your nights. I vow, the thought almost makes me long to cast off my corporeal form."

"How do I know that you are Duncan MacLean?" Kate asked suspiciously.

"I take it that you have not set foot in the portrait gallery?" Duncan asked, silently awarding her a point in the game of verbal fencing. A weak attack, but at this point he had not expected an attempt at argumentative riposte.

She shook her head.

"I thought not," Duncan said, "else you would not ask that question. I am, unfortunately, cast in the wicked MacLean image. Moreover, I have already given you a sample of the savage charm that has made my clan justifiably famous with the fair sex. If that does not satisfy you, I have papers in my saddlebag, which will more than prove my identity. Rejoice, oh widow MacLean, for thy bonny husband has returned to thy bosom."

Kate closed her eyes for a moment, feeling the world whirling around her. They would have to leave, to run once more. All of Daisy's meager savings had been invested in livestock, and they could not very well pack up the cow. There was precious little money, yet there was no choice.

"Dinna play this game again, madame," she heard MacLean saying, "for I am losing my patience."

Kate's eyes began to sting, and she blinked, heartily ashamed of her weakness. She had never in her life been one to weep, despising women who turned into watering pots at the least excuse.

Duncan's expression hardened at the sight of her tears slipping from beneath closed lids. Eve had likely wept after the apple. But when the woman opened her eyes, he was almost shocked by the pain and despair swimming in those green depths and more startled still by her words.

"We will be gone by morning, milord," Kate said, feeling utter defeat. There was no choice but to drive the best bargain that she could under the circumstances. "We would appreciate if you would let us stay the night. The livestock is ours, purchased with our own resources; however if you will give us a fair price, we will leave the animals for your use."

Daisy gasped. "But, where shall we go, milady?" she began. "How—"

Kate cut her off with a warning glance. "The pretense is over, Daisy. I am 'Lady MacLean' no longer, so please give me no titles. We shall pack our things at once."

"And you think that I will simply allow you to go?" Duncan asked.

"We have done you no harm," Kate said, lifting her chin defiantly. "When we came here, this place was unfit for a dog to dwell in. Bit by bit, we have made it a home of sorts. We will leave this place far better than we found it."

"Criminal trespass is a crime, I believe," Duncan said, his voice harsh. His eyes lit on the bow in the corner. "So is poaching. I could bring you up before the magistrate."

Kate blanched, her eyes widening. "No, milord," she whispered. "There is no need. We have stolen nothing. Let us go, and you may keep the animals if you wish. Just allow us to leave."

His curiosity whetted, Duncan pushed his point. "Are you on the run from the law then, madame?"

"We have committed no crime," Kate said, trying in vain to recoup her tactical error. It had been unconscionably foolish to allow him to know that she feared the authorities. "Other than criminal trespass and perhaps a bit of poaching."

Once more, Duncan had raised her score in their verbal fencing match. She had recovered quickly, but not soon enough. It was time to press her. "Who are you?" he asked once more, taking her by the shoulders and looking her squarely in the face. "The truth now."

"I am Kate, milord," she said. "Katherine Smith."

"I would have thought that you would use more imagination," Duncan said, his lip curling wryly. "Surely you can do better than 'Smith.'"

"It was my husband's misfortune, milord, to have a name as commonplace as grass," Kate said. "We had been following the drum with him, and when he was killed at Ciudad Rodrigo, we returned to England."

"What was his regiment?" Duncan barked.

"The fifty-second, milord," Kate answered immediately, naming another regiment that she knew had been present on that January day. So many men's lives had been lost.

"Rank?"

"Sergeant-major, milord. Do you wish to hear just how he died as well? His legs were shot out from under him. I found him there, on the battlefield, barely alive, and I held him until he died in my arms," Kate said, her voice trembling as she wished that she could have been with Adam and comforted him in his final moments. Perhaps he might even have come to value her unusual upbringing had he allowed her to follow the drum, but Adam had insisted that he would not be subject to her fits and starts. Steele's lady would stay hidden in the country where she would cease to be a perpetual embarrassment.

Where did fiction end and truth begin? Duncan wondered. He was certain that she was lying, but the honest emotion in her words was almost convincing. Whether or not the fifty-second had been there or not, he could not say, but it was likely. Still . . . "A touching story, madame," he said, grabbing her by the wrist. "Perhaps you can convince the magistrate of its veracity."

"No!" Kate begged, "please let us go. I will do anything, milord."

"Anything?" Duncan asked with deceptive softness, his eyebrow rising in speculation. *Just how far would she go?*

"Anything," Kate confirmed, snatching her hand from his to stand stiffly beneath his scrutiny.

"I will no doubt regret this," Duncan said slowly. "But being a MacLean, I cannot resist a bargain. You claimed to be my wife, and I find that the idea appeals. This hovel needs a woman's hand."

"No," Daisy said. "Don't make a pact with the devil, milady."

"Shut yer trap, woman," Fred said, clamping his hand over the maid's mouth. "Let 'er made up 'er own mind."

"What duties do you wish me to perform?" Kate asked, a cold dread clenching her insides as she grasped his direction.

"All those that a wife would rightly provide," Duncan

said, his dark hair waving over his patched eye. "House-keeping, cooking . . ." allowing his words to trail off and imply much more. From her expression it was clear that she understood what he left unspoken.

"In return, I will have shelter and protection for me and mine for as long as I will stay?" Kate chose her words carefully.

"Aye," Duncan said, "but you did not allow me to mention the other wifely duty that I expect of you. Come here."

Kate took a deep breath and stepped into the circle of his arms. She had often wondered about Adam's friend, a man as unlike to her stolid, conventional spouse as pudding to porridge. When Adam had written of MacLean's death, she had mourned the rakehell she had never met, but she knew now that she had been lamenting a phantom, an image created from a fabric of gossip glued together by bits of imagination. This unsmiling face, hard and unforgiving as granite, this was not the stuff of idle dreams; this was reality. She could not claim friendship and therefore could not expect mercy. Not from this man. Tears would gain her nothing, and she blinked furiously, trying to stem the flow for the sake of her own pride. "As you wish, milord," she said.

Duncan watched those expressive green eyes in fascination as she struggled against tears. That failed battle for dignity touched him far more than any plea or protestation that she might make. Although he had set the terms of surrender, her quiet capitulation was unexpected. "You must be desperate indeed," Duncan murmured, brushing the warm, wet trail on her cheek. "But why? Tell me the truth, and I may set you free."

The kitchen door burst open, banging like a rifle shot as it caromed against the wall. The indoor barnyard burst into cacophonous chorus as the small fury careened toward Duncan. The child launched herself at his knees, nearly knocking him to the ground. Like a tiny, wild beast she clawed and tore at the stranger who was holding her mother and making her cry. Duncan scooped her up from the floor, ignoring the tiny fists that pounded at his chest.

"Yours, I presume?" he asked, turning his nose aside and

blocking her small hand to avoid a hit. "I believe that I detect a certain resemblance in your pugilistic style."

Kate snatched the child from his arms, holding the shaking body close. " 'Tis all right, Anne. He has not hurt me, and I will let no one hurt you," she crooned in comfort. "No one will hurt you ever again."

Duncan watched his erstwhile wife brush back the girl's golden curls, bits of the puzzle falling into place. The wild green eyes that stared at him in terror were the cut from the same jade as those of her mother. The lioness had been protecting her cub, it seemed. But why did she fear the law so much that she was willing to go to a stranger's bed? The woman looked up at him at that moment, furious, daring him to contradict that pledge of safety, and he knew that she would be capable of doing anything to protect her own. He felt a twinge of envy, wondering what it would feel like to be the recipient of such fierce devotion. "I will leave you to calm the child, Kate, and then we will talk," he said. He nodded to Fred, signing for him to release the other woman from her bonds.

No one will ever hurt you again. The words echoed uncomfortably in his brain. He was out into the kitchen before he realized that there had been a critical sound missing in the pandemonium of the servants hall. The girl had been utterly silent . . . no shouts of "Mama!" . . . no cries, only tears. *No one will ever hurt you again.* A new and utterly foreign emotion filled him—shame.

"She's asleep at last," Kate whispered, rising stealthily from her place beside Anne. The candle flickered by the bedside, the flame dancing to the drafts as Kate paced back and forth across the room, finally giving vent to her nervous energy. There were choices to be made now, and from what she could see, neither of the options had much to commend it. "Stay or go, Daisy. What is it to be?" she asked.

"He was Lord Steele's friend, you was tellin' me when first we came here," Daisy suggested, her voice hushed as she rhythmically smoothed back Anne's guinea-bright curls. "Mebbe if he knew you was Lady Steele?"

"I don't know," Kate said, threading anxious fingers through her unruly hair. "All I know of him is what Adam mentioned in his letters. He is a fine officer, the man to have beside you in the fray. But off the field . . ."

" 'Tis 'Mother watch your daughter.'" Daisy nodded. "Don't need no letter to know that, even starveling and scarred, has that way about him he does. And there weren't a woman within the sound of the drumbeat that didn't know of the 'Mad MacLean.' But he's a lord, milady, a belted earl. Surely, 'tis his duty to help you?"

"Or the 'Mad MacLean' might just feel obliged to deliver us back into Vesey's hands. He is a man, after all. Why would he believe the word of a mere woman?" Kate said with barely suppressed venom, rising gently from her seat upon the bed to avoid disturbing the child. "We cannot take the risk, Daisy. If I did not think it too dangerous, I would steal away this very night. But the terrain is rough, and we would certainly come to grief in the dark."

Cur whimpered softly, thrusting his furry head beneath Kate's hand in a comforting canine gesture, before settling himself once more at Daisy's feet.

"But how far could we get?" came Daisy's anguished question. "Barely even enough for a coach fare, do we have."

"We will get money somehow," Kate said, her eyes hard as gemstones as she watched her sleeping daughter. Anne was still shaking, her breath coming in small hiccups, the remnants of hysteria. "I have always wanted to see America."

"Americay," Daisy said in dismay. "A place of savages, it is. With Indians what takes your scalp right off your head."

"Nonetheless, it is a big country, a place where Anne and I could easily lose ourselves," Kate said.

"And what about me?" Daisy asked suspiciously.

Kate clasped Daisy's hand. "Go back to London. By the time John finds you and questions you, we will be long gone and you can misdirect him. Someday, I will pay you back your savings. I do not know what we would have done had you not put your nest egg at our disposal."

Daisy's face reddened. "You'll not be leavin' me behind like so much baggage. And no more talk of payin' me back, for if there's any what owes, it's me. When my man died in India and left me alone, sickly from childbed and the shy side of sixteen, with no money, the colonel and your ma took me in, they did. I'd just lost my own babe, and t'was I what suckled you. D'you think honestly that I'd leave you and the wee one?"

Kate shook her head, swallowing to ease the constriction of her throat before she spoke. "No, I did not," she said hoarsely. "But I had to give you the choice. T'will be far more difficult to go undetected this time. We were lucky that night; John did not suspect that we would fly immediately with only the clothes on our back. But I have little doubt that his minions are searching for us now."

" 'Tis a pity indeed that Lord MacLean came back," Daisy said with a sigh. "Now there's one what seems that the world'd be better off without."

"He is wounded, Daisy," Kate chided. "And it seems to me his hurts go far deeper than the skin. We _did_ invade the gentleman's home, after all."

"Well, he ain't no kind of gentleman, if he don't see that you're a lady," Daisy said with a sniff. "T'was a slip on the shoulder he was offerin' you and no mistake. 'Tis a blessin' the little 'un came when she did."

"No," Kate said, her eyes lowering before Daisy's re- proachful look. "It was most unfortunate, for I would have accepted his offer otherwise."

Daisy's mouth dropped open. "What would your pa have said? And your husband? You . . ."

"They would have rightly called me a whore," Kate said, completing the sentence, her fists clenching by her sides. "I hope that my father will look down from his place in heaven and know that his granddaughter is safe from harm. As for my husband, I would merely be fulfilling his expectations. He fully believed that I would come to grief eventually. That was the reason that he gave control of our finances and our lives into John Vesey's keeping. No doubt, Adam thought that John would keep my hoydenish tendencies in tight rein. But that water has long rushed beneath the bridge. I will do what I must to keep Anne safe and if that entails walking the streets for passage money, then I shall do so. If you cannot stomach that thought, then you had best go back to Lon- don."

Silent tears ran down the maidservant's wrinkled cheek as

she stood up and clasped Kate's hands. "Do it for you myself, but I could," she said. "But there ain't many what
would want one such as me. I'll stay with you, child, though
it be breakin' my heart."

"Oh, Daisy," Kate whispered, clutching the woman's
hands. "We'll weather this. For Anne."

"Aye," Daisy said, in tones of an oath taking. "For Anne."

Few people were abroad before dawn in the fashionable
Mayfair neighborhood of Portman Square. So it was
scarcely surprising that no one remarked the man slipping
through the garden gate and into Steele House through an
unlocked door. He moved through the darkened rooms
confidently, pausing for a moment at the library door before
entering silently.

"What kept you?" John Vesey said, glaring angrily. "I expected you nearly an hour ago."

"I was waiting for the report from France," the man
replied, his demeanor composed despite his employer's obvious rage. "My man had a rough time crossing French
lines. We are at war, you know."

"Damn your cheek, Roberts," Vesey said. "What does he
say? Has he found them?"

"It seems that they have vanished, sir," Roberts replied.

"What do you mean, 'vanished'?" John Vesey roared,
striking his desk with a meaty fist.

Roberts raised an eyebrow, sorely tempted to mention that
raised voices and pounding were bound to attract attention,
but then thought the better of it. Vesey was paying a pre-
mium price for his services, and although he could not like
the man, his gold was certainly unobjectionable. "They have
not been seen since that day in Dover, sir. My men have
questioned the captains of every packet that day, and none
can recall either of the two women or the child. I have sent
men to the various ports, questioned nearly every smuggler
from here to Cornwall, but there is no trace of them. I have
the account of my peoples' expenses," Roberts concluded,
handing him the bill.

"This is outrageous," Vesey said, his face reddening as he
read the figures.

" 'Tis as we agreed. Expenses as they occur and the balance of our fee upon delivery."

"And when can we expect that?" Vesey asked sarcastically.

Roberts shrugged. " 'Tis hard to say. She has covered her tracks amazingly well. There is even a possibility that she could still be in England."

Vesey blanched at the thought. He was so close to the peerage. Prinny had borrowed a fortune, and the hints of old debts being forgotten for future favors had firmly taken root. All the nods of patronage had been received. It was merely a matter of time, unless that female powder keg exploded before he could find her and cut her fuse. "And have you made any progress?"

"We are making inquiries, sir, but so far they have been fruitless."

"I do not want the fact that Lady Steele is missing known, I told you," Vesey said tightly. "I have put it out that she is ill and has retired temporarily to the country."

"My agency is known for its discretion, sir." Roberts said. "That is why many people prefer us to the more famous Bow Street Runners."

"And a pretty penny I have paid for your skills at subtlety, but I have nothing to show for it." Vesey laced his hands nervously. "Dammit, she could be anywhere, speaks half a dozen languages like a native."

"She has not touched any of her assets yet," Roberts informed him, trying to keep the admiration from his voice. "We have made quiet inquiries among our informants at the banks, the moneylenders. Our sources tell us that she has not attempted to draw on her funds, borrow, nor sell the Steele jewels. A clever bit of restraint on her part, I must say."

"Do not forget the diamond brooch that I described," Vesey said in growing annoyance. "You are on the lookout for that as well?"

"The piece that belonged to her mother? Of course, sir. Though why she would sell that bauble before the others—"

"Less well known," Vesey muttered, thinking of the Steele heirlooms concealed in the back of the vault. She could not sell what she did not have, but he had to make the circumstances of Katherine's disappearance more plausible to the investigator. "Other than the jewels, she couldn't have had more than a few pounds when she left. If she hasn't sold a piece, how in the devil is she managing?"

Roberts coughed delicately. "If you could tell me something more about her reasons for leaving, sir?" he inquired. "Sometimes understanding the motivation can help us determine location."

Vesey rose and faced the fireplace. " 'Tis as I told you. She has been queer in the attic since my brother by marriage died. Dotes on that child of hers so much that I began to fear for her sanity. One night she up and left, taking the Steele jewels with her. My poor wife is heartbroken. She was always invalidish, but this has sent her into a decline. I must find Katherine and my niece, for her sake."

Roberts nodded, not believing a word of it. Each time that he had told the story, Vesey had avoided looking directly at him. It was an absolute rule that Roberts never trusted a man who would not meet him eye to eye. He had little doubt that Lady Steele had run away for some very good reason. Unfortunately, that was not his concern. "We will find her for you, sir, never fear," Roberts said, his expression bland as porridge when Vesey faced him again.

"See that you do," Vesey said, "else you shall not see a penny of that piratical fee you charge."

"As agreed," Roberts said, bowing stiffly before leaving the library. *A pity* he thought as the gate latched behind him with a quiet click. *When 'tis your job to flush the game and your heart is with the prey.*

The rooster perched himself on the servants' hall window and began to lustily greet the dawn. Gold and pink glowed faintly through the mist over the peak of Beinn Airidh Charr. On the courtyard stones beside Duncan's makeshift seat, Fred's blankets lay abandoned. He had gone to the village in the hopes of foraging some food, anything rather than face the "tiger woman" who had nearly bashed his head in.

Duncan's own blankets lay untouched. He had spent the night with his thoughts, unable to rest. From time to time he had seen shadows moving in the castle's single lit window and knew that she, too, was still awake. But he dared not go up to her room. He had done too much harm already.

The events of the previous evening were vivid in his mind. Every obnoxious word he had said, the anguish in her eyes, the stark terror on the child's face seemed to echo in his mind like scenes from an oft-seen opera. But worst by far was the memory of that kiss, haunting his every sense, filling him with a desire that had been strong enough to make him lose every last shred of honor.

Movement in the doorway caught his attention. It was Kate, an old army haversack in her hand. Her hair was scraped back from her face and covered by a shawl of the type worn by old women. Their eyes met with the shock of two people who have seen each other's worst shame. Kate flushed, her cheeks two ruddy spots against the black fabric.

"How is the child?" Duncan asked, rising and walking toward her. Dark circles under her eyes, a redness, bespoke tears.

"As well as can be expected," Kate said shortly. "Daisy is getting her dressed, and we will be off your land as soon as possible."

She was leaving. Duncan had not truly believed that she would. It had been obvious the night before that the two women were destitute and desperate. "I had thought that we would talk," Duncan said. "I was waiting."

"I had intended to come," Kate said, "but my daughter would not let me leave her. She woke up several times, and she would have been terrified if I had not been at her side. I fear that I cannot keep our bargain, milord. For I cannot abandon her to face the night without me so that I might be sport in your bed."

It took every ounce of Duncan's courage to look her in the face. "I am sorry . . ." he began.

"So am I," Kate said bleakly. "For it was the best of the poor choices that I have."

"Even a pact with the devil?" Duncan asked. "Agreeing to sleep with a man who has the face of the monster?"

Kate regarded him silently for a moment, wondering what to say. The harsh light of morning revealed the hollow planes of his face, the gaunt frame that was all angle and bone without the softening effect of flesh. Yet, there was still that indefinable quality about him, that captivating air of danger that promised both delight and doom. Vulnerability and sheer masculine power could prove the most deadly of combinations to an unwary woman. What had happened to MacLean? she wondered. What had made him so terribly bitter, this friend of Adam's? For the sake of that friendship and the temporary shelter she had received, she spoke. "It is not the face that makes the monster, milord. It is the soul. Sleeping with a man capable of coercing a woman unwilling to his bed would trouble me far more than any honorable scars that you might bear," she said, turning to get the rest of their bags.

"Kate . . ."

She felt his hand upon her shoulder and shrugged it off, her hand going to the concealed pocket of her gown. She whirled to face him, the knife gleaming wickedly in the sun's first rays. "You do not have leave to touch me, milord," she said with hushed vehemence, shrugging her shawl aside to free her hands. Weariness and fear had exhausted the last of her patience. Now, as she stood before him, she felt a foolish elation, almost willing him to try his luck. After so many months of sham meekness, defiance was a heady tonic. "Nor have I given you permission to address me by my given name. Now do not force me to add to the damage that the French have done you, for I warn you that I can use this to excellent effect. It is your luck that you reached me last night before I could put my hand on this, else the coffiner would be fitting you for a box."

"And you would be standing trial for murdering an earl," Duncan pointed out.

"Or being carried through the streets of the village as a heroine," Kate retorted. "Your family is not well loved, so they tell me."

"Put your knife by, Kate. You not need fear me laying so much as a finger on you," Duncan said with a sigh. "Besides, you have no need of a weapon with that sharp tongue of yours flaying me to pieces. I have never met a woman who has made an apology so devilish difficult."

"And do you tender your regrets to many women?" Kate could not resist the mocking reply. Nonetheless, she put her blade back in its sheath. The word "apology" had taken the wind of bravado from her sails. This man did not deserve her anger. It was not his fault she felt so helpless, so hopelessly adrift. Where would they go now?

"I have never had to make apologies where any woman is concerned," Duncan said, his lip arching slightly in a rakish grin that underlined his double entendre.

Kate made an exasperated sound of disgust. "A braggart, too."

"My behavior last night was unforgivable." Duncan said, the words coming out in a rush. "I was insufferably rude."

Kate's mouth opened in astonishment. Such directness was the last thing that she had expected.

"I ask your forgiveness," Duncan said, ruffling a nervous hand through his hair as he looked at her expectantly. Her answering smile made him catch his breath. If beauty could be distilled into an essence, it was contained within that enchanted look. "Please stay, Kate," he whispered.

Her smile dissolved in disappointment. "I told you, milord, our bargain is void," she said curtly. "I cannot fulfill it."

"We can amend it," Duncan said, gesturing at the wreckage around him. "If I am to make any headway here, I need help, and there will likely be no female in the village willing to stay under the same roof as a wicked MacLean."

"And with good reason!" Kate said with a snort.

"Keep my house, such as it is," Duncan proposed. "Feed us and you may stay."

"And that is all?" Kate asked incredulously.

"My oath as a MacLean," Duncan said, raising his hand solemnly. "I will not lay a hand on you . . . unless, of course, you should happen to ask me."

"I do not expect to make any such untoward requests, milord," Kate replied primly.

"One can always wish," Duncan said, his voice gruff.

His wistful tone made it clear that he harbored no such hopes. Kate felt a swell of pity. Lord MacLean honestly seemed to believe that his aspect was hideous. But that was no concern of hers. Indeed, if he felt himself unattractive, it was so much the better for her. Heaven help her if he realized how fast her heart was beating, how that smile of self-mockery seemed to squeeze the very breath from her. Even by the measure of Adam's expurgated tales, MacLean had been the very model of the irresistible male who knows his own attraction. She reminded herself that this man did not deserve her sympathy. He would have blackmailed her into his bed. Could any bond that he made be trusted? She would have to tread warily. "You agree not to molest me or mine?" Kate chose her words with care. "You give your word that *all* of us may stay here under your protection?"

"Aye, all." Duncan chuckled as he thought of anyone attempting to trifle with her battle-ax of a maid. "I swear."

Kate put her hands on her hips, cocking her head to one side as she considered. "Very well," she said at last, offering her hand in the age-old gesture of sealing bargains.

He clasped her fingers, feeling as large as a bear as his huge paw curled around her palm. Hers were working hands, chapped and raw with labor. How had she come to this pass? he wondered. She was a lady; every inch of her proclaimed it, soft as a kitten but with claws of steel. Frightened enough of someone or something to face him with utter fearlessness, to bargain herself away for the benefit of his dubious protection. Not for a moment did he believe that her name was Smith, but he could afford to wait for his answers. Solving this riddle of a female would certainly help to pass the time until Dewey fattened the MacLean purse once again.

A kaleidoscope of feelings filled those enigmatic eyes as he took her hand in his. Beyond the confusion was something that appealed to a part of him he had thought long dead. Somehow he knew that this was one oath that would remain unbroken, although it was a deuce of a time to become an honorable man. In all likelihood she would never offer him so much as a finger again. It was a chance that would never be repeated, and Duncan had never been known to waste an opportunity. With a wicked grin he raised her hand to his lips, savoring the delicate feel of her, the flutter of her fingers like a captive bird's wing. Gently, he caressed her palm with a kiss, following the lines and scars that told him a story of hardship. With tenderness he touched the delicate tracery of veins until he reached the pounding pulse beat at her wrist. Slowly, he sealed the bargain that he had already begun to regret with a stolen kiss.

His dark head was bent, and she could see nothing of his expression. He was trifling with her, she knew it. An odd torpor overcame her, a lethargy that spread from the spot where his lips first brushed her skin. Her knees grew curiously liquid, melting in the heat that was flooding her body, all because of a mere touch on the hand. *Am I going daft?* Kate wondered, despising herself for her weakness, yet she could not pull herself away.

When he lifted his head at last, his gaze, a blend of defiance and abiding sadness, held her in thrall. Deep in that grey intensity was a plea for understanding that bound her in a strange sense of kinship, even as his mocking gesture roused her contempt. He raised his other hand as if to touch her cheek, but when he spoke, the spell was broken.

"I swear," he repeated softly.

"There will be no more of that," she said, snatching her fingers from his grasp as if bitten.

"I know," he said with genuine sorrow as she took a step back, her face flushing. "I know."

Chapter Four

" 'Tis near ready we are to go!"

Kate whirled, wondering just how much Daisy had seen. From the vehement tone of her abigail's voice and the annoyance in her eyes, likely too much. Luckily, it seemed that Lord MacLean's untoward gesture had been hidden from her daughter's view. Kate forced herself to relax, trying to wipe away the traces of her own apprehensions. There was no need to add to the child's burden of fears, especially if they were going to stay after all. Still, the events of the previous night had taken their toll. Gone was the confident, laughing little girl of yesterday afternoon. Daisy was struggling to carry a bundle with one hand while keeping hold of Anne with the other. The child was being less than cooperative, clutching at the doorsill, her face tearstained as she struggled to break free. For Anne, this moldering place had been as close to paradise as a child could wish for.

With a sigh Daisy dropped her load and tugged at Anne's arm, trying to detach her grip. "Had to shut the dog in the pantry, I did," she explained, panting as she unclenched the small fingers one by one. "She don't want to leave the beast behind, much as I tell her." She knelt down to sweep the squirming girl into her arms, speaking softly. "We cannot be taking Cur with us, Annie-child, even were he ours to keep. 'Tis a long, hard journey we have ahead of us."

Although she addressed herself to the wee one, Duncan felt the serving woman's smouldering anger. But the older woman's wrath did not disturb him half so much as the expression in the child's eyes when she caught sight of him. Just as it had the night before, the stark fear in those pools of green cut him to the marrow. It was clear that her mother, as an adult, was able to mask her revulsion. But the girl's horrified countenance was as revealing as a mirror. He was a monster now, a man whose aspect was enough to cause children to quake in terror. With a choked sound Duncan turned away. "You need not worry for the lass, Kate," he said, trying to keep the pain from his voice. "She need not see me at all. There's more than enough to do about this place so that I can be out of your way in the daylight hours. Tell her that the ogre will not be troubling her. I came here to be alone. I shall just follow on my original course."

Kate hesitated. Once more her feelings had changed with the capriciousness of a weathercock in the wind. He was actually offering to absent himself for Anne's sake, to consign himself to the darkness in order to avoid frightening the child. To Kate, that meant far more than any oath that the man might make. The defeated slump of MacLean's shoulders told as eloquent a tale as the slight tremor in his tones, confusing her, rousing guilt. He had come to this wreck of a place for solitude, to hide like a wounded animal. How could she allow him to hide himself away in his own home? *But it would be easier for you,* a small voice whispered.

"I could not ask that of you, milord," Kate said, torn between her conscience and her fears. "I do not believe that it will be necessary." Briefly, she considered telling him a bit of the truth, that it was not MacLean specifically that Anne feared, so much as any male who bore the hint of a threat. But Kate hesitated to vouchsafe even that small comfort. MacLean was already too curious by half, someone who would not be satisfied with a mere snatch of the whole. There would be the inevitable questions, answers that might not be credited, even if she could afford to give them.

"What's all this bletherin' about?" Daisy asked, shaking her head in puzzlement. " 'Tis the best of the daylight that we're a'wastin' and miles to go before nightfall."

"We can stay, Daisy," Kate said, crossing the courtyard to touch Daisy on the shoulder. "His lordship has given us leave to remain here."

"And what's the devil demand as his due?" the older woman asked, her brow beetling with indignation. "Same as last night? If it were, than 'tis best that we take ourselves away from here, I'd say."

"No, Daisy," Kate began to explain, shaking her head. "He—"

"Think upon it, my lamb," Daisy pleaded, putting her hand on her mistress's arm. "Time comes when you got to be considerin' of your self. T'aint right, even for little Anne's sake. Think upon what manner of man he is to be forcin' you to this pass. They say in the village that there's a curse upon them, The MacLeans; with good reason, seems to me. 'The sins o' the fathers,' the Bible tells us—"

"I will leave you to finish your sermon," Duncan said, his teeth clenched tight. "If you find you wish to stay after contemplating my illustrious sire's wrongdoings, my man and I will take our evening meal after the child is abed. If not . . ." He reached down and dug into his saddlebag, pulling out the purse that Dewey had given to him. The leather bag flew from his hand with all the force of Duncan's frustration behind it. With a clinking thud the purse burst open upon the flagstones, spilling its golden contents at Kate's feet. "This will more than suffice for the value of the livestock and whatever repairs you have made. Take it and leave me in peace."

He was about to walk away when he heard a burst of barking. Instinctively, Duncan turned.

"How'd he get loose?" the maid asked, lunging to grab at the streak of fur, but the dog slipped past. "Cur, come, Cur," she called in vain.

Duncan raised a shielding hand to his throat, warding off the attack that never came. The collie stopped just short of him, sniffing the air as if in puzzlement. It was not possible. Yet, even though Duncan knew full well that Piper had been long past his puppy days twenty years ago, he could not help himself. "Piper?" he asked softly, slipping to his knees. This dog had the selfsame look, down to the white patch on his left flank. With an intelligence that seemed almost human, the animal cocked his head to one side in an expression of canine disbelief. Giving throat to a whimper that was part greeting and part bewilderment, Piper's great, great-grandson acknowledged the homecoming of Eilean Kirk's master. Duncan felt the rough texture of the dog's tongue against his cheek. For one brief moment he felt like a boy again, reveling in one of the only genuine loves that he had ever known. "Piper," he whispered, wanting to believe the soft fur against his cheek belonged to the one creature that he had wept for all those years ago.

A small shadow blocked the light, and Duncan looked up, reluctantly facing reality. Anne had obviously slipped from the servant's grasp, but when Daisy made a move as if to retrieve her, Kate held the woman back. The girl planted herself opposite Duncan, her hands on her hips in a gesture that made her seem like a charming miniature of her mother. With a pout she stamped her foot.

The collie raised his head at the child's unspoken command, then turned back to Duncan. His feathered tail wagging in agitation, the dog eyed the man and the child as if torn between the two. "She needs you more, old man," Duncan said softly, in the Old Tongue. The collie gave him a look of canine approval, seemingly concurring with Duncan's decision. He padded to Anne's side, and the child's pudgy arms locked about him. Silken curls mingled with mottled fur as she hugged the dog.

"You can take him with you if you would like," Duncan said. "It seems that he prefers you to me."

The corners of Anne's mouth trembled. Had she suddenly realized that she was confronting the gargoyle? For one agonizing second Duncan thought that she was going to cry. Then it dawned, a shy hint of a smile that disappeared so quickly that he knew he must have imagined it. Before he could look again, her face was buried in the animal's furry neck.

"Just like a man, to vex one," the older woman complained with a snort. "After I was tellin' the child how we has to ditch Cur because he ain't ours. What will we be doin' with a dog, I'll ask you?"

Duncan rose and left without a word. He had caused enough trouble. Much as he hated to admit it, Kate's servant was right. His offer of the dog had only added to Kate's distress. They were going to go; there seemed no question now. It would be best if he was gone when they took their leave. A bracing morning swim in the loch might help to put jumbled thoughts in order. Perhaps, when he returned, he would have the solitude that he craved. Why was that thought strangely depressing?

Daisy knelt on the flagstones, for once, heedless of the dirt. Eagerly, she sifted through the debris until she had found every last coin. "The man must have his attic to let. Far more than the animals is worth, he gave us. Nigh on to fifty pounds here, I'd say. More'n enough here to get us to a port. Then betwixt what we could get for your ma's brooch might be enough for passage money. Nothin' fancy, mind, won't be private cabins with places at the cap'n's table, but it'd get us to Americay, and were that signet ring what you got sold, we might even have a bit of a stake left over."

"I thought that you feared for your scalp, Daisy," Kate said, a wry smile touching her lips.

"Rather savages than that 'un," Daisy said, nodding in the general direction that MacLean had followed. "A dangerous man, no mistaking it. Give him so much as a finger, and he'll be to your wrist, and once he's past the wrist, my girl, there's no tellin' where he'll go."

Kate flushed.

"I can see what's what," Daisy continued, heedless of Kate's discomfiture. "Ain't but twice I've come face-t'-face with the man, but it's plain as that scar, the hunger. Looks like a man starvin', and you a prime roast."

"Beef or mutton?" Kate asked.

"Now don't you be mockin' me," Daisy said, wagging a warning finger. "He wants you, wouldn't of said what he did last night if he hadn't."

"Daisy, I spoke to him this morning. He said that we may stay, without any obligation," Kate explained. "He was badly provoked last night, after all we—"

Daisy rolled her eyes heavenward. "It's startin', heaven help us all. Now you'll be askin' me to be puttin' my own self in his shoes. Next you'll be tellin' me how kind he really is."

Kate shifted uncomfortably. "He did leave us nearly fifty pounds."

"Aye,"—Daisy chuckled—"so he did. And seems to me we ought to take it and quit this place while we still can. While he's still willin' to let you go."

"I think you are misjudging him, Daisy," Kate said, re-calling how gently he had treated Anne. "Sometimes wounds run far deeper than scars."

Daisy looked at her mistress anxiously. "Don't be doin' that now. Just like your pa you are. He was a soft touch, and it was everyone from the drummer boy to Wellington what knew it. There ain't a man what came to him with a tear in his eye and a hard-luck story that came away with an empty hand," she recalled. "T'was my milk that suckled you, Katie, and 'tis hopin', I am, that you got some common sense from it. Sometime there ain't no shame in retreatin'."

Kate considered her friend's words, weighing all the pos-sibilies. She was honest enough to admit that Lord MacLean did present a danger, but not because she worried that he would break his word. Somehow, she knew that his oath would bind him. It was herself she feared, this strange reac-tion to a man that she barely knew. But was that small risk worth leaving the isolated haven of Eilean Kirk? It was fool-ish to hope that John had given up on locating them. There was far too much at stake.

Kate looked at Anne, happily playing with Cur, almost as if the night before had never happened. Twice the child had defied MacLean. To be sure, in the first instance, Anne had reacted to a perceived threat to Kate's well-being. But the second time . . . ? Kate regarded her daughter thoughtfully. If Anne were truly frightened of MacLean, then there would be no question of staying. But Kate had watched the con-frontation in the courtyard carefully. If anyone had seemed intimidated, it had been MacLean. The tension in his ex-pression would have been almost comical were it not so pitiable. His anxiety regarding the child's reaction to him had been an almost palpable force. Perhaps that was why Anne had behaved with such odd fearlessness. Kate had lit-tle doubt that even a child could easily read what was so ob-viously writ on his countenance. Besides, if Anne were in terror of MacLean, she would never have dared to approach him, much less remain near him once her objective was achieved.

The wind blew, rattling a loose shingle and causing it to slide to the ground. To be sure, the castle of Eilean Kirk was not a mansion in Belvedere Square, but it was far better than the alternative. Kate's throat tightened as she recalled those first frantic weeks when she had felt like a fox with the pack's breath on her tail. It had taken every stratagem she could muster to evade John's hounds—through the briars and brambles of London's stews, trying to hide their scent at Dover before backtracking and heading north. The journey had almost been beyond endurance, and now they might have to run again . . .

"Anne!" Kate called, beckoning the child.

The little girl hesitated, but after a moment, she led the dog with her to her mother's side.

Kate knelt and cupped the child's face in her hands. "Sweetheart, I want to ask you a question, and I expect an honest answer from you."

Anne nodded slowly, her eyes filled with curiosity and not a little apprehension.

"You know that we are prepared to leave here," she continued. "But Lord MacLean has offered us the opportunity to remain in his castle for the time being. Would you like to stay?"

Daisy uttered a sound of protest, but a look from Kate quelled her.

"Lord MacLean will be living here, too, Anne, as well as his servant," Kate continued, watching her daughter closely for any change of expression. "It is *his* home, but he has agreed to share it with us for now. Do you understand, Anne?"

Once more, Anne nodded an affirmative.

"Do you wish to stay, Anne?" Kate asked. She could almost see the thoughts whirling through the child's head, the same uncertainty and trepidation that Kate herself felt. "Or shall we leave here and find a new place for ourselves?"

"What are you thinkin' to be leavin' this to the wee one to decide?" Daisy asked, unable to contain herself any longer. "We're goin', and that be that!"

"If Anne fears Lord MacLean, then we shall be leaving, regardless of any other risks," Kate agreed, dusting off her skirt as she rose. "I will never allow Anne to lie awake in terror again, Daisy, you know that." Kate felt a tug at her knees and looked down at her daughter. "Do you have your decision, sweetheart?"

The little girl nodded.

"Is it your wish to go?"

Anne shook her head in a vigorous negative.

"We can stay?" Kate asked, to be absolutely certain of Anne's answer.

Anne nodded yes her eyes going to Cur, then back to her mother in an obvious question.

Kate laughed. "Of course you may go back to playing, my dear."

" 'Tis because of the mutt she wishes to stay," Daisy grumbled. "Anne would keep company with Lucifer for that mangy hound's sake, I'm thinkin'."

"No, Daisy, I believe not," Kate said, slowly. "You recall when we ran from Steele House, she left everything behind without a murmur, all the things that she had loved, her toys, even the kitten that I gave her last Christmas. If MacLean truly worried her, I think that the dog would make no difference."

"Aye, like a puppet the poor mite was," Daisy recalled, sadly. "Might have been a bit o' wood."

"It took months for her to come this far." Kate pressed her point home. "She is almost happy here. If we uproot her again . . ." She shook her head dismally.

"But to stay here with that man! Sell your ma's brooch, I say, and the ring, too."

"You know that the ports will still be watched," Kate argued. "As for the signet ring, it is not mine, but Lord MacLean's. The ring and the book of poetry that he left to Adam are in a packet upon my bed. He really ought to have his things back, particularly the ring. He looks as if he is not particularly well to do."

"Might've known you'd do something like that," Daisy grumbled in exasperation. "But that was before his lordship was flingin' gold purses at your feet. Don't seem to me like his pockets are to let! T'would fetch a tidy sum, that ring, with that big ruby in it. Besides, leavin' that behind for his lordship is as good as leavin' a callin' card with your name upon it."

"I had not thought of that," Kate said ruefully. "It would surely give us away."

"Aye." Daisy nodded. "Best to take the signet with us, I'd

say. Don't sell it, if you don't want, but keepin' it against a rainy day seems good to me. The brooch might give us enough."

"Selling Mama'a brooch would be as good as leaving a marked trail behind us, too, Daisy." Kate pursed her lips. "It is a rather distinctive piece, and John has surely given its description. Heaven knows it was the only piece of jewelry that he could not take away from me on the pretext that it was some family heirloom that was too valuable to keep about. How could I have been so very blind, letting him hack to bits any claim to independence that I had?"

" 'Tis not your fault, lamb," Daisy said soothingly. "You couldn't have known."

"Couldn't I have?" Kate said bitterly, watching her daughter fling a stick for Cur to fetch.

"We'll be far enough away from him in Americay," Daisy said.

"There is *nowhere* far enough," Kate said, her fists clenching at her sides. "John would pursue us to the gates of hell, even if he thought the devil himself was sheltering us. We will stay here for as long as we may, Kate, and pray that we have covered our trail."

By the time he reached the brink of the loch, Duncan barely had the patience to shed his travel stained clothing. Clouds were rolling in from the west, carried by a brisk breeze that ruffled the water with white. Without doubt there would be a storm by evening, turning the eastern pass into a muddy sluiceway, but they would likely be well beyond the mountain trail by nightfall even with a child in tow . . . or would they? He hesitated, glancing back up the path toward the castle, then shrugged.

They were likely gone; besides, the old biddy would likely ascribe the worst of motives to any recommendations that he might give. Once they were off his property, the women would cease to be any concern of his. Their leaving was all for the best anyway. All he had wanted was to be left in peace, to be alone. Even Fred's presence had been a grudging concession. Two women and a brat . . . he was well rid of them. No, it would be a waste of time to go back, he told himself as he fumbled with the fastenings of his

worn trousers. Poised at the brink he stood, caught unaware
by his reflection in the deep pool. Since La Purgatoire, Duncan had avoided any form of mirror, knowing, yet unwilling
to see. Until now.

The gaunt man who gazed back at him in bewilderment
was scarcely recognizable as Major Duncan MacLean.
Waves of wild, dark hair fell well past the nape of his neck,
a far cry from the fashionable Brutus that had once framed
his face to perfection. The powerful body of Duncan's recollections could bend a steel bar on a wager; ride, run, and
wrestle till the day was done; then drink most men under the
table before whiling the night away with some wench. The
man in the lake seemed unutterably weary, fragile as thistle-
down. Scarcely a spare ounce of flesh covered that bony
frame.

Strength and endurance would gradually return, Duncan
knew. In that respect, each day was a bit better than the last.
However, some things were forever beyond recovery.
Slowly, the reflection's fingers rose to push back the black
curtain of hair, revealing the scarred track that led from the
edge of his lips to the orbit of his eye. The image's hand
trembled as he slid off the rough patch, allowing the concealing cloth to slither to the ground. The one-eyed creature
stared back in stark horror, the hollow face contorting in a
grimace of pain. A low, keening moan wafted over the waters as Duncan finally accepted the bitter reality. Mercifully,
the marred visage in the pool wavered, blurring with the ruf-
flings of the breeze. He knew that he did not wish to wait
until it returned to clarity.

Duncan's dive cut the water with barely a ripple, bringing
him rapidly to the icy heart of the spring-fed depths. The
cold was a welcome shock, clearing his mind of any
thought. He let himself drift with the tug of the current, carrying him away from shore toward the channel at the center
where his mother had warned him that the water-folk
played. Bred in the Highlands, she was, knowing every invisible danger. Mama had armed him with charms and in-
cantations against the evil forces that craved nothing more
than to snatch a small boy from his mother's arms.

The "ghoulies, ghosties and weird beasties" that Burns
had written of had always been lurking in the darkness just

beyond the quilts during his childhood. But all of Mama's lurid descriptions of hants and the banshees had paled in comparison to his father. The sobs and screams that rang through Castle Eilean Kirk always had earthly sources. Despite the hordes of hell-spawned apparitions that reputedly haunted his home, the only tormented souls that Duncan had ever met were all too human.

His lungs began to demand air, but still he made no move toward the surface. It was a game that he had played often as a boy. He was a selkie, seeking the entrance to the fairie home at the bottom of the loch. They were waiting to welcome him down below, the water-folk, for they knew that Duncan had never truly been The MacLean's son, but the spawn of the selkie King himself. There would be feasting, singing, and dancing all night when he returned to claim his kingdom. They would weave him garlands of lilies and crown him with precious stones mined from the deep.

Suspended almost motionless in the water, Duncan watched as a school of fish slipped within inches of his fingers. It was so tranquil, this silent world, more in focus to his halved vision than the one that he had left behind. What a pity he had never found that selkie portal, he thought as he looked toward the surface. *The light seemed so very distant . . . hardly worth the effort to attain . . . lungs were fit to burst . . . a few seconds more might be cutting it too close . . . why bother? One deep breath was all that was required. No one would care, with the possible exception of Fred. Give a monkey to see the man's face when he realizes that he's the sole heir to the MacLean fortune . . . but then I'll be dead . . . roasting with Papa . . . So dark up there . . . the clouds must have thickened to block the sun . . . storm brewing . . . too soon . . . Kate!*

Powerful kicks propelled him upward as he pushed back arms full of water. Bright spots whirled before his eyes as his air-deprived brain made foolish demands that he open his mouth. With one last powerful thrust, he burst to the surface. Chest heaving, he floated face downward, barely able to lift his head to fill his lungs in gulps.

"Maaajor . . ." Fred's voice floated over the face of the loch.

Weakly, Duncan turned his head and swallowed almost as much water as air. The shore seemed miles away, and his side was aching.

"I'm comin' t'get yer!"

From the splash that followed, it was clear that the damned fool actually meant to pull him in. Duncan would have called out, had he the strength, that there was no sense in the two of them drowning.

"Over wit . . . yer."

Duncan was unnerved when he felt a strong hand pushing him under. He was about to grab his tormentor by the neck when a particle of sense penetrated his panic. Forcing himself to relax, he allowed Fred to turn him on his back. Duncan winced at the sharp pain in his scalp as Fred began to pull him toward shore, using hair as a towline. The current was working against them, and it seemed an age before they finally reached the shingle.

"What'n the devil . . . did yer think . . . yer was doin'?" Fred panted the question as he collapsed on the lee beside his master.

"The . . . backstroke?" Duncan answered weakly.

"Facedown? Lucky . . . I'm . . . a Thames rat," Fred coughed out the words. "Learn ter swim real fast . . . yer does . . . if'n yer pa tries to drown yer . . . six nights outer seven."

"You're . . . a . . . veritable . . . Cockney spaniel," Duncan said, trying to catch his breath. "I . . . take it . . . that your father rested . . . on the seventh . . . day."

"Drunk as a lord . . . by Sunday . . ." Fred smiled weakly, but the grin vanished as he raised himself on an elbow to gaze at his master, sprawled naked in the mud. The bantam shook his head in silence.

Duncan shuddered inwardly at Fred's expression of quiet rebuke. He had expected a tongue lashing, a cesspool of invective at the very least, but this wordless remonstrance was beyond bearing. "Say it, Fred!" he demanded.

Fred sighed.

"Tell me that I am a careless idiot!" Shaking, Duncan drew himself up on hands and knees. "Tell me that I have skated too close to the edge once again. I would have been all right, Fred, I swear. All that was needed was a few minutes to catch my breath."

Fred raised one hoary eyebrow, but said not a word.

"And so what if I hadn't? You were a fool to go in after me," Duncan said, his voice trembling. "I left a revised will with Dewey in Edinburgh. You would have been a wealthy man if you had let me drown, Fred. If I go, everything is yours. Far better you than the Crown."

"Damn yer bloody 'ide!" Fred exploded, scrambling to his feet. "Ain't got th' sense the good Lord gave a flea!"

"I am touched by your gratitude!" Duncan said. "And, as usual, your judgement is entirely correct. I must have been muddled in the mind to think that you would want a blasted fortune."

"Iffen I'd 'ave lived t'enjoy it!" Fred retorted. "Just what did yer think would 'appen if yer turned up drownded with a will like 'at 'un jist made? Finger would 'a been pointed at yers truly, sure as the devil's in Lunnon. Iffen I 'adn't come along when I did an' seen yer dive an' not comin' up . . ." The little man shivered, as much from the thought as from his wet clothing. "I'd 'ave ended me days dancin' from th' nubbin cheat, like as not."

It was chilling to realize that his man was quite probably right. Servants had swung on the noose for far less circumstantial evidence. "I am sorry, Fred, I hadn't considered that," Duncan said, chastened. "If you would prefer, I can alter the terms of the will."

"Aye, Major. Yer can leave me a goodly sum if yer o' mind ter," the servant said. "But not all. Wouldn't be proper."

"Nor, as you say, prudent," Duncan added with a touch of mockery. "How much of a sum would you deem 'goodly'?"

" 'Nuff so's not ter give me no motervations." Fred shook his head solemnly. "Long with what yer owes me in me back pay an' what I won off'n yer in wagers, I ort t'be well set." He gave his master a long look. "Right soon, too, with th' way yer seems t'be bent on stickin' yer spoon in th' wall."

"What in blazes does that mean?" Duncan asked, indignantly hauling himself to his feet.

Fred just rolled his eyes heavenward.

"Just because there have been a few close calls of late

does not mean that I am attempting to put a period to my-self," Duncan protested.

A harrumph of patent disbelief was his only answer. "I did break Selkie to saddle," Duncan asserted. "And got him for only half a guinea."

"Damn near broke yer neck, more like it," Fred retorted. "An' th' beast's marster woulda gived 'im away. Already kilt a stable 'and, an' near bit a groom's 'ead orf. An' what about th' dray, eh?"

"I didn't see it coming," Duncan maintained. Or had he?

"Jist stood in th' middle o' th' bleedin' road. Iffen I 'adn't 'ave pulled you outer th' way . . ."

"Yes, yes . . . I know full well what could have been," Duncan said, his temper returning along with his ability to breathe. "You have saved my skin more times than I care to admit, Fred, but it was entirely accidental this time."

"Aye." The word could scarcely have been more skepti-cally delivered. "An' last night when she could've blowed th' two o' us to Kingdom Come."

"That is absurd. Any fool could see that she is not the kind to pull the trigger," Duncan maintained.

"Any *fool*," Fred repeated, "don't walk up arskin' t'be shot."

"That ancient fowling piece should never have gone off," Duncan mumbled, looking at his feet, rooting out a pebble with his bare toe.

"But yer were 'af 'opin' it would, weren't yer?" he asked. "An' what 'appens if I ain't by next time yer decide to 'ave one of yer accidents, I arsk yer? Damned near lost yer when yer climbed up that bloody cliff, didn't I?"

Those rheumy eyes focused on Duncan, daring him to an-swer. The glint of tears was almost as unbearable as the pain in the older man's gaze. Duncan turned away as he recalled his thoughts on the summit. He plucked a pebble from the bank and tossed it toward the loch's center, watching the rip-ples spread as he tried to find words. There was no denying that the thought of ending it had been tempting.

"It weren't yer fault, Major." Fred broke the silence. "T'was them what chose t'cut n' run when yer told 'em t'stay put, bloody fools. Yer'd think they'd of 'ad th' sense t'mind yer, seein' 'ow you was th' one what 'elped 'em break loose o' th' place. Th' Frenchies picked 'em orf th' beach like bleedin' fish in a barrel."

Duncan clenched his fists as he looked unseeingly out onto the water. "They were my men, my responsibility."

"They were arses!" Fred maintained. "Stoopid arses 'oo dinnent foller orders. Yer weren't th' one what got us in a Frenchie prison, but yer th' one what got us out."

"No, it *was* me that got us into prison," Duncan disagreed, picking up another rock to toss with controlled fury. "Had I not been fool enough to confront Vesey before the battle, we would never have been in that situation. I have little doubt that he was behind the orders that sent us straight into the enemy's lap."

" 'E meant yer t'be kilt, Major. That's certain, an' no never mind 'oo were to die with yer," Fred reminded him. "But yer alive. Seems yer weren't meant to die thrown from an 'orse or drownin'. Iffen yer truly feel yer owes them men somethin', yer got to stay among th' quick."

"Aye," Duncan conceded, focusing on the distant shore. The little man was right. A ghost could not exact vengeance. "Vesey will pay, I swear it."

"Never known yer t'break yer pledged word, sir," Fred emphasized, satisfied for the moment with the vow that he had extracted. He could only hope that the force of that oath might be enough to keep Lord MacLean from stepping off the edge of despair. But once that promise of revenge was fulfilled . . . Fred stifled a sigh. Perhaps by then, Duncan MacLean might have something to live for. "Let's find yer clothes. Yer won't be no good ter no one, iffen yer dead o' lung fever." He put a hand on Duncan's arm.

Duncan reached over and grasped his servant's hand. "How many times now have you saved me from myself?" he asked.

"Not near as many as yer saved me 'ide," Fred said, giving himself up to recollection. "Woulda flayed me to pieces, you 'adn't come along when yer did, plucked me right offen th' whippin' post. An' I mind me o' th' time—"

The man's fingers were like tentacles of ice. "Tell me when we have reached an even score, Fred." Duncan cut him off. "You fetch your horse and get back to the castle to dry off. I shall attempt to locate my trousers and shirt, though I confess it scarcely worth the effort considering their sorry state."

"Ain't goin'; not wifout yer," Fred said, his teeth chattering.

"I will be fine," Duncan said, giving Fred a gentle push. "You need not worry about me now."

"T'ain't you what's th' matter." Fred jerked his head in the general direction of the castle, his teeth chattering as he spoke. " 'Tis *er* with th' skillet. I know 'er kind. Looks t'be a right sweet armful, but an 'art like ter a stone."

Duncan chuckled at the thought of Kate's companion as a "sweet armful." But his amusement faded at the rumble of distant thunder. "She likely won't be there, Fred, so you need not fear," he said, squinting at the sun, trying to ascertain how much time had passed since he left the castle. "When last I saw them, the women were intent on leaving. Kate is likely convinced that I am the devil incarnate."

"Must 'ave more 'air then wits, to quit with a storm brewin'," the older man commented, his brow furrowing. "Is th' way we took o'er th' mountains th' only way 'ere?"

"Aye, 'tis called the Hellgate." Duncan nodded. "And by the feel of it, I'd say the wind is blowing from the north. The pass will become a veritable mudslide when the torrent hits."

"Weren't fit for a goat when we got by," Fred observed.

"And they've a wee bairn with them," Duncan added, worry seeping into his voice.

"I left me 'orse tied up on the causeway," Fred said. "T'was from there that I saw yer. I'll bring 'er up and unload 'er straightway. Got plenty o' time to fetch th' women and babe back afore th' storm 'its."

"I shall meet you at the castle," Duncan agreed.

Chapter Five

Duncan snatched up his garments, pulling on small-clothes and trousers, nearly tripping over his own feet as he tried to hop into his boots at a half run. The squall was moving far faster than he had anticipated, the clouds already hiding the peak of Beinn Airidh Charr.

Deliberately, Duncan forced himself to slow down. Fred was correct, of course, even if the women had left immediately, a man on horseback might easily catch up with them well before they reached the Hellsgate. There was no need for him to rush. If he was to persuade Kate to stay, his chances for success might be improved by a decent appearance. Duncan tied the arms of his shirt about his waist, resolving to change to a clean one. *Aye, and a pair of unsoiled breeches might be helpful. And perhaps,* a self-mocking voice continued, *a shave and a haircut? Might as well put a razor to an ape, MacLean. Dress a monkey in pumps and a chapeau bras and he's still a beast, worthy of mockery at best, pity at worst. Do you honestly think that she would come back, that she would trust a man with a face like yours?*

The courtyard was empty, the bundles gone from beside the door.

Have you no pride, that you would go chasing after a woman who would only have you as the best she could make of a bad bargain? the voice asked. *Are you a dog that you would beg for any bones that she might throw you?*

Duncan picked up his saddle and headed for the stables. Although the stalls themselves were a near-ruin, the sheltered pasture behind was still relatively secure. "Come on, laddie," he said as Selkie whickered a greeting. " 'Tis an errand of mercy that we undertake."

With a snort that was too close to a laugh for Duncan's comfort, Selkie tossed his head. "Remember, were it not for me, you would be a gelding by now, so take care if you think to mock me, m'boy," Duncan said. "I will admit that my motives are somewhat selfish. Dewey said it could be months before the tangle is unraveled. Can you imagine a winter with only Fred and a deck of cards for company?"

The horse whinnied softly. "Aye, you can well afford to affect scorn. Grass and oats are bread and meat to you, laddie. You've no need to endure Fred's cooking; and mine is worse by half. Mayhap we can convince the ladies to stay once we bring them back?"

He was about to hoist the saddle onto Selkie's back when he heard a bark that seemed to be coming from the upper pasture. There was a chorus of angry squawks and the whirr of frantic wings before a covey of birds burst from the cover of the trees. The first pheasant had barely gained the sky when she fell. The second plummeted earthward, landing nearly at Duncan's feet. He picked the bird up by the protruding arrow shaft. Poachers; more than one, most likely, considering the two shots followed so nearly one upon the other. While Duncan had no objection to a hungry man taking a bit of game, he could not like anyone hunting so close to the castle.

The rustling noise from the far corner of the pasture sent Duncan seeking for cover. Bow hunting was often a poor man's means of conserving precious shot. However, there was a fair chance that the poachers had more than arrows at their disposal. Unarmed and probably outnumbered, it would be extremely unwise to confront his crofters now and ring a peal over their heads. Considering the legacy of regard that his father had cultivated, they would be more likely to shoot their new laird than listen to him.

Kate leaned her bow and quiver against the ramshackle fence before scanning the pasture. There was no sign of the fallen bird, but the sight of the stallion capering near the stables was almost enough to make her forget the game. Such a magnificent creature! Even though Adam's stables had been accounted excellent, they had contained nothing to match the sheer power that was apparent in the animal's every move. Besides, she thought glumly, even if Adam had owned that stallion's match, she would never have been permitted to ride him. How she had loathed it, scorned those timid lady's mounts, hated riding confined to discreet trots at the proper hours, perched on sidesaddle, dogged by grooms. But she had endured for Adam's sake, trying to be the wife that he wanted, the porcelain doll, wrapped in the cotton batting of convention. But that cozy world had been an illusion.

The stallion had noticed her, and he galloped toward the gate.

"Ah, you are a handsome brute," she crooned admiringly.

Her voice carried clear across the open field. Kate? It was Kate! Duncan took a measured breath, trying to understand this contradictory feeling of elation. It was beyond the bounds of reason this strange vacillation. What did it matter to him that she had chosen to remain? The solitude that he had craved so strongly would be entirely spoiled. But this was no time for contemplation, he reminded himself, not with poachers skulking about. However, before he could step from his concealment and warn her, she spoke again.

"Did you see where my pheasant fell, my beauty?" she asked the stallion. "I know that it must have hit ground nearby."

The huntress? Although the idea seemed absurd on its face, somehow it fit. Duncan peered cautiously beyond the crumbling stone wall that shielded him from view. Kate was half hidden by the brush and the fence, but he could see the bow leaning against the gap. He still could not quite believe that she had gotten off two arrows in rapid succession. Then again, the woman seemed to be a veritable quiver full of surprises. The stallion ceased his capering, stopping just short of the fence to rear and paw the air. But instead of drawing back in fear, Kate laughed. The sound was wonderfully startling, wholly at odds with Duncan's expectations. This was not the shallow chime of bells, the polite tinkling that he had heretofore defined as female laughter. Slow and mellow, her mirth rose from some source deep in the very heart of that small body. Never before in Duncan's experience had there been anything like it, incredibly sensual in its earthy contralto range, running up his spine like fingers on a pianoforte. Her head was thrown back, her neck a long column of sun-gilded alabaster. Though he knew it was madness, he allowed himself to recall the feel of her skin, the silken touch of her hair.

"You are a show-off, to be sure. Do you think to impress me with your airs?" she asked with a grin that seared Duncan to his core. By thunder, was he jealous of a horse now? There was no deceiving himself any longer. It was neither fear of Fred's company nor his cooking that was causing this insanity, Duncan knew as he watched her hungrily.

"Do you want an apple?" she asked, rummaging in her pocket. "They are rather small, for the orchard was near to ruin. I always carry a few with me when I hunt. One never knows how long it will take, but we were lucky today."

"We were lucky." So, she did have a hunting companion. Somehow, Duncan could not picture Daisy in the role of a stalker. One of the men from the village perhaps? An oddly annoying thought, but the direction of his ruminations were altered abruptly as Selkie trotted closer to the fence. Duncan was about to call out, to warn Kate away. The stallion had more than once been known to bite the hand that fed him, but Selkie nipped the proffered apple with the daintiness of a dowager at tea.

To Duncan's amazement Kate scrambled onto the fence and began to rub Selkie's mane. Even after nigh on two months, the balky horse would not let Fred come close to him, but in the space of a few minutes Kate had the stallion close to purring like a contented cat. However, the horse's reaction was less oversetting than the sight of Kate herself in breeches and a boy's shirt. Why was it that those ill fitting garments so disturbed him? They covered as much as the most modest of gowns. Yet, the masculine cut somehow served to emphasize the feminine charms beneath, hugging curves, suggesting softness.

Kate knew that she ought not to. The mount must certainly belong to The MacLean. Yet, the horse seemed to be taunting her, butting himself playfully against her shoulder, nearly knocking her from the rail as if encouraging her lunatic thoughts. The temptation of freedom was beyond resisting. To gallop, to fly on horseback if only for just a few moments would be more than enough, and Duncan Mac-Lean need never know of it. As if the stallion somehow understood, he sidled closer, standing stock-still. Grabbing a handful of mane, Kate used the fence as her mounting block, sliding herself on to the horse's bare back in a swift motion.

Disbelief held Duncan rooted. She could not be so utterly reckless, to ride an unknown horse with neither reins for guide nor saddle for grip. But by the time he was convinced that his vision was telling true, it was too late. Beast and woman became a single creature, a melding of hair and hide, horseflesh and skin that was almost seamless as they cut through the tall grass, gaining speed.

As they rode beyond the narrow pale of his view, Duncan stepped from his concealment and watched them soar effortlessly over a fallen log. The air filled with a childish whoop of glee as her long braids flew behind, the plaits of copper mingling with Selkie's light mane. They turned at the corner of the pasture with the precision of a crack regiment on parade and he caught a glimpse of her face.

It was as if he was truly seeing her for the first time. The weight of care and wariness was gone, her face wholly open and unguarded. She wore the joy of the moment, shedding the mantle of mistrust that cloaked the fire of a untamed spirit. Green eyes glowed bright, lit like faceted emeralds by the exhilaration of her smile. A wild thing she was, in the freedom of that untrammeled flight, as much girl as she was woman.

Still as a lead soldier, Lord MacLean stood by the stables, his shirt tied carelessly about his waist, despite the growing chill in the air. Freed from its queue, The MacLean's damp hair curled at his shoulder, the sunlight shading it the many-hued dark of a raven's wing. His arms were folded across his torso, throwing the night-colored whorls on his chest into shadowed relief. As she drew closer, she tried to read his expression, but his face was an impassive mask. The horse danced to a halt before him, but he made no move, said not a word to break the damning silence.

There was no choice but to dismount on her own. Apprehension made her awkward as she slid from the stallion's back and she nearly fell in a heap on the ground. There was no excuse that she could think of as she scrambled to her feet. How could she hope to explain the impulse that had grown to a need? Surely, no man could understand what it was to spend a life shackled by convention.

Did she realize the eloquence of her expression? Duncan doubted it, else she would be much better at masking her emotions. Although her back was ramrod straight, her eyes were green pools of uncertainty. He moved forward and, involuntarily, she took a step back. That small gesture of fear cut him like a whiplash, releasing all the anger that he had tried to rein back. "Are you mad?" he shouted. "You could have bloody well killed yourself! Selkie is no Hyde Park hack, not the compliant pieces of cat's meat that ladies are wont to ride, my girl!"

My girl, the phrase reverberated in her mind, but she heard Adam's voice. *You are being childish, my girl . . . Have you no concept of proper behavior, my girl?* Always those two hateful words tacked on to every rebuke, simultaneously reducing her to both chattel and child, usually followed by a sigh, a look of regret that told Kate that she had failed once more to meet Adam's lofty standards. *Ah, whatever shall I do with you, my girl.* "I am *not* your girl," Kate said, her fists clenching by her side. She saw Lord MacLean, but it was not to him that she spoke. "Moreover, you have likely surmised that I am not of that vapid breed known as 'lady.' "

Duncan's anger diminished as fascination came to the fore. Her voice was quavering with obvious emotion and her eyes blazed bright.

"I have survived, milord, although I once thought that nothing could be a worse ordeal than a Wednesday night at Almack's," Kate declared, reaching beyond the shame, the feelings of inferiority. That woman, the weak dependent female that Adam had wished her to become, could never have reached this place, never have brought herself and his daughter to safety, she reminded herself. "I have survived."

Somehow, she had grown in the space of a few moments. Gone was every trace of the irresponsible girl, playing the tom in borrowed breeches. Her voice was soft, but there was considerable dignity in that quiet declaration, justifiable pride if the pain in her eyes was any indication. He saw terrible knowledge in those depths. "Aye," Duncan said, jarred by the recognition. Other than Fred, his companion in hell, Duncan had never before encountered anyone who understood. "I too, know something of survival . . . and its cost."

"Indeed," she agreed, recalling herself to the here and now, "endurance has its price."

"And its limits," Duncan added, looking pointedly at his horse. "No matter that you might show them a trick or two at Astley's Amphitheatre, you cannot depend on luck."

"And you have never been tempted to try the bounds of your luck?" Kate asked. To her surprise, a red flush spread beneath the unshaven stubble on his chin. Fearing that she had roused his ire once more, she hastened to apologize, trying to tell him that she was not some untried greenling who might bring a horse to ruin. "I should not have used your stallion without leave; for that, I am sorry. However, the chance that I took was not a great one. Papa was always telling me that I spent too much of my time about the stable yards. Selkie has a bit of the devil in him, true enough, but there is not a horse worth riding that does not. And he is a champion, milord, as good a piece of blood and bone as I've ever ridden. 'Tis like flying, I vow, a wondrous, smooth gait." Her lips tilted in a wry grin. "But you know that."

"As false an apology as I have ever heard," Duncan said gruffly, but he could not hold on to his anger. How could he in the face of that small, self-deprecating smile and her enthusiasm? "You would do it again in a minute, 'Mrs. Smith.' "

"I am sorry, milord," Kate repeated lamely, her head bowing as she cursed her foolish tongue. How could she have been so stupid as to endanger everything with her fits and starts? Perhaps Adam had been right after all. "If you wish us to leave now, I understand. I cannot blame you for taking me into contempt."

"Leave"— the word hit him with the force of a blow. In less than a day, the solitude of a hermit's existence had suddenly lost its savor. "Why would you think that you are deserving of my disgust?" he asked.

Was there any means of salvaging the situation? Kate wondered. She should have simpered, affected meek subservience, the air of helplessness that she had learned at great cost. That was what men truly wanted; she ought to have taken that lesson to heart by now. Although it was likely too late, at least she might try. She had managed well enough to dupe most of Society. The London hostesses had looked tolerantly upon her, although she never achieved the brilliance that would have satisfied Adam. Even John had regarded her as a cipher.

But when Kate dared to look up, she knew that the timorous facade that had fooled others would not deceive this man. His dubious inflection upon "Mrs. Smith" had been a warning, a line drawn in the dust. There was only so much that he would leave unquestioned. That steely slate eye penetrated too far, told her with a look that there could be no more deception. Caught out at last, Kate gave a brittle laugh.

"Do you roast me, milord?" she asked, drawing at the baggy knees of her breeches and sketching out a mocking curtsey. "Do you see that I am the epitome of genteel womanhood? La, sir, you do jest, surely. Well, I freely admit that what I do to a pianoforte could set the milk to souring, but I can shoot the pip from a card, milord, set a snare, or tickle a trout, then clean and cook what I catch. Titter at me behind your hand at the Prince's levee when I make use of the wrong fork, but I can tell which foraged mushrooms would soon have you sticking your spoon in the wall and which roots could satisfy your stomach. Put me on a fine horse and I vow, I can lead you a dance, but you waltz with me at risk of your toes."

"Would you, 'Mrs. Smith'?" he asked, softly.

"Would I what?" she asked in confusion. Her eyes were starting to sting. She would not cry.

"Waltz, of course; were I willing to put my feet at hazard, that is," Duncan said, noticing the telltale glitter, the furious fluttering of that fan of lashes as she struggled to maintain control. This was the second time that she had refused to use tears as a weapon. No female in his past acquaintance had ever been restrained by that compunction.

"Why are you trifling with me?" Kate shook her head. "I am by no means a proper type of female. Heaven knows Ad . . . my husband told me so often enough."

"Did he indeed?" Duncan snorted, watching as she self-consciously tucked in the trailing ends of her shirt. How small the span of her waist seemed; he was certain that his two great paws could easily encircle it. Not a proper female? Had the man been blind? Could there be anything more feminine than those delicate features, the sculpted planes of her cheeks, the generous lips that seemed made to smile or to kiss? What could be more womanly than the body that he had held all too briefly the night before, the soft flesh, the clean female scent? Yet, although this pocket Venus seemed as fragile as spun glass, she was made of stronger stuff and therein, perhaps, was the answer. "Then your husband sounds like a bloody fool. Did he wish you to become a Dresden figurine, Kate? To live upon his shelf and be admired?"

His perception was wholly disconcerting, much too close to the truth. Kate opened her mouth to deny, but thought the better of it. Far wiser not to speak at all. She had already betrayed too much.

"Did he fancy himself Pygmalion then?" Duncan sensed his advantage and pressed the point. "I had always thought that the gods did Galatea no great favor when they brought her to life. 'Tis an easy thing for marble to maintain perfection, but when Pygmalion's creation became flesh and blood, I warrant she was bound to disappoint him. Is that who you are running from, 'Mrs. Smith?' Did Galatea suddenly find that she had dreams of her own, a will that would not be chiseled to suit the sculptor who would shape her to his own image?"

"You are a fanciful man, milord," Kate said, trying to conceal her sudden confusion. "I had always thought that rogues were of a pragmatic frame of mind."

"And how did you become aware of my rakish history, 'Mrs. Smith'?" he asked, advancing slowly.

She had made a grievous tactical error, in fact, several, she realized as she rapidly tried to recall what else she had let slip. It was so long since she had allowed herself to be carried away, to give vent to her true feelings. What magic did this man have to make her so reveal herself? "Your behavior is common knowledge . . . the crofters . . ." She left the words dangling, hoping that they would be adequate.

They were not.

"I left this place at the age of fourteen," he said. "As far as the crofters were concerned, I might as well have fallen off the rim of the earth and good riddance. The last news to reach beyond the passes of this corner of Wester Ross was likely the Bonnie Prince's defeat."

"Very well then, if you must know." Kate gave a shrug of feigned indifference, knowing that any retreat could be fatal. "The 'Mad MacLean' was something of a byword in military circles, milord. Your exploits both on and off the battlefield gained you no little notoriety."

Her use of his sobriquet gave the explanation credence, but he knew that it was not of whole cloth. Something was missing, and he pressed the attack once again. "Almack's, military circles, dining with Prinny does not add up to 'Mrs. Smith' poaching off the land and existing hand to mouth. I find myself tiring of this 'Mrs. Smith,' nonsense. We both know it to be a fiction, so I refuse to call you by that last name any longer. Tell me, why are you here, *Kate*?"

Once again, she found herself scrambling to maintain her position. "If you think me a liar, milord, perhaps it is best if we go," she said, facing the possibility that the battle was lost.

"Is he a brute, Kate? Did he hurt you? Or the child?" For a brief instant he saw something flare in her eyes, then disappear as quickly as it came.

"No," Kate said, meeting his gaze squarely, "there is no husband searching for me, milord. Anne's father is more than a year in his grave and he would never have knowingly harmed his daughter or me."

That was truth; there were no lies in that straightforward look. "Then why? Why have you abandoned the world of Mayfair and the beau monde? Were you left destitute? Is that why are you hiding at the edge of nowhere, living in a crumbling ruin?"

"It was not truly my world," Kate said. It was a private opinion that she had never voiced to anyone except for Daisy. Why was it so easy to tell a stranger of her grievous failure? "With my husband gone and my funds limited, there is nothing for me there now. In honesty, I sometimes wonder if there ever was. As for your question, I turn it back to you, milord. Why have you returned here? To a crumbling ruin?"

Duncan lifted his eye beyond her toward the stone turrets

of Eilean Kirk. "Why? Aye, well you might ask! Why would I leave London when Lady Jersey and all her fellow patronesses were fair to swooning at the sight of me? Abandon Town though His Highness would have me at his right at his next Carlton House fete to thank me for the service I gave my country? T'was my duty as The MacLean to hie to my auld ancestral home, to enjoy the splendor, the adulation of my clan," he said, the burr adding bite to his sarcasm. "My mother would be calling it destiny, that this hanted place is the only thing that is left to me. We Scots are great believers in the forces of fate, you know. Do you put credit in destiny, Kate?"

Thinking of the twists and turns that led her to Eilean Kirk, Kate nodded. If she had not gotten Ian Dewey's belated letter that accompanied the inheritance that MacLean had left to her dead husband . . . if Dewey had not chanced to mention that the castle was deserted and inquire if there might be any possible interest among Adam's friends . . . Her father had always held that every step was guided by providence, but Kate had hitherto been convinced that the attentions of fortune were capricious. Now her opinion was decidedly a mixture of the two. She was a wealthy woman, but she dared not touch a penny of her funds lest John trace her. She was beyond her brother by marriage's reach for the time being, but well within touching distance of her late husband's unusual comrade. It made that sea-wracked space between Scylla and Charybdis seem quite comfortable by comparison.

"You never answered my first question, though I've answered yours. Why did you decide to come here, of all places?" Duncan demanded, continuing to advance.

He was *close*, within a hairsbreadth of breaking his promise. As for her, if she so much as lifted a finger, she would graze that bare expanse of skin. For a brief instant she was tempted to tell him everything, to rely on the strength that seemed to radiate from him. But with so much at risk, Kate could ill afford to gamble on the integrity of a rogue. "Ah, but you have already given the answer, milord." Her mouth curved in a poorly attempted smile. "Fate."

"And if I demand a more precise explanation?" Only strength of will kept him from closing what remained of the gap between them. She seemed so vulnerable, her fear pal-

pable despite her brave front. Although there had been many
women in his past, he could not ever recall feeling this urge
to comfort, to hold and protect. Never had a sworn oath
seemed so fragile a barrier.

"Do you wish us to remain here?" she countered, wondering what the answer would be. He could not like it, for
MacLean seemed the sort to dictate terms, not accept them.
Yet, she could see the hesitation in that singular core of grey,
and she began to hope. But there was something else in his
gaze that was oddly unsettling, something undefinable but
undeniably dangerous.

"Stay . . ."

The word seemed torn from his throat.

"Please . . . stay . . ."

There was a sound from the brush, and Cur came loping
toward her, the other lost pheasant cradled in his mouth. She
bent and took the bird, glad of the excuse to turn away from
that raw force that beckoned to her, drew her like iron to a
lodestone. "Good boy," she murmured, stroking the collie in
approval. No, it was not lust in Duncan MacLean's expression, for Kate had already seen him wearing his rakehell's
mask of desire. The emotion in that glimpse was far more
disconcerting. It was need that spoke . . . the raw, desperate
need of a man who has suddenly discovered himself to be
entirely alone. "Cur is a most excellent gilly, is he not?"

"Your hunting companion?"

"Yes," she said, avoiding the scrutiny of that lone eye as
she reassessed her position. Every instinct cried danger, told
her to cut her losses and retreat. She had already said too
much. Daisy's warnings echoed in her head, but as long as
the threat was to Kate alone, it was tolerable. He had given
an oath, she told herself. If the game got too deep, they
could always pick up stakes and go. It was still the best of
bad choices. "Since you will still allow it, we shall stay.
Now, milord, if you will forgive me, my partner and I will
flush a few more birds before the storm hits."

Clearly, he was not invited. "Aye, Fred will be needing my
help unloading." Reluctantly, he turned back, pausing moments later at the promontory that overlooked the loch. There
she was, directly below him, still as a marble sculpture as the
collie flushed the game. As the birds rose into the air, she drew,

sighted, and shot so swiftly that the arrow was in the air before he could blink. He had been fairly good with a bow once, but even before his eye was lost, he could never have laid claim to such skill. Now give him a pistol or a rifle . . . doubt assailed him. He had not fired a shot since the escape from La Purgatoire, and those recollections were numbing. The man who could be three sheets to the wind and shoot the cork from a wine bottle could barely sight a target. Fred had been the one to place the shots where they were needed.

A bark from below sounded as Cur plunged forward to retrieve the birds, the woman moving behind him with the feline grace of a stalking predator. Duncan closed his eyes and envisioned whirling Kate around a ballroom, imagined her seeing him as he had been, dressed in regimentals, his face whole and handsome. If she had seen him then, when he had been able to make a female smolder with a mere look . . . but he was no longer an incendiary man, and he could not blame her for avoiding the sight of him, looking anywhere but directly at him. After all, he could barely stand his own reflection.

Yet for a moment, for an all too brief snatch of time, he could swear that she had forgotten his disfigurement. She *had* looked at him directly, even smiled at him, and, he reminded himself, she had decided to stay of her own free will. Perhaps she was not as terrorized as he supposed.

Or, his inner voice gibed, *she fears what is out there more than she dreads you, MacLean*. Once more, he was fooling himself. With a stifled sigh he started slowly for the castle. His thoughts were interrupted by the sound of raised voices. Duncan groaned as the yard came into view.

"Put that biscuit back, or I swear, I'll pop you one, I will," Kate's woman declared waving a cast iron skillet threateningly. "You'll eat with the rest of us!"

"Can't." Fred got the single word out of his full mouth then swallowed, but his cheeky grin disappeared as the angry female advanced. "Ain't never 'it a mort," he declared as he backed away. "But I'll defend meself, I will. Now let me be about me business, woman." The little man gave a resounding sneeze, punctuated by a rattling cough.

"Bad enough, you stealin' the food out of our mouths. You'll be the death of us too!" she declared. "Just listen to you, sounds like it's gone to the lungs already, it has. Don't think I'll be nursin' the likes of you, you thievin' jackanapes."

"Rather be dead," Fred called, shaking his fist. "All this fussin' 'bout a wee bitty biscuit an' a few wet clothes."

"Must be somethin' about bein' born within the sound of the London church bells rings all the sense out of them Cockney heads. Next time you go takin' a bath, you might try undressin' first. Shakin' like a leaf you are, 'tis a wonder your hand was steady enough to snatch that food from under my nose," she said, lowering her skillet and voice. "I got some hot soup in the kitchen. Now take them wet clothes off, little man."

"Yer'd like that, wouldn't yer," Fred said with a leering smirk. "Don't see many fine figures o' men 'ere do yer?"

"And I ain't likely to see none now," the woman retorted. "I've seen scrawny roosters that'd do better than you for the dressin'! Though I must say, you have somethin' of the look of a drippin', plucked chicken."

Fred's rubbery lips fell into an indignant scowl, his fists clenched at his sides. Amusing though it was, Duncan decided to put an end to the Punch and Judy show. "I will unload the supplies, Fred," he said. "It looks as if you've already finished with most of it."

"Ain't done nothin' yet, 'cept kept me noggin from bein' bashed," Fred said with a frown as he gestured toward the paltry array of sacks. "That's all there is, barley, bit o' oat flour, some sugerloaf, salt; couldn't even git yer a razor to take place o' th' one what yer lost and with mine broke this mornin' we'll both be lookin' like 'ermits afore th' week is out."

"What else happened, Fred?" Duncan asked, reading more in his servant's expression. "Obviously there is something that you are not telling me."

"Nothin'," Fred mumbled. "Ain't much t' spare in th' village. 'Ad t'show 'em th' coin first, sir, afore I saw so much as a grain of barley."

Duncan skewered him with a look. "What else happened?"

"The sot brain told them that he was from the castle," Daisy informed his lordship. "Gave them the glad news that you was still this side of hell, milord. T'was a wonder that they didn't hang him on the spot."

" 'Ush yer bleedin' mouth." The bantam-faced man shot her a threatening look.

"He might as well know of it," Daisy argued. "Better to know where you stand with the folk here, I say. Tell him."

"I believe Daisy is right, milord," Kate agreed as she led a small donkey into the courtyard, a brace of birds slung over the blanket on its back. "I fear you will not find much of a welcome down in the village."

"I expect no joy at the sudden resurrection of the house of MacLean," Duncan said, his tones clipped. "But I will not suffer my servant to be abused."

"I weren't 'urt none," Fred hastened to reassure him. "No man what I know of ever got killed by a lick o' spittle in th' face. I'd 'ave learned 'em a bit o' respect for their betters, though." He shook his fist. "But I ain't one to be strikin' at no Methuselahs."

Duncan frowned, knowing how much it must have cost the prideful little Cockney to swallow such gabble, even from old men.

"You mustn't blame them, milord. 'Tis a poor place," Kate explained, "a worse hole, I would warrant, than some I have seen on the riverside streets of Lisbon."

"Surely you exaggerate," Duncan said, recalling the filthy warrens and tavernas that abounded near the Tagus. Some of them had made the sewers of Whitechapel seem like Mayfair by comparison. "The village was fairly prosperous when I was a boy. I know that my father was in the habit of taking what he would without a thought to paying back the tradesmen, but they seemed to do well enough nonetheless. Even though they knew him to be from the castle, Fred had gold in hand."

"Gold will not buy what is not to be had," Kate said, responding to the puzzlement on his countenance. Perhaps she had misjudged him; it appeared that he was genuinely unaware of the state of his people. "There is but one shop left in the village, and that hardly stocked with a few staples. You will find little to spare here and naught beyond the barest of necessities."

"What caused the change?" Duncan asked.

"You are aware of the Clearances?" Kate asked cautiously.

"No need to beat around it," Duncan said, his jaw tightening as he realized what she was getting to. "When I was a stripling, my father was well on his way to fencing and claiming any bit of bog that he could for sheep grazing, and woe to the crofter who stood in his way."

"Then you know that there was an exodus then, not just from here, but from much of the Highlands. Many of the young men left," Kate explained, nodding "When your father died and you were presumed dead, the flocks were sold. That left almost no means of making a livelihood. Entire families headed for the cities, and from what I understand, a good many of Eilean Kirk's boys are in Canada now. I sometimes read the letters that they pay someone to write to those that they left behind. 'Tis mostly old people who eke out a bare existence as your tenants, milord, grandfathers and grandmothers, those too timid or too weak to seek a new life or those who fear that their leaving would be the sentence of death on those that they love. Perhaps they think that you intend to dun them for the rent that they cannot pay."

Outrage blended with sadness in her voice. Did she dare to blame him then? It was not his fault, he told himself, but his father's. Duncan had not set foot here since he was a boy. "You seem to know a great deal about my crofters, madame," Duncan said.

Kate shifted uncomfortably. "They thought me your widow."

"They must have accounted you as something of a heroine," Duncan murmured. "Few and far between are the MacLean women who managed to survive their spouses."

"I was a great disappointment, actually," Kate said. "They believed that I had returned to rebuild, to fulfill some kind of prophecy and make Eilean Kirk prosper once more, but they soon realized that I was as poor in the pocket as they themselves were. Still, I have done the best that I can to help. I owed them that much, considering how I have deceived them."

"Charlie's bloody curse again, but then you would know nothing of that," Duncan added sarcastically, heaving a sack onto his shoulder. "Were you playing at noblesse oblige since you were, after all, The Lady MacLean?"

" 'Tis no game that I play here, milord," Kate said in frustration. "They are good people who deserve far better than what they have had. I do what I can as a human being. The blind toleration of suffering diminishes us all. No matter what name or title we may hold, we are obliged to help where we can."

"No wonder you did not take well in London," Duncan remarked, setting the sack down beside him. "Such dangerously republican sentiments would likely put you straight in scandal broth were you foolish enough to voice them publicly." His annoyance changed to surprise at the sight of her face, suffused pink with consternation. "I would swear that you did!" he chortled. "Did you defend the Luddites, too?"

"Do you justify the penalty then? To kill a man for breaking a weaving machine so that his family will not starve?" Kate barely choked the words out. How did he manage to do find all the scabs and pry at them? "We have only to look to France to see what can happen when people are driven to desperation.

"'The starved mechanic breaks his rusting loom
And desperate mans him 'gainst the coming doom,'" she quoted. "Though I hate to admit it, I find myself agreeing with that reprobate Byron."

"Ah, but he has the advantage of being a charming scoundrel," Duncan said, "he can get women to agree to almost anything from what I recall."

"A characteristic which you share," Kate retorted.

"I did—once." Duncan stared at her, daring her to look him full in the face. He had to know; it was important to him to see the disgust that she was masking so successfully, to accept that he was loathsome to her. Surely, that would stop these absurd flights of fancy. He had spent half the night imagining her in his arms. Such dreams were a distraction that he could ill afford. "I find now that I cannot get women to agree to much of anything, especially you, Kate."

She knew neither the stakes, nor the rules, but a hand had just been dealt to her, and somehow she was aware that the next play was the critical one. Kate searched the rough shadowed planes of that square-set jaw, followed the straight unsmiling shape of his mouth, the wounding line that reached far beyond the surface of his skin, that single grey eye that was bleak as a storm-beset crag of stone. His expression yielded no clue.

That frank search was agony, looking at him, through him, the shallow man that he had been, the hollow man that he had become. The examination of those jade eyes seared at the remnants of his soul and asked questions that he dared not answer, not even in silence. But she did not look away. She did not look aside, even when she spoke at long last.

"If you cannot get me to agree, it is because I have always been a most disagreeable woman, milord," she said, her lips curving gently. "Or so I have been told, so you need not fear that all is lost."

That soft smile was like a healing balm, and Duncan wondered what manner of man her husband had been, what fool could have such a woman and value her so lightly. If only he had found her before . . . no, there was no lying to himself beneath that crystal gaze. He would have used her if he could and discarded her eventually, just as he had so many others. The "Mad MacLean" would never have thought to search beneath that pretty surface, to see the courage and decency of the core of her. Then again, a woman like Kate would have stayed well clear of him. She might not abhor the sight of him, but she had precious little respect for the man that he had been.

"Well, leastwise we don't 'ave to go chasin' yer up to the 'ellsgate now," Fred said as he picked up the sack at Duncan's side.

Kate's look of bewilderment prompted Duncan to explain. "We feared that you might attempt the mountain pass. Fred and I were going to go after you."

"We was." Fred punctuated his agreement with a sneeze. "Sewercide, t'would be, with th' rain like to be comin' by the bucket."

"So it is called the Hellsgate, an apt name for it," Kate said, touched that he had planned to come after her. She watched as Duncan untied the shirt from his waist and draped it around the shoulders of the shivering man. The simple gesture told her far more about Duncan MacLean than he could ever have imagined. It was something that her father might have done, one of those many small acts of kindness that his brother officers had often derided. Yet, Papa's men would have followed him through the true gates of hell.

Indeed, in the end, they had. For if ever the devil had gained dominion on earth, it was at the battle of Rolica. It was hard to believe that the stupidity of one man had led the 29th to disaster. But Papa and his men had followed orders and followed Lake up that narrow gully to their doom. According to the accounts not a one of Papa's men had faltered or fled. From the look of near worship upon Fred's face, Duncan's servant would likely do no less if called upon. "Has the rain already fallen in the village?" Kate asked. "You are soaked to the skin. How odd, since the storm seems to be turning. I suspect that we might not get so much as a drop here."

To her surprise the little man turned as bright as a lobster on the boil.

"There are just some things that are beyond prediction," Duncan said hurriedly. "Eilean Kirk is known for its unusual atmosphere."

"Aye," Fred agreed, giving Duncan a measured look. "And th' fishin', too. Never know what yer kin haul out o' th' lake."

"I caught a salmon that must have weighed at least four stone," Kate agreed.

Duncan gave a strangled gargle that sounded to Kate like a smothered guffaw, but that was nigh to impossible; Duncan MacLean seemed incapable of laughter. Obviously, he did not believe her. "Well, I did," Kate said defensively.

"I'm sure you did, milady," Fred said, his brow wrinkling as he smiled. "Mighty big fish in them waters. Ahr . . . Ahr . . . choo!"

"No more fish stories, Sergeant Cockney and bull," Duncan said, taking the burden from the small man's shoulder and gave him a gentle push. "Dry off and get something warm in you; consider that an order."

The Cockney cast him a dubious look, nodding his head significantly at the woman who stood in the kitchen door.

"Do as your master says," Daisy said, setting her skillet on the windowsill. "So long as you don't go touchin' nothin', I won't bite you, little man."

Fred cocked an eloquent eyebrow. "Wonder what yer got to touch to get bit?" he asked in an undertone for Duncan's ears alone.

Duncan shook his head at the glint in Fred's eye. There was absolutely no explaining tastes.

"Let me give you a hand, milord," Kate said, undoing one of the knots that held one of the larger sacks in place.

Duncan's look plainly spoke his doubt.

"My strength would surprise you," Kate said, her expression amused as she easily hefted the burden from the saddle.

"You are a woman of many surprises, Kate," Duncan said, putting his own load down to firmly take the sack from her hands. "If it is your aim to make me feel inferior, I must vow that you are succeeding. You have already proven you are my peer as a rider and my master with a bow. I have no doubt that you could school Gentleman Jackson in the science of boxing, paint pictures to rival Lawrence's portraits, fly a balloon higher than Sadler, and explain natural history to Faraday. However, *I* will do the hauling, madame, if you do not mind. Leave me that small illusion of superiority at the least."

"I am hopeless with a paintbrush," Kate confessed with a smile.

"I am most comforted to hear it," Duncan said in mock relief as he lifted both sacks, trying not to grunt at the effort. "Now if you truly wish to be of assistance to me, you might go and exercise Selkie. In fact, consider his care to be one of your daily duties. He and Fred never got on very well together, and I doubt that I will have the time for such mundane chores."

Her grin spread from ear to ear. "You cannot mean it, milord!"

"What, do you go womanish on me at the thought of stable dung?" Duncan hid his amusement behind the burden. "If you feel that the stallion might be too much for you—"

"Oh, no, milord," Kate interjected. "I would account it a privilege."

"Saying that you actually enjoy mucking stables is doing it a bit brown, don't you think?" Duncan asked.

Kate groaned.

Chapter Six

Vesey's eyes adjusted quickly to the dim light. Of late, Chloe always preferred to keep the shades drawn. In his estimation it was an excellent sign that the drug was taking its course, causing a slow but inevitable decline. The doctors, of course, were easily fooled, unwilling to admit that they could neither diagnose nor treat his wife's supposed ailment. They clucked their tongues, quacked her with a myriad of nostrums, and presented their bills. Unfortunately, the price of getting away with murder was proving to be high, but then he could well afford it. It would be said that John Vesey had spared no expense to cure his unfortunate spouse.

"My darling," Vesey murmured, forcing himself to take hold of his wife's bloated fingers and bringing them briefly to his lips.

"John," she whispered, blinking as if not quite sure of his presence. "Have you had any word?"

"Nothing, my love," Vesey said, bowing his head in feigned sadness to hide his anger. "There is not a trace of Katherine or the child."

"I vow, I nearly wept when 'Silence' Jersey asked about dear little Anne today . . . or was it yesterday?" Her voice trailed off in confusion.

How in the devil had Lady Jersey gotten in to see Chloe? He had given strict orders that his wife not be disturbed. It was most unfortunate that she had found out about Katherine's disappearance. The servant that had let it slip had been dismissed without reference. However, most of Society still accepted the story that Lady Steele had retired to the country and thus far, Chloe had supported the Banbury tale, eager to avoid scandal. Nonetheless, with Chloe's deteriorating condition, there was no telling what she might say. If word got out, people might start to wonder, begin to ask questions . . .

"John, I meant to ask you . . ." His wife flitted to another topic. "About the maid, the one who was found floating in the Thames . . ."

This time Vesey allowed his anger to show. "Who told you?" he exploded. "I vow, they will be out on the streets by day's end."

"John!" Chloe exclaimed, putting her fingers over her ears.

"I am sorry, my love," Vesey soothed. "It is just that I would protect you from these sordid realities."

"And keep me from knowing what is taking place in my own household," Chloe said with a trace of her former shrewdness. "T'was Lady Jersey who made mention. It would seem that her abigail was the chit's aunt. She was barely fourteen, John, though she appeared much younger, more of little Anne's age."

"The lower orders," John mumbled, as if that were all the explanation necessary.

"Poor Anne." Chloe's mind wove back to her former topic. "I cannot believe that Katherine would do such a horrible thing. To steal my jewels was a foul deed, but to take the Steele heirlooms as well! They are part of the entail, Anne's inheritance."

"Yes, 'tis hard to believe that Anne will inherit a barony in her own right," Vesey declared, his fists clenched.

"The Steeles are an ancient family," Chloe said, warming to one of her favorite topics. "It is quite unusual that a title can descend through the female line."

As Chloe droned on about Charles I, royal charters, grants, and William the Conqueror, Vesey's thoughts were running in circles. The female line . . . a pity that Adam had not gotten himself killed sooner, before he married and sired a pretty little obstacle. Once more, Vesey examined all the possibilities. Chloe would die of course, though he dared not increase the dose beyond its present level, and then he would be free to marry again. Katherine. His tongue slipped stealthily over his lips as he thought of his brother-by-marriage's widow. She had refused his attentions before, but what of a licit liaison? Would she agree if it was marriage that he offered this time? Was that why she had run away? Or was there another reason? Could she have discovered . . . Vesey shook his head. It was impossible of course. He had been so very careful, made absolutely sure that the secret would be kept.

". . . do about the maid, John."

Something in his wife's voice brought his attention back to focus upon her. "Dear?"

"Your attention is wandering," Chloe said peevishly. "I was just saying that the maid ought to be replaced."

"I will see to it myself, my love," John promised. Younger, this time, with curls and green eyes, innocent green eyes.

It was wet, cold and wet. Anne's eyes flew open, glowing emerald in the light of the bedside candle. Cur whined softly, his rough tongue licking her fingers with canine urgency. Grabbing the cloth of her nightrail, the collie gave a gentle tug.

Her mother stirred and sighed, "Duncan," the Sad Man's name. Poor Mama, too tired for even a bedtime story, yawning out the words to Anne's favorite poem about the tiger. Lucky Mama knew it by heart, 'cause her eyes were half closed when she turned the pages. It was all *his* fault. Since the Sad Man came, Mama was always working. She said it was because they had to get ready for winter, but Anne knew that Mama just didn't want to be where the Sad Man was. When the Sad Man was out fishing, Mama was in the garden. When the Sad Man was fixing the goat pen, Mama went out hunting. Mama didn't seem to mind the Smiling Man, neither did Daisy, though she was forever telling him that he was a nuisance and underfoot. Daisy liked the Smiling Man, that meant. Wasn't she always calling Anne a nuisance and telling her that she was in the way?

Daisy turned on the truckle bed. Mama had wanted her to sleep on the big bed when she had moved into the room when the Sad Man and the Smiling Man had come, but Daisy said that wasn't her place to sleep with the mistress. Anne had been glad that it wasn't Daisy's place since Daisy snored really loud. Even from the floor near the fireplace, Anne could hear the harsh, rasping in-and-out sound.

Cur whined softly, tugging once more at Anne's gown. Stealthily, the girl slipped out of bed, her bare feet quiet on the cold stone floor. She took the candlestick in her hand, glad that it hadn't burnt itself down to a nub yet. It couldn't be too late, that meant, since her mama had lit a new one just before bed. Anne hated the dark, feared it, but with the glow of the light and Cur to guide her, she stepped into the corridor.

There was no sound in the shadowed hall, save the rhythmic click-click of Cur's paws on the stone, until they were midway down the stair. Then it came, a slow moan, echoing upward, rising then dying into silence. Anne clutched at the collie's furry coat tugging him back, but the dog would not halt. Instead, he seemed determined to pull her onward, down toward the bowels of the kitchen to confront whatever it was. Given the choice of facing the darkness with dying candle or a ghost in Cur's company, Anne chose the latter.

The dog led her to the door of the cramped room behind the kitchen that was once Daisy's place, before the Sad Man and the Smiling Man had come. There was little light from the window in the chamber, but she could see the hulking shadow of the Sad Man tangled in the sheets. There was no sign of the Smiling Man, save a disarranged mound of blankets on the floor. He was gone! Had the ghost got him? Perhaps that was what Cur wanted, for her to wake the Sad Man.

It began as a whimper, then rose in pitch until the aching sound of loneliness and loss filled the small room. Anne moved closer and watched the Sad Man's sleeping face twist; he was hurting. The sliver of moonlight touched his cheek and made it shine with wetness. The Sad Man was crying in his sleep. Anne suddenly understood. Poor Sad Man, with no Mama to chase the bad dreams away.

Kate blinked, instantly awake, her insides knotted as a clenched fist. Daisy's snore echoed across the room, strong and reassuring. It was the dream, Kate told herself, that idiotic dream that had woken her. Once more, she had been in Duncan's arms; once again, he had been holding her, his mouth hard upon hers with an all-consuming hunger. Although she had been able to partially avoid him by day, Kate could not evade him at night. Shameful though it felt, she did not want to. Two kisses were the sum of her experience, yet over the past three weeks, imagination had woven those brief moments into a tapestry of emotion, the feel of his hand, the texture of his tongue, the taste of his lips, the deep rumble of his voice, and every shade of grey from laughter to desire in that single mocking eye. Far better to dream of him than to face that reality.

As the drowsiness dissipated, Kate began to feel that something was wrong . . . missing . . . the gentle sound of Anne's breathing. Frantically, she pulled away the cover beside her. Anne was not there. "Anne?" The chamber pot in the corner was unoccupied. Kate drew a deep breath as she tried to arrange her thoughts. The candle by the bedside had been taken. Surely, the child would not have gone outside by herself? Not with her fear of the dark and of . . . Daisy murmured softly, turning on her side and her sawing ceased momentarily.

At first, Kate thought it was the wind howling so mournfully or the distant melancholy baying of a lone wolf, but this sound was not coming from the window; it came through the open door.

"No," the Sad Man cried. "Leave him alone . . . he's only a boy. *Il est un enfant.*"

Anne cocked her head, watching the Sad Man, wondering what he would do next. He was sitting bolt upright, his eye open, but she knew that he didn't see her. He was seeing the boy.

"Do not dare touch him. Stay behind me, Colin, lad."

The boy named Colin.

Kate heard Duncan's voice from the stair. "*Non . . . non* . . . aren't you men enough to find yourself a woman? He's only a child for heaven's sake."

"Anne?" Kate called, seeing the glow of candlelight. She turned the corner and was startled to find her daughter standing by MacLean's bed, with the candlestick trembling in her hand. He was sitting bolt upright, his bare chest slick with a sheen of sweat. "Lord MacLean?"

But there was no reply, just a cold forbidding stare, a look that held both terror and threat.

The girl ran to bury her face in the soft flannel of her mother's gown.

"You bastards! You buggering bastards. If you want him, you will have to come take him," Duncan roared, his arms thrown wide as if to bar a path. "Stay behind me Colin; they will have to get past me, laddie."

A nightmare; he was in the throes of a horrific dream. Kate moved forward, ready to pull him from the grips of his imagination's conjuring.

"No, ma'am, don't be wakin' 'im now." Fred came from behind Kate and put a restraining hand on her arm.

"He's in pain," Kate said, her eyes upon that agony-contorted face. "You must wake him."

"Aye, I will, but not jist yet, else I'll 'ave a fist in me face," Fred said, putting himself between them and his master. "Won't know yer, nor me. Stay clear o' 'im, ma'am an' keep back the l'il miss. 'Ee don't see yer, 'tis Frenchies 'ee sees. Mosttimes, I wakes 'im when 'ee gets ter tossin' and moanin', afore it gits this far. But devil take it, I counnent close me eyes and got ter longin' for a pipeful and went walkin' and smokin'. Best that yer take th' little 'un an' go."

Duncan was panting, his breath coming in great heaves, his eye dark with terrors that Kate could only imagine. "Who was Colin?" she asked Fred in low tones.

The Cockney shook his head. "A drummer boy what was taken when we was. A Welsh lad, couldn't 'ave been more'n a dozen years in 'is dish, sommat o' th' company pet. 'Ee were a pretty boy." The small man glanced meaningfully at Anne before he continued. " 'Ad blue eyes an' lashes long as yer own, ma'am, I swear. Pretty as a lass, poor lad."

Though his words were garbled by haste and heavy accent, there was no misreading the unspoken message in the little man's eyes. Kate felt the blood draining from her face as she recalled Lord MacLean's words.

"The major put 'isself twixt th' boy an' th' Frenchies. Goes wi'out sayin' 'ee counnent do nuthin' o' course, 'gainst men wi' bayernets. But 'ee tried, th' only one o' us what did,

I'm blamed to say. 'Ee bloodied 'em though," Fred said with pride, "bloodied two o' them Frenchies afore 'is eye got put out."

"Non passent." Duncan's eye narrowed as the enemies in his mind advanced.

"T'was Lucifer's own luck, 'ee lived through it. 'Ad a Welsh doctor taken wi' us in La Purgatoor. T'was 'im what saved th' major. Counnent do naught fer Colin though." Fred's mobile face twisted in sadness. "Th' boy wounnent eat, wounnent sleep, wounnent talk when th' Frenchies brought 'im back. Ever seen a locust 'usk, ma'am? Colin 'as like that. There weren't nuthin' left after those bastids got done with th' boy, savin' yer presence ma'am." He glanced down at the child. "Best to git th' wee lass gone, ma'am. She might get scairt wi' what's t'come."

Kate nodded and drew Anne toward the door, the dog following. So far it seemed that the child was more fascinated than frightened. Thankfully, Anne did not seem to understand the drama that was being reenacted before her. "Let us go upstairs to Daisy, love," she said softly, taking the candlestick from the child. "Lord MacLean is having a bad dream."

The girl looked back over her shoulder as if reluctant to leave. Kate knelt beside her. "Do you want me to stay and see if I may help?" Kate asked.

To Kate's surprise, Anne nodded a slow, unspoken assent.

"You will go then," Kate said, accompanying her daughter out the door, "and Cur will go with you. Now get right in to bed, and I shall be joining you in a trice." She watched Anne scramble up the stairs, Cur at her heels.

"Cowards! You won't take him!" Duncan's chin thrust out in challenge.

"Thought I gived yer marchin' orders," Fred said as Kate reentered the small chamber.

"Anne is upstairs; I came back to help," Kate told him. "I have some experience dealing with nightmares."

Lord MacLean's voice grew in volume as the phantom attackers grew closer. He struggled with the empty air, screaming strings of oaths and imprecations in English, French, and Gaelic.

"Ain't nothin' what kin be done, 'cept wait till th' storm

blows by," Fred said, his face relaxing enough to accord Kate a half smile. "Though 'tis right good o' yer, ma'am, t'be offerin'. 'Tis comin' ter th' end now. Might shake th' rest o' th' bedclothes, an 'e's nekkid as Adam were when 'e first oped eyes in th' garden. Gets worse from 'ere on and t'would be shamin' him ter see yer 'ere when 'e wakes."

The urgency in Fred's voice propelled her from the room. The potential for embarrassment far outweighed any possible benefit of her remaining on the scene. Nonetheless, even though she knew the little man to be entirely correct in his reasoning, Kate lingered at the door, torn between leaving and staying. Then it began, the final onslaught. Even though she knew that he fought with shadows, the desperate, brave terror in his voice was beyond bearing. Kate fled.

Halfway up the stair, she faltered as she unraveled the Cockney's earlier words. "La Purgatoor." It could be none other than the fabled La Purgatoire, Fouche's personal ground of torment. Some officers had used it as a goad to their troops, the one threat that would make even the most cowardly of men fight like a berserker rather than be taken. Like hell, it was a place from which no one had ever returned, yet no soldier doubted its existence. And Duncan MacLean had survived it, escaped it.

"Anne!" As she looked up from the landing, Kate could see the candle casting shadows. The child sat whimpering, huddled by the railpost, Cur's head resting on her in an attitude of canine comfort. Kate was up the last stairs in an instant, scooping the girl into her arms. The sounds from below were growing in volume, the terrible shadow battle coming to a close.

Kate had little doubt that Anne had heard it all, every graphic word of the horror that had played itself out in Duncan MacLean's threats and shouts. The child burrowed her head in her mother's shoulder, the bones in that small body quaking. Kate held her daughter close, praying that the little one would not understand his meaning as he invoked both God and the Devil. For a few brief seconds there was an eerie quiet, then a wavering scream that was both rage and anguish.

Kate wanted to weep, to mourn, but she could not, not with Anne depending on her. "Hush love," Kate whispered to the trembling girl, brushing back tangled curls. " 'Tis but a dream, and dreams do not have the power to hurt us. Remember Anne, remember how you would wake in the middle of the night? Your bad dreams went away, and Lord MacLean's will too, in time. Now, hush, and do not be afraid. He is a good man, a very good and brave man, and he has his Fred to help him." Kate picked up the candle.

Anne raised her head, her eyes awash. How much had she comprehended? Kate wondered as the child stared back at her solemnly. Seemingly little, for by the time they had reached the bedroom, the tears had stopped flowing and the girl was sucking her thumb. Daisy was half awake, clumsily groping for the tinderbox.

"Thought I heard the little one, I did," Daisy mumbled drowsily. Kate looked fondly at the older woman. A barrage of rockets could not rouse Daisy, but let Anne so much as mewl, and the older woman would be instantly aware. Long before Kate herself, Daisy had argued that there was something wrong, that Anne's slow transformation from active healthy child to silent wraith was not the natural result of losing a father that she had seen seldom.

Cur jumped up in the bed, placing himself protectively beside the child. "Off with you, you mangy mongrel," Daisy grumbled, moving to shoo him from the mattress.

"Leave him, just for tonight," Kate told her, pulling the cover up and tucking it carefully around Anne.

"Lie with dogs, rise with fleas," Daisy gave the dire warning.

"I will risk it," Kate informed Daisy with a speaking glance before turning her attention back to Anne. "Close your eyes, love," Kate whispered, stroking the soft velvet cheek. "And do not be afraid to dream. Mama and Daisy are here with you." Perhaps that reassurance was enough, for within a few moments, the girl was asleep.

"What happened?" Daisy asked, her voice low. "Where were you?"

"I awoke and found Anne gone," Kate said, rapidly explaining what had occurred.

"Well, don't that beat all," the older woman said, shaking her head in disbelief. "That Anne would go by herself and

stay by a stranger's side. Mebbe she was too affrighted to
leave?"

"I think not, Daisy," Kate said, rearranging the blankets
about the sleeping child. "She was concerned. Anne sent me
back to tend to him. Heaven knows, the child has had more
than her share of horrific nightmares."

"But he's a fearsome-lookin' man, he is," Daisy persisted.
"No less with that beard that he's growed. Makes Fred look
like a picture of a leprechaun I see'd once, but makes his
lordship look like a great big bear. 'Tis a wonder she ain't
quakin' at the sight of him."

"Yes, it is, isn't it?" Kate said, her fingers drifting to cra-
dle her chin and cheek in a thoughtful attitude. "She avoids
him, but she seems to be watching him all the time from a
distance, almost as if she is trying to get his measure. Perhaps Anne's yardstick is a more accurate one than mine,
Daisy, for her assessment seems to be on the mark."

Daisy shook her head in bewilderment.

"I measured the man by the gauge of gossip. I did not
even attempt to see beyond his reputation," Kate considered.

"Well-deserved, from what I heard," Daisy maintained.
"The 'Mad MacLean' was a byword from Bristol to Bengal
and back again."

"And would you have thought that the 'Mad MacLean'
would risk himself in a noble, futile gesture?" Kate asked.
"To place himself in harm's way with no hope of success?"

"Mayhap you misunderstood?" Daisy posed the question.

Kate shook her head. "There was no mistake, except on
my part. He has done nothing but help us these past weeks,
repairing the pens and stable, clearing ground so that we
may get in some late planting, and I have been avoiding him,
as if he were some lowly untouchable. I did not see him
clearly."

"Or you're letting yourself be blinded by one grand gesture, I say," Daisy disputed, settling herself down next to
Anne. "Even the most forsaken man can do one bit of good
and get himself a ticket to Kingdom Come. Could be that
was his lordship's. One minute don't change a lifetime, I'd
say. As for the fixin' and the plantin', 'tis his property and
his belly."

There was no denying the sense of Daisy's argument. But

Kate could not quite reconcile what she had just witnessed with the wild reputation of the "Mad MacLean." The friend that Adam had described was a vain coxcomb, a gambler, a charming scoundrel who viewed women as a challenge and life as a lark. However, the haunted man below had dared to fight a hopeless battle, had paid an awful price for that moment of doomed courage. Which one was he then, the hero or the reprobate? Kate pulled her wrapper tighter around her and went to the window, hugging herself against a chill that had suddenly touched her despite the unusual warmth of this Highland night.

He was out there; the glow of moonlight touched him, wrapping him in a lambent silver sheath.

"Are yer back to yerself, sir?"

She heard Fred's voice.

"Aye, unfortunately," came the reply. "Every time, I find myself hoping that the Frenchies will finish me and put me out of my misery, but lamentably, even my dreams run afoul of luck. Get yourself some sleep, Fred."

"Might be well t'take yer own advice," the Cockney told him.

Kate caught a harsh bark that was not quite laughter.

"There's no sleep for me tonight, Fred, so you can stop playing at Nanny. I'll not be going back to that stifling room. 'Tis too much like a cell for my peace, even sharing it with just one instead of a dozen others. I think that I'll be making my bed out of doors from now on. After two years of not seeing the stars, I still have not got my fill of open skies. I've my blanket and some bottles to keep me company. What more can a man ask?"

The little man sighed, and Kate heard the sound of retreating footsteps echoing against the stone. She went to the wardrobe and pulled out a shawl.

"Where you goin'?" Daisy asked, her lids half drooping.

"To get some air," Kate said. "If Anne calls for me, I shall be right below in the courtyard."

"In sight o' the window?"

Kate concealed a smile. Even partly asleep, there was little that could get past Daisy. "I am not a green girl, my friend."

"I know, but don't you be forgettin' either what he is.

Seen a hundred like him, you have, in your pa's regiment, bold as the brass buttons on their uniforms; playin' with hearts like they was so many draughts. 'Tis a game to him. But 'tis you who have all at stake."

"I am not likely to lose sight of just what is at risk here, Daisy," Kate said, affection mingling with annoyance. Really, the woman was forever treating her as if she were just barely out of swaddling clothes.

Daisy sighed. "I know that, lass."

"I shall return shortly after I have made certain that his lordship has not come to grief."

" 'Tis not *his* grief that brings me to worry," Daisy mumbled under her breath as she watched Kate light another candle and go out the door.

The whiskey seemed to get smoother with every swallow. It was a crime, Duncan knew, to be drinking fine aged Scot's whiskey like so much water, but that was not, by far, the worst trespass that the MacLeans of Eilean Kirk had ever committed. "To you, dear Father," he said, raising the bottle to the sky in a mocking salute, "for having the foresight to lay this in your cellar and the grace to die before you drank every dram."

"Blasphemy, milord?" Kate asked softly.

Duncan spun round. "Well, well, what have we here?" he asked, drinking in the sight of her, the candle in her hand casting a nimbus of light round her face. Her hair fell simply about her shoulders, glowing molten copper with a seductive flame that made a man wish to singe his hands. Kate, with an air of innocence that was breathtaking in its allure, yet entirely at odds with the experience of a widow. Her dressing gown caught the dull moon-glow with an unmistakable gleam. As many light-skirts as he had franked, Duncan knew the sight and sound of silk and marked it as one more inconsistency among the many he had upon his list. Silk and flannel, luxury and poverty, porcelain and steel, fragility and strength, the woman was a walking contradiction.

He took another swig of the bottle, but it did nothing to extinguish the burning sensation that seemed to radiate throughout his body. "No, 'tis the mother's milk of the

Scots, not sacrilege, my erstwhile Lady MacLean," he answered at last. " '*Uisgebeatha*,' we call it, 'MacLean's Gold,' a rare brew, famous throughout the Highlands for its taste. My grandfather filled many a purse with the profits from this liquid gold." He held the bottle aloft in salute. "This batch was distilled before the Prince ever set foot on Scot's soil and there has not been another to match it since Culloden."

"Another aspect of Charlie's curse?" Kate asked.

"Aye, so 'tis said. Now you may either leave, or douse that damned candle. I came out here to enjoy the stars, and you are spoiling it with the light." He did not want her to see him like this, bestial, wallowing in the full measure of his darkness. With better than half a bottle down the hatch, the last thin veneer of civilization had already begun to peel away. He had to make her leave before that meagre facade was entirely gone, before he went down on all fours and bayed at the quarter moon.

The light went out with a gentle puff. Foolish woman, not to know her imminent danger. "I am being behindhand as a host; would you care for a swallow?" It was not so much an offer as a command. No gently bred female would countenance passing a bottle with a half, no, a three-fourths sotted rake. He fully expected her to run.

Trust Kate to do the unexpected.

"Only a dullard would disdain a well-ripened Scot's whiskey," came the reply.

"And you are no dullard, I take it," Duncan said, deciding to give her another chance to retreat. "However, we have no glasses."

"Did I request one?" Kate asked. "You seem to be doing well enough without a proper vessel."

"Half seas over, without a vessel, but well-pickled in the brine," Duncan remarked, "and three sheets to the wind."

He heard a groan.

"Drunkenness is not an excuse, milord, for such word-mangling atrocities. Are you trying to drive me away?"

"Are bad puns the talisman that I must employ as the means of keeping my oath then?" Duncan asked, raising the bottle to his lips once more, hoping to blur the last outlines of her features, to make her but a voice in the dark, but damned if his eyesight did not seem to grow sharper, seeing every plane of her face with impossible distinction. Despite the lack of light, she seemed to glow more beautiful by the moment. "Very well, did you hear of the dolphins who took to abduction and kidnapped gulls for immoral porpoises? Or when Rowlandson published his caricatures of His Highness and his brother Cumberland sans corsets, otherwise known as the 'Prints of Whales.' "

"Spare me." Kate giggled, her eyes growing accustomed to the scarce light, but try though she might, he was nothing more than a disembodied outline, a shadow within the shadows.

The chuckling sound touched his spine with heat, and suddenly the night became uncommonly warm. "I am trying," Duncan said, hoarsely. "Though it is driving me half mad, I would spare you, but you do not seem to understand, Kate. If you want whiskey, here!" He thrust the bottle into the night and felt her take it from him. "Take the rest up to your room and share it with your woman."

Kate cradled the bottle, still warm from his hand and put the lip to her mouth. It was strangely disconcerting, an unexpected communion as she took a slow, small sip and felt the simmering sensation on her tongue. It slipped down her throat lightly, without a trace of harshness, spreading its heat with a languorous touch.

"Excellent," she commented, handing him back the bottle. "I have never tasted the like of it."

Duncan accepted it without comment, then himself took a long, hard pull. Was it imagination, or did the taste of her linger on the bottle's mouth, mingling with the flavor of the spirits? The potent mixture of woman and whiskey became suddenly difficult to swallow and he found himself choking.

"Such whiskey is a treat to be savored, milord. Not guzzled like gin or swallowed in hasty gulps like cheap claret," she commented, coming round behind him to pound on his back.

"And what do you know of whiskey?" he sputtered, catching his breath. Surely he had to be entirely cast away if a few thumps on the bare back could feel so incredibly sensuous. What if he were to turn, to reach round that waist and pull her close, to feel those hands upon his chest? But before he could pursue that ill-advised course, the hammering of her hands ceased, and she stepped back, out of arm's reach, but dangerously within the scope of his senses. Even above the liquorous fumes, Duncan could smell her scent, attar of night, essence of woman.

"Good Scot's whiskey was one of my father's few weaknesses," Kate admitted. "He could pass by even the finest of ports, and would drink an occasional sherry just to be sociable, but a whiskey of quality was ambrosia to him. When he came upon a particularly excellent bottle, he would nurse it along, doling it out to himself dram by dram. Sometimes, when I became older, he would let me taste and explain the qualities that made that particular bottle choice."

Her voice was tender, filled with the fondness of memory, but there was an undertone of sadness. "He's gone, isn't he, your father?"

"Rolica," Kate confirmed.

"A botched business if ever there was one. Even in India, we heard of Lake's charge. Shows the kind of damage an officer can do when he takes too much on himself." Duncan shook his head. "So your father was a soldier as well as your husband."

"I was raised upon the drum."

Her voice was a like the lapping of waves on a distant shore, and Duncan gave himself over to the peaceful sound, letting it soothe the turmoil within.

"Papa wanted a son; I suppose all men do," she said, giving voice to a long-held realization. "But there was only me. Mama was scandalized, of course, but there was no denying Papa when he had the bit between his teeth. He taught me to hunt, to shoot, to ride, and to know when the cards are marked."

"And recognize good whiskey, all the essential skills for a young gentleman," Duncan remarked.

"Aye, I suppose so."

From the tone Duncan could almost see her self-deprecating smile.

"To be fair, Mama did her best. She and Daisy both tried to make me a lady, as well, but it was an unfair competition. Fine needlework and furbelows cannot compare with handling the ribbons of two high-steppers and a phaeton. And skirts and sidesaddle are a blamed nuisance if one wishes to keep pace with the hounds. But I did try to be a lady, for their sakes."

"And succeeded," Duncan noted. "You achieved the ultimate objective—marriage to a well-born man, a family . . . What went wrong, Kate?" At that question, she stepped back. Clearly, she did not wish to talk about that part of her past. But even though he had found the lever that would move her, that would get rid of her, he did not want her to go. "You need not name names," he told her. "Give me no clues. Surely, you realize that if I really wished to, I have enough information to find out who you truly are. How many women have abigails named Daisy and a child of six or seven who is as silent as a doorpost? You are obviously genteel, you hated Almack's, and are not overly fond of Prinny. When we add the facts that you are the oddly indulged child of an army officer, raised as a daughter of the regiment, I am sure that it would take but a wee bit of investigation to uncover your real name." He could hear the intake of her breath and cursed the whiskey for loosening his tongue. He had frightened her. "I won't, Kate, I swear. I won't seek out what you are unwilling to tell me. I just want to understand. All considered, is that too much to ask?"

He felt a mixture of regret and relief when she turned away.

"I was a failure."

Her voice was faint, almost a whisper.

"My husband's grievances were entirely legitimate. I was a wretched excuse for a female. My hoydenish ways were a constant source of embarrassment to him."

She stopped for a moment, framing her words carefully before she went on. "When I found myself increasing, he was monstrously relieved. My father was his superior officer, and it was just the excuse that my husband had been seeking to ship me back to England, you see." She could hear no reaction of recognition from him, but that was not surprising. Her late husband had told her often enough that she was less than a source of pride. It was doubtful that his wife had been the subject of fond reminiscence. "I was hidden away in the country to whelp. Yet another disappointment."

If it had not been for the darkness, he might have taken her words at their surface, given the detached tone of Kate's voice and the fact that her countenance was hidden from him. But he was listening carefully, weighing every nuance, and there was no mistaking the pain beneath her deliberate nonchalance. "I take it he had hoped for a boy?"

"What man does not wish for a son to succeed him? My own father had the same desire, after all," Kate said, omitting the fact that Anne had inherited her father's title in her own right. There were so few exceptions to the rule of male heirs. It would be almost tantamount to revealing that it was Adam Denton, Lord Steele, that she spoke of. "Perhaps we could have made things right, had there been time. I was very young, full of childish expectations. If I had tried a bit harder, perhaps—"

"Ah, poor Galatea," Duncan murmured, "you blame yourself."

"If I had done different, we would not be at this sorry pass. If we—"

"If, if, if," Duncan mocked. " 'If wishes were horses then beggars would ride,' my auld nurse would say. What is the use of dwelling on 'if'? There is no certainty that you could have changed your husband's attitudes. Even if you had made yourself into the perfect statue of a spouse that he so obviously desired, what would have been the cost to you, Kate? Would you have so willingly destroyed everything that you are?"

He rose, taking a step toward her, but halted just short of reach. "You would have died by inches, woman, a part of you perishing with every insipid afternoon call, every banal ball, every commonplace remark. The words that you really wanted to say would stick in your craw and choke you. Your cogitations would crowd your mind until it was fit to burst, but you could never give your boiling thoughts vent, for fear of angering Pygmalion."

Duncan's hand lifted, to touch that shining fall of moonlit flame, but he recalled himself. "The fool thought that you were his creation, saw only that beautiful shell, that silken marble skin that can be found in a heart of stone by any sculptor of skill. But it was not he who gave you life, Galatea, t'was the gods. You were blessed in bow and saddle by Diana, the huntress; given understanding by Athena, the wise; and it was Aphrodite herself who granted you the capacity for love. For a statue cannot love, Galatea, and heaven knows that the assembly halls of London are filled with walking statues."

He could see the shimmer of silk. She was shaking, and when she turned round to face him once more, he could see the silvered trail of tears on her cheek. "Do not live in 'ifs,' Kate," Duncan told her. "Else you will make your life a hell. I know." It was all he could do to keep himself from gathering her into his arms, from letting her spill her heart on his shoulder. He wanted to calm that trembling body, to soothe that wounded spirit, but he could not. Duncan lifted the remnants of the whiskey in silent offering. Unfortunately, liquid comfort was all that he could give.

Kate took the bottle, raising it to him in gesture of salute before draining it to the dregs in a single swallow. "That was unconscionably selfish of me," she said, her voice hoarse with tears and liquor. "To put period to a man's last lick of whiskey is an unpardonable crime, milord."

Her gallantry touched him, as did her ability to make light where any other woman would sink into a morass of weeping and emotion. He could do no less. "A terrible trespass," Duncan agreed, "as your father no doubt taught you, to exhaust your host's spirits. Far worse than daring Almack's without proper breeches, more lacking in manners than asking Lady Hertford after dear Mrs. Fitzherbert's health. As a penalty for your misdeed, I demand that you will address me as Duncan." Kate gave a reluctant smile, and Duncan's heart soared. "Luckily, there are over a dozen more bottles of this down in the cellar, pipes of excellent claret and veritable oceans of sherry and French brandy that was laid when Louis was still King of the Frogs. We could drink ourselves into oblivion and still have plenty to spare. No one thought to try the cellars when they were stripping this place of valuables. There is a drunkard's dearest dream down there in the bowels of the castle."

"You could sell it, Duncan," Kate said in growing excitement, scarcely noticing how easily his given name tripped off her tongue. "Surely, such a collection of fine spirits could easily find a buyer. You could start with a flock of sheep, perhaps, and make some repairs to the crofts. Within a few seasons—"

"Hold, Kate." Duncan raised his hand. "You would have me part with the only solace that I have? Nepenthe of this quality is not easily found."

"And what of your obligations to your people, milord?" Kate asked, slipping back into cool formality. "Or is it your intent to share that bottled surcease with the men and women who depend on you for their livelihoods? Do you intend to let them drink themselves into indifference as well?"

Duncan stiffened. There was no need to sell the cellar's contents, not with the Treasury in mourning due to his untimely resurrection. Even though she did not know about his fortune, it was not her right to interfere. "That is none of your affair."

"I see," Kate said. "How hypocritical, milord, and so typical of a man. You imply that you value my thoughts, yet when I am so foolish as to give my opinions expression, you demand that I not mind your business. But then that should not surprise me. The 'Mad MacLean' is reputedly an expert at cozening women with what they want to hear."

"And who are you to judge me, milady?" Duncan asked, anger broaching the last barriers of control. "You occupy my home under false pretenses, then have the audacity to tell me what I owe people who hate me sight unseen! You claim to know me, profess to understand my motivations, yet, to my knowledge, we have never before met. What do you know of who I am?"

"You are Duncan MacLean," she said, the whiskey freeing words that were perhaps better left unspoken. "You are a player of cards, a warrior, and a slayer of hearts."

"No longer," Duncan said, stepping out of the shadows. "You mock me. Light your candle and look at this face. I am my own hant, a macabre joke of fate. Look at me and honestly tell me that I am still that man."

"No, not quite the same," Kate said, gazing past the traces of his scars, looking beyond all the scandalous stories. "He was a paltry sort of fellow, Duncan MacLean, a soldier's soldier, 'tis true, but proud and vain."

"And now, I have precious little reason for vanity," Duncan said, "and I fight no more."

"Untrue, milord Duncan, untrue," Kate said, all caution vanishing at the sight of his stricken face. He honestly believed that all his worth lay at the surface. "You fight still a battle with the past, a war within."

Her words struck him sober. *"You heard,"* Duncan said, his gut tightening in mortification. How could he have hoped that she had slept through his banshee cries? Somehow he had convinced himself that her walk in the night was a mere coincidence, and now he was grateful for the darkness, thankful that he could not see the pity that was surely in her eyes. "Did you come to comfort me, Kate?" he asked, keeping his tone steady. "Is that why you are here?"

"Is that so shameful?" she asked. "To want to give comfort?"

"I do not need your sympathy!" Duncan exploded. "If you wish to play Lady Bountiful, then go down to the village and do your good works. Go down to the cellars and give them all a bottle, then leave me here with mine." He took up another bottle and pulled the cork with his teeth. With a mocking salute, he raised it to her and drank till he was breathless, letting oblivion pour down his throat. But the roar of his own voice was still echoing in his ears when her reply came, so quiet that Duncan barely heard.

"We all need sympathy and understanding, upon occasion. You gave me yours; I was hoping only to return the favor. May your bottles bring you sweet dreams, Duncan MacLean."

Before he could frame a reply, she slipped silently into the night.

Chapter Seven

K ate paused in the kitchen doorway, looking back toward the lone shadow. Glass glinted briefly against the night, sailing in a moonlit arc to shatter somewhere in the darkness. Empty or full? she wondered; then wondered why it mattered so much to her. If Duncan MacLean chose to drink himself into a stupor, it was not her right to interfere. He had told her in no uncertain terms that he did not desire her presence, yet she did not want to leave him to himself, not when despair floated around him like a miasma. Not when he had been so kind to her.

Kind? A strange attribute for a rakehell, but Duncan MacLean's innate decency could not be denied. Kate was beginning to realize that it was as much a part of him as the cleft in his chin, or the sardonic arch of his brows. His concern for Anne; his willingness to refrain from prying into the question of her past, tolerating a stranger whose identity was a known charade; the indulgence in allowing her to ride his horse; these were but a few of his acts that bespoke a character wholly at odds with his reprobate reputation.

Kate began to count the many small, unasked favors, the way that he had quietly shifted minor burdens from her shoulders, dressing the game, chopping the wood, making their part of the castle more proof against bad weather. It was all very well for Daisy to claim that he worked as much for himself as for others, but if he were indeed so selfishly motivated, he would be driving everyone harder, not easing their way.

Kate sighed. It was something of a shame that the "Mad MacLean" had not lived up to his sordid stature. She had dealt with her share of rogues; any number of them had worn England's red coat. If Duncan MacLean had proven to be one of the usual run of scoundrels, she would have used him without qualm or conscience and dismissed him entirely from her thoughts. Unfortunately, Kate was forced to acknowledge that those quiet acts of kindness were proving far more seductive than any of the rogue's usual catalog of lures. As she watched the shadow of that powerful figure stalking to and fro in the night, she knew that she was losing her struggle. She did not want to like him, but she did. He made no claim on her emotions, yet she had given him her sympathy.

"Don't yer be frettin' yerself, ma'am."

Fred's whisper startled her. The little man had blended so completely with the darkness that she had not noticed his presence.

"Nor mind what th' major might o' said. Ain't no reasonin' with 'im when 'ee's like this."

"Do these dreams occur frequently?" Kate asked, recalling the early days of their flight. Anne had wrestled with her terror almost nightly, her cries waking the other occupants of the various inns they had frequented. More than once, they had been shown the door and had been forced to take a tortuous route for fear that someone would speak of two women with a little girl who screamed the night away.

" 'Ee's gone weeks since th' last un." Fred scratched his head thoughtfully. "Th' nightmares 'ave come less an' less since we got 'ere, seems ter me. T'night were a bad un though, don't know what sets 'em off. Mebbe th' 'eat. It were powerful 'ot t'day and 'ee was workin' out in th' field in th' worst of it. Couldn't get 'im t'stop."

"He's a stubborn man," Kate said. "Anyone with any sense could see that it was not a day for hard labor."

"Didn't see yer stintin' on th' work either," Fred remarked, "Daisy were sayin' 'ow she were thinkin' ye'd bake yer brains into a puddin' out in th' garden. Seems to me yer two o' a kind. I figger twixt th' sun on 'is 'ead all day an' th' fact th' room were so stiflin' 'ot it put 'im in mind of La Purgatoor."

Kate decided to let the first part of his comment slip, although she intended to let Daisy know what she thought of being gossiped about. "You were prisoners at La Purgatoire?"

"Aye," Fred acknowledged. "Twelve men in a cell what would barely fit 'alf th' number. Took turns sleepin', we did. It were th' major what worked it out, took care o' us all, be it enlisted or officer, made sure we got th' same share. There were a lot o' grumblin' 'bout that, let me tell yer, but th' major kept it fair. T'were 'im what figgered out 'ow we could get loose. Took us all, even those we would o' been better off leavin' for th' monsewers."

The little man clearly had more to say, so Kate asked the question that he was obviously waiting for. "Why would you wish to leave anyone behind?"

"They near t'got us kilt. Soon as we was beyond th' walls, them other 'igh rankers bethought themselfs o' their own plans. 'Eaven 'elp th' private when there's too many officers, I say. Wouldn't take no orders from Major MacLean. Them sons o' Mayfair swells knowed better, they thought then some Scots savitch. My major were all for 'eadin' inland, layin' low in th' countryside."

"What the Frenchies would least expect?" Kate conjectured.

"Aye," Fred agreed, looking at Kate with newfound respect. "But them nobs wouldn't 'ear of nothin' but 'eadin' straight fer th' coast. Told th' major t'let them fools walk into Jacque's waitin' arms, but 'ee wouldn't leave 'em; 'oped t'make 'em see reason. They was 'is men, fer all that they were follerin' th' cavalry charlies. Now anyone knows that twixt a Hussar an' 'is horse, 'tis the horse what 'as th' greater wits."

"The Hussars have ever been known for the cut of their uniforms rather than the sharpness of their minds," Kate said, wondering how Duncan had managed to bear it, to follow even in the knowledge that he was likely being led to his death. "I suppose the French were waiting for you?"

" 'Alf a regiment by th' look o' it," Fred said bitterly. "Iffen th' major 'adn't fallen an' twisted 'is foot on th' cliffs, we would o' been cut down on th' beach same as th' others. But 'ee told 'em t'go on without 'im, 'ee did. An' devil take 'em all, they left 'im behind with no more'n a fare-thee-well. One of 'em even 'ad th' cheek ter order me t'come with 'em, crack marksman, what I am. Told 'im where I'd put me rifle, I did."

"With or without the bayonet?" Kate asked and was rewarded with an appreciative smile. "A hanging offense, to threaten an officer."

"Good fortune then, that 'is bloody lordship never got t'report me. For that matter not a one o' them did. Eight men, ma'am, cut down afore our eyes, an not a blasted thing could we do to 'elp 'em," Fred muttered. "Weren't nothin' what could be done, I keeps on sayin', if we'd o' fired a shot, th' Frogs woulda' picked us off like flies on an 'orse's back."

Even among the shadows, Kate could see the change of expression as the little man told his tale, the anger, the bitterness, the profound sadness. She could only imagine what he and Duncan had felt as they had watched that slaughter. Once again, her eyes sought him. He stood silhouetted against the pale silver glow, another bottle in his hand. "Does he always drink away these dreams, Fred?"

Fred shook his head. "Can't, I fear. Sometimes, I be thinkin' if all th' sea was blue ruin an' 'ee could swaller it all, 'ee'd still be 'alf sober. 'As an 'ead like Gerbralter, 'ee does. Why, 'ee could drink Lord Steele 'isself under th' table, and Steele was a toper few could 'ope to match."

Kate blessed the lack of light that concealed her reaction. "Lord Steele?" She made the name into a question, keeping her tone under careful control.

"Yer ain't 'eard o' 'im, an yer follered th' drum?" Fred's bewilderment was obvious. "A reg'lar Lord Thirstington 'ee was, but rare 'ee ever came th' worse for it. Never touched th' bottle afore a battle though. 'Ee weren't one o' those 'oo 'ad t'be pot-valiant on th' field an' got their guts from a bottle."

It was hard to imagine Adam even mildly muddled. He had always been so totally in control of himself.

"Aye, a man's man, Lord Steele, th' very devil wi' th' ladies, too," Fred reminisced. "Why I recollect . . ." But the little man trailed off as he recalled his companion. "Savin' yer presence ma'am, I do beg yer pardon."

Adam? A drinker? Unfaithful? Kate was torn, but decided she wanted to hear more. "Why, I do seem to remember something now, but you could not be speaking of Lord

Steele. He was a married man, was he not?" she asked, praying that her voice would stay steady.

"Aye," Fred conceded, "but 'ee wouldn't be th' first ter ferget what 'ee told th' parson. Beside, t'is said 'ee married beneath 'im. 'Ee wed Colonel Braxton's brat, if yer would credit it. Sure yer 'eard o' that 'un, a real spitfire th' colonel's girl. Wed 'er on a wager, t'is said. Bet five 'undred guineas that 'ee could make 'er into a lady. 'Ee won the five 'undred quid, they say, 'ad 'er dancin' at Almack's."

"Like a performing dog," Kate murmured, the pain of the revelation slicing through her like a blade. The last veil was ripped from her eyes, and she looked back upon her marriage with painful clarity. How naive she had been. All this time she had wondered why the great Lord Steele's eye had fallen upon her, why so lofty a being, who could choose any well-bred female for a bride, had taken a hellion as a wife. "Braxton's brat"; she had known of the name, of course, taken a perverse pride in it, convinced herself that it did not matter, though it had. Till Adam. A wager . . . he had married her upon a betting whim, and if Duncan's man knew it, then all the world was aware as well. That first waltz at Almack's had been a shining moment for her, but now she knew that the look in Adam's eyes had been neither love nor pride, but triumph. How many people had been tittering behind their hands as she had danced with delight in Adam's arms?

She had honestly believed that her husband had seen the woman beyond the breeches, discerned qualities past the foolish badges that were reserved for those with an odd kick to their gallop. That supposed esteem had been the hope that had sustained her, through the long absences, through the numerous small cruelties that only Polite Society could contrive. And she had endured, for Adam's sake, striven to make him proud because, after all, he had chosen to elevate her. She had told herself that the failures of her marriage were entirely her fault because she did not love him enough, because she was not good enough. Kate stared up at the wavering stars as the underpinnings of her past crumbled.

"Milady!"

The cry that rose to punctuate the urgent tone of Daisy's

summons made the reason unmistakable. Kate's ruminations would have to wait, and Duncan would have to wrestle with his demons alone. Anne's nightmares had returned.
"Keep an eye on him, Fred," Kate said. "I must see to my
daughter."

"Aye, I will . . ." Fred promised, adding softly when she
was beyond hearing, "milady."

At first Duncan thought that he had become disconnected
from his body, that the small voice that he sometimes heard
within had finally freed itself. The thin, high wail pierced
the heart of him, found an echo inside the recesses of his
soul that keened like the winter wind through the barren
wastes. All of his horror, the sum of all his deepest fear was
contained in that reverberating shriek. He put his hands over
his ears, knowing in the whiskey-sodden recesses of his
mind that it would do no good; it never had before. But to
his amazement the sound was muffled, and he slowly came
to the realization that the scream that he heard came from
without, not within. Once that had been determined, Duncan
tried to discern the source of that agonized cry, comparing it
with jug-bitten judgement to every similar noise that he had
ever heard. A wounded man about to go west? An animal in
a trap? A damned soul in torture? His own screams. Aye, a
combination of all of those and yet unlike any of them. Like
the cry of a *bean sith*, those ghostly heralds of death, this
was, high, thin, reedy . . . like a child. No, not a banshee, a
little girl.

He turned toward the castle, toward the direction of the
din, his eyes rising to the lit window above the courtyard,
and somehow, comprehension dawned. Pain instinctively
recognized pain, torment understood torment. Duncan knew
that the silent child was silent no more. He ran toward the
castle.

"Mebbe 'tis best that yer didn't go up," Fred told him,
standing before the door. " 'Tis but th' little 'un 'avin' a bit
o' a bad dream, 'tis all, Major."

The major gave no answer, but the expression on his face
made his intent clear. Fred stepped aside, then followed his
master's charge up the stairs.

It seemed almost like a Rembrandt painting that Duncan

had once seen. Light spilled from the wide-open door, framing the women and the child upon the bed in a softly illuminated tableau, momentarily tranquil, until an ear-piercing shriek tore the temporary fabric of peace.

"Hold her, Daisy," Kate said, grabbing Anne's flailing arm.

"Hard t'credit the little un's so strong," Daisy grunted as she held the other hand fast. "Get the leg if you can, else she might twist her shoulder right out of its socket."

"Anne, Anne, listen," Kate said, desperation in her raised voice. "Mama is here! Daisy is right beside you. We will let nothing harm you, love. We will protect you. 'Tis but a dream you fear, only a dream."

But the squirming did not diminish as the child struggled against the arms that held her.

"Got to pare her nails again," Daisy observed, looking ruefully at a red slash along her wrist. "Gotten lax, I fear, since we ain't had none of these nights for a while."

"Oh, Daisy," Kate said, struggling to keep Anne's fingers from scratching her own face. "I am sorry."

"I know she don't mean it," Daisy said gruffly. "Just fear that she might succeed in gougin' herself, like she done before, poor little mite."

At that moment Duncan wanted nothing more than to go back to his cache of bottles and find solace in whiskey, but then Kate chanced to look up at him. The weary sorrow in her eyes made him ache with compassion.

"Do you dare to pity me, Duncan MacLean?" Kate challenged when the cries had stilled to a guttural whimper. "Or my child?"

There was a second of stillness as her expression dared him to deny it. "Both," Duncan answered, "I pity you both. Is there aught that I can do to help?"

"There is hope for you yet, Duncan," Kate said, warmth lighting her eyes. "I thank you for your honest concern, but there is nothing you can do. When Anne gets like this, we cannot waken her."

"Why? What is wrong with her?" Duncan asked, stepping into the room.

Anne began bucking about violently.

"If it's helpin' you want to do, get yourself out!" Daisy

Rita Boucher

yelled, bracing herself against the child's shoulder. "T'was you that started it, with her seein' you yellin' and tossin'. 'Tis no wonder that the sound of your voice is settin' her off. Get out!"

Duncan backed away in confusion, pulling Fred with him to the end of the corridor. "The child saw me, Fred?" he asked, grasping the Cockney by the shoulder. Fred's sudden concentration on his feet was all the answer Duncan needed. "How much did she see? Hear?" Duncan demanded, bunching the fabric of his servant's shirt in his fist.

"Shh!" The little man put a finger to his lips, nodding his head toward the open door. The cries had died momentarily.

Duncan nodded, hurrying down the stairs and out the kitchen door. But if Fred had hoped that the question would be forgotten, he was doomed to disappointment.

"How long?" Duncan asked, clasping Fred by the arm. "How long was the child there?"

The little man shrugged his skinny shoulders. "Can't rightly say 'ow soon they came."

"They?"

"Th' babe, 'er ma, an' th' 'ound—"

"A regular Bartholemew Fair crowd," Duncan said from between clenched teeth.

"Came to 'elp yer, they did, not to gawp," Fred said, his voice rising in annoyance. "She's a right 'un, th' lady. An' them Frenchies must o' blinded yer in more'n one eye, if yer can't see it."

"I do not need anyone's pity."

"Nay, don't need nobody's pity, do yer?" Fred shook his head. "not mine, not 'ers, not nobody's, not when yer got so damn much for yer own self. Pity ter spare."

It was as if the Cockney had upped and slapped him in the face. Duncan looked at him, startled. "Sergeant Best," he began.

"Ain't no sergeant no more, an yer ain't no major. Yer a man, same as I, alive an' breathin' if yer don't go to pullin' no more stupid larks. Yer alive, man, *alive* an' yer got a hell o' lot o' cheek cryin' over it! 'Oo cares what they saw, 'ceptin' that it might o' been cause ter *that*."

That rasping childish wail rose once more to break the peace of night, and Fred felt his master's silent shudder.

Duncan looked at the small man uncertainly. "Do you think that I . . . ?"

"No sayin', lad." Fred's tone was kinder, as he answered the unspoken question. "If I knowed what brings bad dreams an' what makes for good, wouldn't a' had to take the King's shillin', would I? Open me a shop on Bond Street an' make me a fortune, I would. But I'd give 'er a few on th' 'ouse, poor lass."

"And me, Fred?" Duncan asked, his mind growing clouded, the effects of restlessness and alcohol draining him.

"Aye, lad," Fred said, picking up the blankets that he had left by the door and spreading them on a pile of fresh straw that had been piled away from the cow byre. "I'd save th' best dreams for yer. Now lay yerself down."

Obediently, Duncan lay down and closed his eyes. He did not even feel the rough blanket as Fred tucked it carefully beneath his chin.

They were pounding the nails in his coffin. The steady clink of metal upon metal felt as if it were directly atop Duncan's head. Cautiously, he opened his eye, then rapidly squeezed it shut again as the sunlight stabbed at him. It wasn't the whiskey. Unfortunately, he had not imbibed nearly enough the previous night. Indeed, the muzziness of the totally sodden would be infinitely preferable to this awful clarity of memory and thought. Every single blasted word that he had uttered, each foolish move that he had made the previous night was recalled with unshakable distinction. Duncan forced himself to float, to breathe steadily in rhythm with that hammering tattoo until he felt the throbbing recede into the back of his head. When the sound ceased for a moment, he rose and pulled off his shirt, then made his faltering way to the pump. He worked the handle with self-punishing vigor, putting his head directly under the icy, spring-fed flow until he wanted to scream at the cold.

Duncan came up sputtering, shaking his head to and fro like a sopping dog, sending rivulets of water coursing down his back and chest. Dripping, he wiped the hair from his eye and faced the light, letting the sun's warmth take away the water's chill. As he looked up, he saw the source of the odd noise. In horrified wonder, he watched transfixed as Kate trod delicately along the ridgepole, her steps sure and dainty as a dancer's.

She stood momentarily limned by sunlight before she bent to hammer a shingle into place. The beams that broke through the clouded sky transformed her into a glorious pixie creature of red and gold, feminine and delicate for all that she was dressed in her breeches. As she rose again and moved further along the roof, he wanted to call out, to demand that she get down, but he dared not break her concentration, and continued to watch, torn between amazement and fear.

It was neither sound nor movement that alerted Kate to Duncan's presence, just a strange feeling that ran the length of her spine. Somehow she knew that he was there, watching her. Despite all her assertions that a man's attire was the most sensible garb for roof work, Daisy's oft-repeated admonitions about propriety came flooding into Kate's mind. What would he think of her? she wondered, even as she told herself that she did not care in the least. He had seen her in men's clothes before. It did not signify. She would not allow any man's opinion ever to matter to her again, not after last night's painful truths.

Nonetheless, as she knelt and hammered in a shingle, Kate stole a look through the veil of hair that had loosened itself from its scraped-back severity. Sure enough, he was there down below, his shirt flung carelessly over his shoulder, his hair shining a polished ebony with moisture. Beads of water trailed down his neck and chest. It appeared that Daisy's meals had worked wonders; the gaunt hollows and spare angles were no more.

As he lifted a hand to shade his eye against the sun, Kate abruptly realized just how many muscles were involved in that simple action. Hard sinew rippled across his chest in a fascinating display. She knew that she ought to turn her attention elsewhere, but she could not. Perhaps it was the dark tangle of his beard that made him appear so utterly barbaric; or it might have been the uncivilized bronze of his skin, but all at once he became the embodiment of secret dreams. Warrior, pirate, conqueror, every fantasy that Kate had ever imagined abruptly became Duncan MacLean.

Her throat suddenly felt parched; Kate half choked as she attempted to swallow. Deliberately, she turned her attention back to the roof and began to hammer relentlessly. It was the heat, she told herself. The heat, lack of rest, lack of water, lack of common sense. She had known that it was within him all along, the power that had beguiled so many women into his arms, but never before had she felt that sheer magnetism so strongly. *Please*, she begged wordlessly, *put on your shirt before I tumble off the ridgepole*. But another furtive glance confirmed that he was still standing there like a pagan statue. She brought down the hammer. "Damn!" She put her throbbing thumb in her mouth.

"What are you doing up there?" Duncan demanded. "Other than cursing and pounding your fingers?"

"I am practicing the pianoforte!" she said, sending him an angry glare. It was, after all, his fault that she had missed the nail. Kate pulled another from her pouch and sighted it carefully. *Inconsiderate lout* Thwack! *Going about half naked* Thunk! *As if there were no ladies present* Whump! *Had no one ever taught him manners?* Bang! *Common decency?* Kerthwack! *Going about in a ragtag fashion; why his trousers were torn nearly up to his . . .* Her face was afire.

"You must be halfway to baked up there," Duncan said. "Your cheeks have ripened to cherry."

"If you will let me get about my business, I will soon be down," Kate retorted. "These shingles are in need of replacement. It is clouding up again, and I thought to take advantage of the good weather. A few more and there will be two bedchambers snug against the rain."

"I have told you before that I am content with the present arrangement," Duncan said. She was avoiding his eye; no wonder, considering the events of the previous night. A half-drunk, half-wit was what he had been, throwing her concern back into her face. It was astonishing that she could bear to speak to him at all. "Fred and I are just fine as we are in the butler's pantry."

"Are you, indeed?" Kate asked, keeping her eyes firmly fixed upon the next nail. "Is that why you were sleeping out in the hay last night, Duncan?"

Duncan groaned inwardly. Of course, she had noticed. "I

prefer the open when the weather is fine," Duncan said shortly.

"That is as may be," Kate agreed, gesturing with an up-raised hammer toward the mountains, "but you ought to know that clear skies are a tenuous prospect to depend upon in these parts. There are thunderheads upon Beinn Airidh Charr."

"Get down off the roof, Kate," Duncan told her, his heart pounding at his throat as she rose and stepped casually along the ridge.

"The master's suite is rather large," Kate informed him, making no sign that she had heard his command. "In fact, I had considered repairing it first, since a great portion of the roof above it is sound. However, it will be the very devil to heat because of its huge size. I vow, you could carpet it with grass and raise sheep in there."

Although her remarks seemed offhand on the surface, Duncan became more than a little suspicious at the third reference to the room's spaciousness. Had Fred been talking too much, telling her how much Duncan loathed confined spaces? "Then bring up the sheep, by all means," Duncan said. "For I dinna have intention of moving."

Kate shrugged. "You are the master here. If it is your wish to sleep with the cow, who am I to deny your bovine preferences?"

"Who, indeed?" Duncan asked.

"However, since I have taken the obligation of caring for you upon myself, I cannot allow you to risk your health to ill weather," Kate continued, wondering whether she was crossing the boundaries of prudence by challenging him.

The obligation of caring for you. Duncan turned the phrase over in his mind, trying to decide if her use of *caring* outweighed the employment of *obligation.* "*You cannot allow!* When did it become your province to naysay me, madame?"

Although it was difficult to discern from his expression, there was something in his tone that encouraged her. "Naysay you, milord, I would not dare!" Kate said.

Duncan softened at the tentative smile that accompanied the denial. Perhaps she did not hold him in contempt as much as he feared. "I had thought that we had dispensed with the use of 'milord,' Kate," he ventured.

"If you wish to act the seigneur, sir, then I shall address you as one," she replied.

"Saucy wench, get down from there."

"Stubborn mule, I shall not until I am done!" she replied, the anxiety within her gradually dissolving. The revelations of secrets, the exchange of confessions was always a chancy affair, either the cement that bound or the blow that shattered. She had spent a good part of the previous night worrying that he might wake with regrets or take a perverse disgust to a whiskey-swilling hussy who would follow him into the night.

"I am your employer," he reminded her.

"And I am doing my job of housekeeping," Kate explained, setting another nail in place. "It was not my intent to dispossess you, Duncan. T'will take but a few more minutes, and then we may all rest in comfort."

"No, not a few minutes. Now. Get down, Kate, immediately," Duncan commanded. "I will move the ladder closer."

"Not quite yet, milord," Kate said, frowning at his dictatorial tone. "I have no wish to sleep with water dripping on my head tonight. A few more shingles and I shall be done."

"*Now,* Kate!" Duncan said. "It is far too dangerous."

"Nonsense, 'tis no more than fifteen feet up, but a hop compared to the roof above the tower," Kate retorted, pointing to the steeply pitched roof that sloped to gird the small turret above the servants' hall.

"You were up there?" Duncan asked, the pit of his stomach roiling at the thought of Kate climbing on that perilous incline. It was at least forty feet to the ground.

"T'was not nearly as difficult as it might seem." Kate laughed, edging her way to the next loose piece of roofing. "I have been climbing trees since I was knee high to a grasshopper. My papa often used to say that the monkeys in India must have tutored me."

She and her father had lived in India. Duncan added that bit of information to his store as he went to get the ladder. If she would not come down, he would have to go up and get her. However, the moment he set his foot on the first step, the wood splintered.

"I would not attempt it," Kate warned. " 'Tis a miracle that rickety old thing can bear my weight."

Duncan eyed the aging ladder in disgust. "Do you often rely on miracles?"

"When I must," Kate said solemnly, bringing a skewed shingle back into position before fastening it in its place. "I have lately found that miracles seem to occur in direct proportion to need. There! That is the last of them." Her foot felt for the rung and found it. Edging herself off the roof, Kate was on the third rung when she heard a cracking sound. She threw herself forward, trying to grab hold of the ridge, but it was too late. She was sliding, then falling. From the bedroom window overlooking the courtyard she heard Daisy scream.

"Kate!" He reached for her, bracing himself as she dropped, but when the force came, it still knocked him from his feet, taking the breath out of him.

"Milord!" Kate rolled to her knees, totally unhurt. "Milord . . . are you all right?"

"Milady! Katie!" Daisy called anxiously from above.

"No harm done to me at all," Kate said with a wave of her hand. "Barely a bruise. 'Tis his lordship that I fear for." She gently smoothed the side of his face.

Having determined that Kate was uninjured, Duncan kept his eye closed, enjoying the touch of her hand on his cheek. He could feel her breath as she bent nearer.

"Duncan, please look at me," she begged. "I am sorry, so very sorry."

The guilt in her voice forced him to open his eye, but her closeness was a temptation. Her scent was sweet and fresh, like the heather that bloomed on the hillside. How he wanted to lift his fingers to feel the softness of her cheek, to smooth away the tension in her mouth. But if that was not allowed him, he could at least keep her near for a few minutes longer. Surely, he deserved that much. He moaned softly.

"Can you speak?" she asked, her eyes green pools of anxiety.

"Closer, Kate," he whispered with a grimace. He was in some pain after all—his ribs ached; there was a rock digging into his left buttock; and the stone was cold against his bare back. Her hair fell loose, brushing like silk against his chest as she leaned forward to listen, her fingers splayed above his heart. "Does this . . . make me . . . a . . . miracle . . . Kate?" he asked, softly.

"Yes, I suppose you are," she said, reassured by the strong steady beat beneath her hand. "I could have come to serious harm had you not been there to catch me." She found herself momentarily trapped by his gaze, but she forced herself to look away and began to examine him, running experienced hands over his limbs in search of broken bones.

"Oooh," he moaned as she touched his thigh, "there . . . right there."

"Does it hurt?" Kate asked anxiously.

"Aye, there's an ache," he told her, closing his eye and enjoying the sensation as her fingers explored for the wound.

Neither of them noticed as Daisy came running up beside them. The small smile that was playing at the corner of Duncan's mouth was the first thing to catch her attention.

"Will you kiss me, Kate?" he choked weakly. "Just once before I die."

At those words, any doubt that the older woman might have had was replaced with certainty. The man was definitely drawing the bow a bit too long. As for her mistress, Kate seemed utterly befuddled. She looked up at Daisy and shrugged her shoulders.

"Nothing seems to be broken," Kate said.

Duncan moaned once more. "Just one kiss, is all I ask."

Daisy put a finger to her lips and knelt, elbowing Kate aside. As far as she was concerned, if Kate saw no injury, then like as not there was none.

Kate's eyebrow arched in a question mark. The servant shook her head and bent, cupping Duncan's chin firmly before bussing him on the cheek.

Somehow the kiss was not quite what he had imagined it would be. Duncan's eye flew open at Kate's gurgling laugh.

"Weren't one of my best," Daisy said, fluttering her lashes, "but if you feel another kiss would help . . ."

"Another miracle," Kate said, her fact alight with suppressed laughter. "You drew him back from the verge of death, Daisy."

"Aye." Daisy chuckled. "Just call me Mrs. 'Elijah' Kent."

"If that was the method that the prophet Elijah used for

raising the dead, then oblivion might be preferable," Duncan complained, stowing the name Kent in his memory.

"Aw, now milord, t'weren't so bad. I was accounted a fair kisser in my day, I was," Daisy said, drawing back in mock offense. "Just weren't what you was hopin' for, I expect."

A strangled sound of embarrassment issued from Duncan's throat. The older woman's knowing look left little doubt that she had understood exactly what he had been about.

"Are you still in pain?" Kate asked, trying unsuccessfully to stifle her laughter as she rose and dusted her skirts. "I am sure that Daisy could be persuaded to continue with her restorative efforts."

"I would not presume to ask Mrs. Kent to compromise herself once more," Duncan said, holding out his hand to Kate.

Kate hesitated, then grasped it, helping him get up, but once he was on his feet, he did not relinquish his hold.

"You could have been killed," Duncan said, his voice deep with emotion.

"Aye, he's right, he is," Daisy agreed, her chuckles ceasing. "Time and again, I've told her that a bit o' water ain't worth riskin' life and limb for, but does she listen to me, I ask you?"

"Of course not," Duncan said, matching her indignation. "Kate never listens."

"But I was not hurt," Kate said, glaring at her treacherous companion.

"Ah yes, miracles." Duncan shook her head. "Do not gamble on good fortune again. I may not be there to break your fall next time. I do not wish to see you on the roof anymore."

"Then I hope that you do not snore, milord," Kate retorted, attempting to tug her hand away. "For if you open your mouth in a rainstorm, you might drown with the state these slates are in."

"No, I've been told on Fred's excellent authority that I am not destined for drowning." Duncan kept her wrist imprisoned firmly. "Now, I want your promise Kate, that I will not see you up on that roof again."

Kate looked at Daisy, but saw that there would be no support coming from that quarter. The older woman was nodding in agreement. "Very well," Kate said reluctantly. "You shall not see me on that roof anymore." *Because I will make damned sure you are nowhere near when I do my repairs.* she added silently. "Now will you let me go?"

"No," Duncan said, smiling at the careful wording that had made her intent more than transparent. "Not until you give me your promise that you will do no more roofing work."

"I already have," Kate complained.

"Then it will make little difference if you will repeat after me. I solemnly swear . . ." he inclined his head, waiting.

"This is incredibly foolish!" Kate said. "Need I remind you of your oath? Unhand me, sir!"

"T'was you who gave me your hand, Kate," he reminded her. "And I'll not give it back until I have your word that I will not have to spend my days fearing that you will tumble on me unawares."

"Oh, very well," Kate grumbled. "I solemnly swear . . ."

"Never to set foot on the roofs of Castle Eilean Kirk."

"Never to set foot on the roofs of Castle Eilean Kirk," she parroted, concealing a secret smile.

"Nor its outbuildings," he concluded.

Damn! "Nor its outbuildings," Kate repeated reluctantly.

"Well done, that was milord," Daisy said, picking up his fallen shirt from the ground and shaking it before handing it to him. "I tell you it fair put my heart in my throat every time she climbed that ladder."

"I can well imagine," Duncan said.

"May I have my hand back?" Kate asked in a small voice. "There is a great deal to do before the foul weather hits."

Just as Duncan relinquished his hold, Anne burst forth from the bushes, her eyes wild with fright.

"She must o' heard me scream, poor lamb," Daisy said. " 'Tis all right, child. There is naught to fear."

Kate bent and gathered the child, knowing full well how Anne must have viewed the scene. This was not the first time that she had seen someone laying an unwelcome hand on her mother, and it would not be well to let any misunderstanding linger. "Anne, there is naught amiss," Kate crooned softly. "Mama is fine and nothing can harm you."

Anne looked accusingly toward Duncan."

"Perhaps, I had best leave," Duncan said.

"No, milord, please stay," Kate said. "Lord MacLean saved my life, Anne. He caught me when I fell from the roof."

"Aye, 'tis true, Annie my lamb. Look at his poor back." Daisy pointed, clucking her tongue. " 'Tis all scraped and bruised from when yer mama fell upon him. If you'll come into the kitchen, milord, I can be puttin' some of my salve on it. It'll be stingin' somethin' awful, less we do."

Anne stared, looking from Daisy to her mother and finally to Duncan.

"I shall surrender to your ministrations, Mrs. Kent," Duncan said, stirring uncomfortably beneath the little girl's gaze.

Anne tugged her mother's sleeve, signifying that she wished to get down.

Duncan watched as Kate set the child upon the ground, standing rooted as Anne walked toward him. The little girl looked up at him, her eyes asking a question that he could not quite understand, and the two women provided no guidance. From their expressions, it was obvious that they were just as puzzled as he was. Then, without warning, the child threw her arms around his knees, giving him a fierce hug that nearly knocked him from his feet. Then she turned and ran into the woods, the dog barking at her heels.

To Duncan the child had blurred into a hazy red dress running amidst a watery haze of brown and green. A strange warmth spread within him, like the first rays touching the winter snows, gentle with the promise of spring.

"She were sayin' thank you, milord," Daisy said, her voice quavering.

"I know," Duncan said, hiding behind a mask of gruffness. "I will collect that salve later, Mrs. Kent. I er . . . have to see to my horse." He moved stiffly, his body still sore from the impact. Lucky it was that Kate was such a wee thing, so small, so very fragile. If he had not been below to break her fall . . . He shook his head, not daring to think of the possible consequences, as he strode toward the path, hoping that his obscured vision would not cause him to stumble.

Only Kate saw the glistening single tear that ran down his cheek. Indeed, she felt like weeping herself. Before, Anne had been such a friendly little girl, so warm and charming that even the frosty Mrs. Drummond-Burrel had warmed sufficiently to urge Anne to sit upon her lap during one afternoon call. Now, however, even the merest contact, the chance jostling of a crowd was sufficient to make the child flinch. Kate recalled the carter, who had been kind enough to give them a ride from Dover. When that man had patted Anne upon the head, she had cringed before bursting into tears. Perhaps Duncan MacLean *was* a miracle, if Anne could willingly trust him, touch him. Whatever the consequences to Kate herself, she was now certain that the decision to stay had been the right one. Perhaps Anne could learn to put her faith in people again, and perhaps then she would speak once more.

"We'll be needin' to get the livestock into shelter," Daisy said, glancing anxiously at the sky. "Glad his lordship made the coops tight again, or we'd be playin' at Noah's ark once more."

"There is yet time before the storm breaks," Kate said absently, watching as Lord MacLean retreated around the bend. He was walking awkwardly, stirring her to guilt. She should have been expressing her thanks, but instead, she had made light of him. Some of those scratches on his back had been nasty ones, and he was likely in pain. "I will assist his lordship first, Daisy. He might be injured and not yet realize it."

"Aye," Daisy grumbled dryly, "and the fall just might have addled your wits, milady."

Kate lifted her chin, not deigning to reply to that blatant bit of disrespect.

"Now don't you be looking at old Daisy like that," she chided. "You know yourself that that man is trouble on two feet."

"He saved my life," Kate said. "Or do you forget that so quickly?"

"Aye, he did, most like," Daisy admitted. "And I'm grateful for it."

"So am I, and was it not you who taught me that I ought always to express proper appreciation?" Kate asked.

"Aye," Daisy admitted grudgingly.

"Then that is what I intend to do," Kate said, turning to set off down the path. "And Daisy," she added, casting a look over her shoulder, "do not call me 'milady,' please. It is too much of a risk."

"Risk," Daisy muttered glumly at her mistress's retreating figure. "You're a good one to talk o' risks, milady."

Chapter Eight

Duncan heard her before he saw her. The hasty tread was far too light to be the footfall of the Kent woman, but too purposeful for a child. For a moment, he contemplated flight, eyeing a nearby tree and wondering whether his tree-climbing skills had survived the years as well as Kate's. Facing her was not something he wished to do, not now when he was too confused to think clearly.

The little girl . . . Anne . . . Duncan had never considered himself a man who was naturally at ease with children. The little ones had never flocked at his knee. Yet silent though this child might be, she spoke to him in her own strange way. She was obviously intelligent, understanding all that was said. Those wide green eyes were impossibly expressive and way too wise for a child who could be no more than seven. He could feel that terrible sadness, understand it with an aching clarity.

She reminded him of those sombre brown-eyed urchins of Lisbon, the war-tossed orphans who would sell their souls for the price of a herring. The child's tossing, screeching, wild fury of last night haunted him because those screams had been the reverberations of his own torment. And now the girl had spoken again, albeit without words; the pressure of those small arms had said as much as the look on that luminous face. Trust. A wondrous gift from such a child, both favor and burden.

Had Anne always been thus? he wondered, trying to piece together the puzzle. Or was her present state the result of that "hurt," her mother had obliquely referred to more than once. What terrible calamity could befall one so young that it would haunt her hours of sleep?

"Duncan, please wait."

The very sound of that breathless call seemed to paralyze him in his place. Duncan schooled his face into a stony expression, his hand rising to wipe away the last trace of the tears that he had only just realized had fallen. But while his countenance was the picture of composure, inside he was a mass of befuddlement. What confounded imp had caused him to behave with such incredible stupidity? Even though he had known Kate for less than a few weeks, every rake's intuition had warned him that he would have to move carefully with a woman like her. She was far too canny a female to be won on the strength of charm and a handsome face.

His face, unfortunately, would never be what it once was, and now it seemed that every other rogue's art had deserted him as well. How could he have resorted to so callow a ploy, not even worthy of a junior officer, for a kiss, a mere touch of the lips? He knew full well that she could not want him, but at least he had begun to gain her respect, and now he had likely forfeited that hard-won regard.

Was that the measure then, of his desperation? How the mighty had fallen! Although Duncan had always prided himself on his discretion, his exploits with the ladies had acquired the patina of legend. If only Adam, Lord Steele, could see him now. No doubt he would consider Duncan's present state of decline the height of ironic humor. Adam . . . Duncan had not thought of him for days. Would the course of events have changed if Adam had not taken leave to go back to England? Duncan wondered. But there was little use in wishing the past undone.

"Duncan?"

Her face was flushed. It was obvious that she, too, was embarrassed by what had just occurred. Desperately, Duncan cast about for something to say. Luckily, his years among the English had provided him with the perfect expedient, the weather. He cast his gaze at the sky. "It will be a heavy storm when it comes, Kate," Duncan said, retreating behind the social bulwark of formality.

She made her own slow survey of the heavens, "Surely it will not reach us before evening. There is plenty of time to treat your back. Why don't you go to the kitchen and let Daisy put some of her salve on while I collect the animals.

It is a most excellent concoction, I assure you. And quite worth enduring the smell, for the soothing effect it has."

So much for the storm as an excuse, Duncan thought, surprised that her own evaluation of the approaching blow coincided so nearly with his own. He had never met a woman before with an ounce of weather sense, but then again, he had never met a female before who, within the space of less than a month, had threatened him with blunderbuss and knife point, ridden an avowed killer mount, scaled rooftops with utter fearlessness, and looked absolutely enchanting in breeches. "I can do without your Daisy's ministrations," Duncan declared, seeking refuge in curtness.

But Kate was not to be put off. "If you wish, I will chaperone," she offered solemnly. "That way you need not fear for your virtue." Duncan searched her countenance carefully, but there was not a trace of the pity and contempt that he had feared. Although her face was entirely composed, there was the definite glint of a twinkle in her eye, and the hint of laughter in her voice could not be denied.

At his look of consternation, the hint turned to a full revelation. Kate could not help but laugh.

Even though Duncan had heard her laughter before, this was somehow different, reaching into the core of him, despite its teasing tenor, echoing within like the notes on a scale of emotion. It was then he realized that her laughter was an invitation, not to make mockery of him, but to release the strain, the fear that had been building within him. He did not know when his frown had turned to a smile, but it had. Nor did he realize that the explosion that seemed to be building inside of him was bursting forth, until it finally happened.

It sounded like a rusty hinge at first, protesting after long disuse as a forgotten door opened. How long had it been since he had laughed? Beyond recent memory, certainly; there had been precious little occasion for humor in La Purgatoire. But this . . . this was unlike anything that he had ever experienced, this shared sense of the ridiculous that was like an invisible cord, twining them together. Perhaps it might have happened before, but never could he recall enjoying a genuinely humorous moment with a woman.

Once the door was opened, there was no closing it again. The chuckle grew to a guffaw that rose from his gut.

"If only you could have seen your face," Kate said, shaking with laughter herself.

"Daisy was . . . not quite . . ." Duncan stammered between gales of merriment.

". . . what you had expected," Kate admitted in gasps. "It was as much as you deserved."

"I suppose it . . . was," Duncan owned.

"You had me truly frightened, you know. Luckily, Daisy saw through your cozening tactics."

"Aye, just my luck," Duncan said wryly. Kate had been frightened for him? It was a novel occurrence, to have someone who had actually been concerned on his behalf. "Instead of comfort in my pain, I get a smack on the cheek by a woman old enough to be my mother."

"I would have you know that Daisy is considered a rather handsome woman. She is quite the object of courtship."

"I find myself in fear that Fred might call me out. Is she going to claim that I have compromised her now," Duncan said. "Or am I now compromised?"

At this, Kate fell into another fit of giggling. "Wholly beyond the pale. They will never let you waltz at Almack's again."

"Alas!" He put his hand to his forehead. "I am utterly ruined."

"But you were the instrument of your own destruction, milord. With such outright deception, what did you expect?"

" 'Expect' is too definite a word. 'Hope' is more the like of it, and what I was hoping for was you," Duncan admitted with a crooked smile. "You see, I merely wished to ascertain if my memory was damaged by the fall. Surely, no lips could feel as soft as yours, Kate. And I knew for a certainty that no woman could possibly taste of heather and sunshine. But alas, I had no opportunity to compare reality to memory."

His words were blatant concoctions, and she knew it. Nonetheless, they evoked unbidden recollections of that first night; memories of fear and forbidden longing had melded in that fraction of a moment when she had lost herself in his kiss. Did passion have a taste? Was there a flavor to yearning? Or was it just the potent mingling of strong emotion, darkness and imagination that lingered on her tongue, evoking those few seconds where her every sense had been roused? "You are a complete hand, Duncan," Kate said, trying to cover her confusion. She wanted to look away, but there was a spell in that one-eyed gaze of his, holding her enscorceled.

"Not a *complete* hand," Duncan reasoned, taking a step closer. "Else I would now be savoring heather on my lips." The laughter was gone from her face, replaced by a beguiling innocence. But although those moments of humorous sharing had passed, the bond created seemed to linger. It was a strange sweet intimacy, rivaling anything that he had ever experienced with a woman, more powerful, in some ways, than the ultimate union that two could share. He was loath to spoil it, yet the temptation to move closer was beyond resisting. "Ah, Kate," he asked softly, "do you really taste of heather or was it just a foolish fancy?"

They were barely a hand-span apart, attracted like two poles of an unexplained magnetic force. But the bemused look in her eyes was not consent to break the pledge that he had made. Yet, for all its intensity, the need within him was surprisingly simple, not a burning, but a gentle, warming flicker. He wanted nothing more than to hold her, to be held by her, to feel the soft texture of her hair against his shoulder, to breathe in her scent and savor her lips. Then, as if moved by the intensity of his will, her hand rose. Slowly, her fingers moved tentatively toward him, almost like the limb of a marionette manipulated by invisible strings. Duncan held his breath, unmoving, unwilling to break this bewitched moment.

He had changed somehow, and Kate suddenly realized that she had never heard his laughter before, never seen him smile without that twist of the lip that was closer to sneer than grin. For once, his expression was unguarded, an open path to the very depths of his emotions. The longing, the loneliness that she had sensed, were there for her to see, like words on a printed page. A silent plea. *Let me comfort you. I know you are in pain, so am I. I am drowning inside myself,* the silver eye told her. *I need you. I want you. I am afraid.* She wanted nothing more than to step into the circle of those arms, to accept the terms of mutual surrender.

But once that temporary truce came to its end, she knew that she was bound to be a casualty, a victim of her own emotions. Still, the temptation was strong. But it was Duncan's fear that held her in check; his air of vulnerability frightened her almost as much as the sudden force of her own feelings. Rake though he might be, Kate could not believe a face could lie so convincingly. If there was any truth in that gaze, the passion that he promised was a blade with two edges. Inevitably, they would both be wounded when she left here, left him.

The clip-clop of steel-shod hooves against stone rang like a church knell, its hollow echo cutting through the silence. Potent imprecations in a half dozen languages slipped wordlessly through Duncan's mind as Kate blinked, then backed away, eyes wakening in realization of what had nearly occurred. Those slender fingers flew to her mouth in horror, whether at him or at herself he could not determine. Her cheeks were aflame. There was no hope of salvaging the moment. Someone was crossing the bridge over the stream. It would be no more than a few seconds before the intruder rounded the bend.

Duncan's thoughts were veiled within a winking, quick as the closing of a shutter. The scarred side of his face with its unseeing eye was inclined away from her now, as if he had just recalled his wounds. That unspoken appeal that had drawn her despite every instinct and sensibility had been snuffed like a candle without so much as a wisp of feeling to mark its passing. Had it been the invention of her own imagination, or had she merely succumbed to the blandishments of a man that her late husband had somewhat enviously described as a wily seducer?

Far simpler to credit the latter of the two possibilities. Much easier to believe that this man was a rogue and treat him with all deserved disdain, than to allow for the complications of genuine sentiment on his part. But try as she might, she was too honest to dismiss what had just occurred as entirely one-sided or the aberration of a moment. Indeed, it would be dangerous to stay willfully blind to this strange fascination. He could no more stop himself from charming women than change the color of his eye. She would just have to remain wary and keep her distance.

A colorful curse trumpeted Fred's appearance. If he had come a few seconds later, or happened upon them unawares . . . Kate shuddered, deliberately ignoring a niggling twinge of regret. Nonetheless, she could not help but wonder how reality would have compared to the conjurings of her dreams.

When Fred rounded the bend, it was easy to see why the Cockney was profaning the sacred. One eye was nearly swollen shut, and his lip was bleeding. He pulled up the reins at the sight of the duo on the path. Duncan was beside him in a few long strides. "What happened?" he asked, raising a hand to gently touch the small man's lip.

Fred winced and shook his head. "T'weren't nothin'," he said. "Shoulda' known better'n t'try th' village again. Ain't nothin' there nohow, t'buy or t'beg. T'was just that Daisy were talkin' o' biscuits. Now yer know 'ow partial I am ter biscuits, sir."

"Fred once crossed the French lines to steal a pan full of biscuits," Duncan explained with grim humor. "Nearly joined his Maker for a bit of fried flour."

"They was good!" Fred remembered. "Best I ever et! Now th' woman was goin' on an' on, she was 'bout 'ow 'ers could all but fly iffen they weren't tethered t' th' ground. 'So,' I says, 'why don't yer make 'em?'" Fred's voice rose to a falsetto. "'Ain't got th' flour,' says she. 'Got ter 'ave wheaten flour,' says she." The man sighed. "So's I arsk 'er where kin I get me some wheaten flour? and she says 'Sometimes yer kin get some from Tam in the village but it costs dear.'"

"And biscuit connoisseur that you are, off you went in immediate pursuit of the ingredients," Duncan said, stifling a smile. Fred's imitation of Daisy was right on the mark, tone and expression.

"Well," Fred said sheepishly. "Seein' as 'ow we was needin' a few things else, we was, aside o' flour; salt so's we can lay by some o' th' game milady 'as been catchin' an' such. Figgered I'd take care o' it all, save me a traipse, fool as I was."

"Who struck you, Fred?"

Duncan's voice was deceptively quiet, but it was easy for Kate to discern that he was a powder keg on the verge of ignition. "Perhaps the question to ask is why?" Kate added hesitantly.

Fred's expression was pained. "Didn't start no fight, I didn't. T'was this feller name o' Tam."

"Tam who keeps the store?" Kate shook her head in disbelief. "It cannot be; Tam is almost as old as the Mad King himself and as amiable as a lamb."

"A ram is more th' like," Fred muttered. "No sooner as I sets foot in th' shop when 'ee goes for th' throat. Says as 'ee don't want no one from th' castle settin' foot in 'is place. Says 'is lordship . . ." Fred's voice trembled in outrage.

"Go on, Fred," Duncan demanded.

"Says 'ow 'is lordship kilt 'is wee grandbabe and near to kilt his darter as well. When I asked 'im 'ow 'ee reckoned that, 'ee jist kept sayin' t'were yer fault."

Kate groaned softly. "Maeve's time must have come early. Why did she not send for me?"

"You have been acting the midwife?" Duncan asked.

"There was no one else," Kate said, meeting the challenge in his look. "Old Marie, who likely saw you into this world, milord, is too weak to leave her croft. She appealed to me as your, er . . ."

"My widow," Duncan supplied, enjoying her discomfiture.

"Yes . . ." Kate flushed. "She begged me to take over the task. I know something of herbs and simples; any army wife worth her rations is aware of the rudiments of caring for the wounded and ill, the relief of pain. Old Marie taught me what she knew, and I have been doing that duty ever since."

"Ever the gracious Lady MacLean," Duncan said.

It was almost easy now to convince herself that the other Duncan had never been. Anger whirled about him, thick as the storm clouds over Beinn Airidh Charr. The sneer had returned along with the biting sarcasm. "What would you have had me do?" Kate asked. "Stand aside and play lady of the crumbling manor? There is sore need here, Lord MacLean, if only you would bother yourself to see it!"

"I fully intend to," Duncan said, his jaw clenching. "Perhaps it is time that Lord MacLean has a word or two with his loyal clansmen. Go back to the castle, Fred, and get yourself cleaned up. I will go to the village."

Fred cleared his throat. "Beggin' yer pardon, sir, but yer cannot be thinkin' o' goin' now."

"A little rain will do me no harm," Duncan said.

"What he means, milord," Kate said, reading the servant's discomfort, "is if it is your intent to lambaste the crofters into submission, then you might wish to change your clothing. I have seen chimney sweeps better attired."

Duncan looked down at himself, noticing for the first time his lack of shirt and the shabby state of his trousers. He reddened beneath his beard, and without a word, bolted for the castle.

Kate sighed. "Let me examine those cuts," she said.

"Ain't nuthin' but a scratch 'ere n' there," Fred told Kate as she inspected his hurts. "Daisy kin patch it up, she will. Wounnent o' even made mention o' it, milady. Bad luck it was, meeting up with yer both like that."

Bad luck, indeed, Kate thought, recalling what might have occurred between her and Duncan. "Please do not call me 'milady,' Fred. I feel bad enough about the deception that I perpetrated. Indeed, it seems to have caused even more problems than I could have imagined. Why did Maeve not call me when the baby was on the way?"

Fred shrugged. "Dunno, but 'er father were right griefed about it."

"I have to go to the village and find out what happened. Perhaps I can get matters in hand before your master arrives in all his avenging fury, and Maeve might need me still. If I could borrow your horse?"

Once more there was a vigorous bobbing of the Cockney's Adam's apple in a loud attempt to discreetly gain Kate's attention.

"What is it you wish to tell me, Fred?" she asked. "Or did someone knock some teeth back that you wish to clear from your gullet?"

"Tain't my place to tell yer, but Daisy's . . ." he began hesitantly.

"I give you leave to speak for her then," Kate said with growing impatience.

"Don't know right how to say," Fred began.

"Say it just as she would, Fred, since you do so credible an imitation. And do it now," Kate told him. "I will have to ride like the very devil to get to the village and back before the rain starts to fall."

Fred grinned and put one hand on his hip in womanly mimicry. "Milday, 'ow can yer be thinkin' o' showin' yerself dressed like an 'oyden! I vow, 'tis to o' a kind yer are, yerself and 'is lordship, goin' about like paurpers."

"Thank you, Daisy," Kate murmured with a rueful look at her soiled ill-fitting breeches. "If I attempted to visit Maeve looking like this, they would think that the hobgoblins had come calling. I had best go change." She flew down the path.

Fred chuckled, then winced and composed his face into a mask of woe, determined to let Daisy tend to his wounds. However, his dreams of feminine comfort were short-lived, as he approached the castle.

"Where in blazes are my shirts?" Duncan demanded, pointing down to his pants. "And what happened to my good pair of trousers? These ragged things are all that I can find."

"Those what you teared *was* th' best," Fred explained mournfully, dismounting and making his way toward a small patch of white midst the sodden ground near the pump. "As fer yer shirts, ain't got t'mendin th' other yet, an' looks ter me like there's th' one yer 'ad on yestidday." He held the length of linen up distastefully between the thumb and forefinger. "Got warshed in th' mud. Seems ter me that yer ought t'be stayin' close ter 'ome till I kin get yer lookin' decent, sir."

"What do you mean, I cannot wear the blue?" Kate's voice rang in the courtyard as she strode out the kitchen door.

"Thought you meant to wear those nasty breeches all the day," Daisy said defensively, following her mistress. "It seemed a good idea to give your dresses a cleaning, though a decent burial might serve those two rags better, it might! Ooh, when I think of what you left behind, milady, I could just—" The older woman caught her tongue as she spied the two men in the courtyard. Her eyes went wide. "Fred! You poor lamb! Whatever happened to you?"

"Tain't nuffin," Fred said in a sombre tone that put him somewhere between agony and death.

"Come into the kitchen," she said, hurrying to brace him

up beneath her beefy shoulder. "Let me take care o' that handsome face."

Kate and Duncan watched in astonishment as the two servants disappeared indoors without so much as a backward glance at master and mistress.

"And thus we are firmly put in our place," Kate ventured.

" ' . . . take care o' that handsome face,' " Duncan mimicked. "Is your woman blind or merely cozening him?"

"Daisy hasn't a deceptive bone in her body," Kate said. "If she calls his face fair, then it must be so in her eyes. The eye of the beholder is what makes the difference."

Duncan turned away from that frank gaze, bewildered by what he saw in those troubled green eyes. Was she wary of him now, because of what had occurred on the path, or was there something else in those emerald depths? *And what do you see, Kate, when you look at my face?* he wanted to ask. Strange, how a woman who had perpetrated a massive fraud was possessed of an inherent integrity. He knew that she would not lie to him if she could help it. Therefore, he would not ask the question for fear of outright evasion or the answer that she might give.

"It is sopping wet!"

Kate's exclamation caught Duncan's attention. She had gone to the wash line and was fingering the bunched blue fabric with obvious dismay.

" 'Tis the only thing I have fit to wear to the village," she said.

"You are not going to the village," Duncan told her, "not after what happened to Fred."

"That is why I *must* go," Kate said, wringing her hands. "Something has obviously happened to Maeve and her baby, and they are blaming you for it. Were it not for me . . ."

"Were it not for you, Kate," Duncan admitted, "they would likely be even less kindly disposed toward me. They hate their chieftains and with good reason. 'Tis an awful heritage that we have, we MacLeans."

"Yes, yes," Kate said impatiently. "I have heard whispers of this terrible curse. What utter falderal! To live one's life in fear of a few angry words said half a century ago. It seems to me nothing more than an excuse for wickedness and wallowing in self-pity."

"Perhaps," Duncan agreed. "But words have power, Kate, more than you would ever credit. There was a wisdom in what the Bonnie Prince said. He understood the MacLeans, you see, knew what has ever been in our blood, ever been in the murky depths of our hearts. Know you the story of the MacLean who set his Campbell wife on a rock in the Sound of Mull, expecting the tide to drown her?"

Kate shook her head, unable to speak, trapped by the grey look that was as bleak as the sea.

"Luckily, some fisherman rescued her. And Campbell of Cawdor avenged that bit of cruelty by knifing his brother-by-marriage to death. And do you not believe me, you have only to ask the fisher folk to point out the place they still call the Lady Rock. 'Tis a story known from the crofters to the king along with other tales of the MacLean leanings to cruelty." The old pain flooded him, the burden of his blood, the darkness of his thoughts. It was madness to want her so much, especially knowing that she could never want him in return. And the most puzzling thing about it was Kate herself. She was certainly not of the type that he usually favored. Yet, even as she was, mud-stained, her hair atangle with bits of twig and leaf, she was no less desirable, a nymph to his satyr.

Duncan's throat was tight as he continued. "So do not mock at curses, Kate. When he uttered his bane, Charlie was well aware that we would have to go against our very nature to break his curse. There is a darkness in our sept of the MacLean line, Kate, a blackness of the soul that fouls all that we touch, all that we love. 'Tis that shadow of melancholy that drove my mother from her home, and then it killed her."

"But I thought that she had left your father," Kate said, startled.

"Aye, she did," Duncan said, gazing beyond her toward the ruins of the castle as he recalled that day, remembering standing at the Hellsgate and wondering if he would ever see home again. "But it was too late. If she had left me behind, it might have saved her. But Mother had chosen to take me with her."

"And you were the heir," Kate murmured. "It must have taken a great deal of courage for your mother to leave, especially with you in hand."

"Aye, my father never suspected that she had the backbone in her," Duncan said, surprised that Kate had discerned just how much fortitude it had taken. "Mother was the mildest of women, full of fairy tales and dreams. My grandfather was a rich man, and his clan is a powerful one. Once she had left him, The Munroe kept my mother from my father's clutches, but my presence galled him. I am my father's image, or at least *was* once." His laugh was bitter as his fingers rose to absently trace his scar. "By choosing not to forsake me, she had brought the MacLean curse to her family's bosom. If a babe was born deformed, if the milk's gone sour, t'was no one's fault but her MacLean son's. But she would not let them return me to my father, despite his demands and my grandfather's dislike. Her family made her life miserable because of my presence, never let her forget that it was her own foolish choice to wed a man with a curse upon his head."

"Why did she marry him?" Kate could not help but put forth the question, although she knew it was none of her affair. Despite his even tones, the pain ran like a refrain through his narrative. Although he spoke of his mother's anguish, it was clear that the child that he had been had suffered far more.

"I asked her much the same, though I could never understand her answer. She had honestly believed that she would be the one to break the curse," Duncan said, his lips twisting in a wry mockery of a grin. "She loved my father, fool that she was, loved him enough to blind herself to everything but his charm, to be deaf to the rumors that kept every girl of respectable family at a distance. Mother was fey, and she claimed that when she met my father, she saw great joy in the future. T'was the only time, I think, that the Sight failed her. In the end, t'was Charlie's bane that broke her and not the other way around. My grandfather couldna wait to be rid of his MacLean grandson, so much so that he even parted with a bit of his precious gold to purchase me a commission in the army. On the day that I left, my mother took her own life."

"Coward." The word was out before Kate could stop it, forced from her lips in an unreasoning surge of anger at the woman. Surely Duncan's mother ought to have guessed that her son would blame himself, as he clearly did for everything else.

"How can you call her courageous in one breath, then name her coward in the next?" Duncan asked, annoyance patent in every staccato syllable. "She knew that I was safe. Her note said as much." Why was he babbling on about this? he wondered. He had never before divulged the contents of that last note, forwarded by his grandfather without so much as a phrase of condolence to accompany it. But somehow, the words kept tumbling out. "It was I who was the coward for leaving her. I should have stayed."

"It was what she wanted, Duncan," Kate said, but he went on with his narrative, as if he did not hear her.

"I was so desperate to get away," he said. "I did not realize how by shielding me, she had put herself in the line of fire. Once I was gone—"

"It is a parent's sacred obligation to protect a child," Kate cut in before he could blame himself any further.

The vehemence in her voice roused him from his recollections. Her green eyes glittered, fierce and feral as those of an angered tigress.

"Your mother did what she had to to preserve you against evil. As a child, it was not your duty to protect her, but the other way round." She could not stop the tears from forming, and she focused her attention on the distant hills. "I apologize, milord, for I had no right to name her a coward. She likely thought that her job was finished once you were out in the world. She had succeeded in her goal, and I envy her that."

"Why?" came the soft question from behind her.

"Because she was able to protect her child, and I could not," Kate whispered, slowly turning toward him.

The shimmer of her tears and the deeply etched sorrow on her face roused a long-dormant emotion, something that he had not felt since his mother had died all those years before. He wanted to wipe away that sorrow, to ease that terrible hurt. "Kate, if I can help . . ." he began.

"There is nothing that either of us can do to unravel the

tangle of the past," Kate said with an air of finality. " 'Tis today we must deal with and, if we have the strength, tomorrow."

"Very well," Duncan agreed. "Today, then. I must take myself to the village, Kate. My people have just grievances, I know, but I cannot allow poor Fred to take abuse on my behalf."

"I will go with you," Kate said.

"Dressed like that?" His dark brow arched in question. "Or are they already accustomed to a Lady MacLean who wears breeches?"

"No more than a lord who appears a shirtless tatterdemalion," Kate retorted. "Unless . . ." A hint of a smile appeared. "I may have a solution to both our problems, Duncan. However, if it suits, you must agree to allow me to accompany you."

"Kate . . ." His tone was a warning.

But she was not to be put off. "Do we have a bargain?" she insisted.

"Aye, a bargain," Duncan agreed warily, "probably as good a one as the last deal that we MacLeans struck with the English. That one led to a curse. I wonder what this will lead to."

"I shall show you," Kate said. In her excitement she grabbed him by the hand, towing him along behind her like a bark hauling a ship of line.

Bemused by her sudden touch, Duncan allowed himself to be dragged through the kitchen. He noted in passing that Fred and Daisy were nowhere in sight, licking wounds in private no doubt. But before he had time to speculate, Kate had moved on to the servants' hall, pausing only long enough to pull a key from the ring at her waist. The great brass lock on the tower door turned with a rusty clatter, and Duncan found himself in the cool stone heart of the well room. A battered oak lid at the center of the chamber marked the ancient, spring-fed water source, one of the primary reasons that the MacLeans of Eilean Kirk had proven well-nigh unconquerable and MacLean's Gold smooth as mother's milk.

"We always keep this room locked because of Anne," Kate explained. "Most of the uppermost story is totally unsound, but the middle floor, while somewhat shaky, is safe. Come along."

It was quite disconcerting, those fingers twined with his, and he could barely keep from stumbling at that insistent pressure as she ran up the stone staircase. Light spilled from the south-facing window, illuminating the room. Motes of dust stirred as Kate bustled him along to a darkened corner.

"There it is," she said, pointing toward an old leather trunk. Abruptly, she realized that she was still holding Duncan's hand; she had never realized how very large it was. As she let his fingers slip from hers, she turned hastily toward the trunk and knelt beside it. "I had meant to keep this till winter, when I had time to use my needle, but we can make do," Kate said, talking rapidly to cover her confusion. The warmth of his hand lingered, filling her with an aching regret that she had let that comfort go. What on earth could have possessed her to put her fingers in the fire? Kate opened the chest with the panache of a magician. "Violà!"

"Moths?" Duncan asked, his nose wrinkling at the strong scent of camphor, but as Kate pulled the top covering away, he saw a verdant field of fabric. Eagerly, he reached in and pulled out the folds of the garment, shaking away time. He held up the cloak to the light, letting the sun burnish the rich red and black checks that distinguished the tartan of the MacLean clan. The faint yellow stripe that designated the Eilean Kirk sept was faded but discernible. "I had thought these long gone," Duncan said in wonder. "After Culloden, my grandfather thought it politic to put the plaid aside, since he did not wish to stir the memories of our Scots brethren or his English masters."

"You will wear it then?" Kate asked, watching as he pulled forth the garments and laid them out with loving care. "It is against the law, still."

"Is it you threatening to call the law on *me* now, Kate?" Duncan asked.

He was actually teasing her! Kate nearly dove into the chest headfirst to cover her flaming face. "I had thought that I might wear this, Duncan," Kate said, digging through the clothing below. "It is a riding outfit, woefully old-fashioned, I fear. My grandmama was painted in one just like it, except hers was not a Scots plaid. See, 'tis rather cunningly divided, so I will have no need of a sidesaddle."

"It is just the color of your eyes," Duncan said, admiring the effect of the deep green against her skin. "You will look magnificent."

"Do you think so?" Kate asked, holding up the dress for examination. "I suspect that I will look rather ridiculous."

It was startling to realize that she actually credited that absurd statement, that a mere garment could make her look anything other than beautiful. "Do you dare call The MacLean a liar, Kate?" Duncan put on his most fierce expression. "You are fortunate, indeed, that there are no tides or rocks in the Loch Maree."

"And you are too lazy to take me to the coast so that you might dispose of me in true MacLean fashion?" Kate asked in delight, seeing the laughter in his eye.

"Aye, our slothfulness almost outweighs our treachery, milady," Duncan said, finding himself caught once again like a creature in amber, her smile bathing him in a golden warmth. He had to get himself away before he was trapped forever. There was a dirty smudge on her cheek that could be wiped away with a fingertip. She was looking up at him, the pulse beating at the base of her throat. Somehow, he had to make her understand her danger, make her see what he could become. He was a MacLean, as his grandfather had often told him, worse than the beasts of the field, for at least those animals had the excuse of lacking reason.

"If we would be at the village and back before the storm, I suggest that we proceed with all due speed." Duncan hastily snatched the garments from the chest, then sped downstairs as if followed by all the hounds of hell.

Chapter Nine

The view from the hilltop recalled the aftermath of a battle. Duncan reined in Selkie, pausing at the top of the road to scan the tiled roofs that he recalled from childhood, seeing in his mind what had been once, even as his eye denied the reality of now. Silently, they rode on, meeting not a soul on that single lane as they rode into the valley. The signs and decorations that had previously proclaimed the contents of the row of shops were gone. Only part of the vintner's sign remained. Where the hand of a jolly Bacchus had once squeezed a huge bunch of grapes into a goblet, only the cup remained, waiting forever to be filled as it swung mournfully. The happy god was gone. There was no door on the baker's shop, and the hearth before the farrier's barn was cold.

"Angus Munroe?" Duncan asked, shaking his head in disbelief.

"The blacksmith? He was gone to Canada before I arrived," Kate said. "There were no wagons to fix and even fewer horses to be shod, so he took his anvil and his kin to try his luck there."

"It would seem that everyone else followed," Duncan said, listening to the keen of the rising wind. "Used to be that there was scarcely room in Kirkstrath on a Thursday, betwixt the animals and the people. Market day, it was. Anyone who did not wish to make the trip up to Loch Ewe and the coast would come here to sell their wares or buy what they needed. You could barely hear the sound of Angus's hammer on the iron above the babble of the auld market wives, hawking 'herring and salmon fresh caught, still twitchin.'" His voice rose to counterfeit the peddler's cry. "Or *uisgebeatha* distilled in the glens, aged in oak since the

Bonnie Prince was a babe. I hope my father is roasting in hell, for what he has done!"

"T'was not he alone who was responsible," Kate said, moved by the desolation of his countenance. "At least he was not as cruel as the Countess of Sutherland. 'Tis said that she hired armed men with dogs and set torch to the crofts of those who would not leave the Strathnaver glens."

"Aye," said a cracking voice, "but men and dogs woulda been costin' him gold, an' the auld laird was never a one for partin' wi' the blunt, milady, could he help it. The MacLean just let his people starve and suffer till they could be takin' nae mair. Cost him not a pennypiece." A white-haired man dressed in a weather-beaten plaid stepped into the lane. "So 'tis ye comin' back at last, young MacLean. Knew ye would, sure as the Devil mun return to hell."

"Indeed, Tam, t'was time and fitting. But is that just reason to put your fists to my servant?" Duncan dismounted and walked toward the old man.

"Aye, that sorry cockerel." Tam spat contemptuously, studious aim bringing the shot just short of Duncan's brogues.

"That sorry cockerel," as ye name him, is not in the habit of fighting auld men," Duncan said. "Besides, yer quarrel is nae with him, but with myself."

Slowly, like wisps of fog, people had begun to trickle outside. Kate remained on Fred's horse, transfixed as Duncan seemed to change before her eyes. Although Kate was familiar with the plaids worn by the Highland regiments, the regalia that Duncan wore had seemed almost outlandish in its brash splendor. The chieftain's bonnet had appeared somewhat absurd with its full, rich trim; and the checkered hose with its bright patterns along the bold colors of the plaid itself had seemed an assault upon the eye.

Now it suited him, as fitting and right as the broadening burr in his speech. A shaft of sunlight broke through the clouds, making the rubies in his jeweled brooch flash blood red against the heavy gold. He was The MacLean, the Laird, and she could hear the murmur of angry voices as memory stirred old grievances, ancient wounds and wrongs.

"Is it to lesson me, ye've come then?" Tam mocked, putting up his fists. "The finery of yer grandda' yer wearin'. When last I seen it, I was but a wee laddie; our chief's

feileadh-beag with the great bonnet and the sporran. Seein'
it, I be recollectin' muh da and his pride, a distiller by trade,
t'be the piper for his laird for the True King. *Fear eil air son
Eachainn*, they was cryin'."

"Another for Hector," Duncan translated the clan motto.
"Aye, so you told me, laing time ago."

"But I did nae tell ye' how muh father came back a
shamed man, a broke man, muh puir da? How dare ye to
dress in the MacLean sett, laddie? With the dishonor yer father and his father heaped on our clan's name. Takes more
than *breacan triubhes* to make a chieftain." He nodded at the
tartan trousers. "There now, 'tis said, and 'tis ready I am to
die."

Kate could hear an undertone of approval at those brave
words and the collective gasp as Duncan reached down into
his patterned trews to pull his *skean dhu* loose from its place
against his calves. The small deadly blade glittered as Duncan turned the hilt outward, silently offering it to Tam.

The old man's fists dropped wearily to his sides as he
stared at the weapon.

"Do ye truly have a quarrel with me, auld Tam?" Duncan
asked softly, letting the knife fall to the ground. "If so, I
wouldna hae it told o' me that I dinna fight fair. Should I
bare my throat for ye then? Would that undo what my kin
hae done? For I canna return ill for good, auld man, for all
that I am a bloody MacLean. I recollect a lonely young lad
and one kindly man who let him tag by, for all that he was
cursed spawn."

Tam stared at the weapon in the dust between them, and
then turned his glistening gaze to Kate. "Why did ye nae
come, milady, to see to muh lassie's lyin' in? With her mon
gone to Americay and me alaine to give comfort the laing
night through?" he asked, his voice breaking. "The bairn's
for the kirkyard, and Maeve's heart fair to broken. Why did
ye nae come? Would he nae let ye gang then to tend to the
birthin'?"

"If I had been summoned, I would have come," Kate said,
pained that he could believe that she would have deliberately stayed away. "And how can you speak such evil of
Lord MacLean, Tam, that he would keep me from your
daughter in her time of need?"

"But Robbie himsel' went to bring ye, milady. Did ye nae Robbie, lad?" Tam motioned to a young boy who stood before the shop. The lad came reluctantly and stood before his grandfather. "Tell the lady what ye tol' me, laddie. How ye knocked at the door and were tol' she would nae come."

The boy's eyes dropped. His voice, when it finally spoke, was a shamed whisper. "There were banshees, Granda, screamin' an yellin' like all th' hants o' hell were loose. An' then I kenned this fearsome beast, prowlin' about the dark, the *bean sith* itself. I could nae get past it, Granda, and then a she-ghoulie started to wailin' and I was afeard." The lad began to sob.

There was a murmur in the crowd, then a long silence, which was broken finally by Tam. " 'Tis pardon I'm askin' to ye both," the old man said, looking at his grandson sadly. "Should hae kenned that ye were not that kind, milady, nor are ye yer father, milord." He bent and retrieved the *skean dhu*, cleaning it with the fold of his plaid before holding it out to Duncan. "I wouldna blame ye were ye to use it on me, milord, for the insult to yersel' and yer lady."

The old man's sincerity touched him deeply, and the words resonated . . . *nor are ye yer father* . . . Duncan took the knife and bent to return it to its place within his stocking. Black and red and green and yellow, the MacLean pattern from beyond memory. All his life he had been told that the sett of his life had been fixed years before he had been born, the warp in a loom with a curse running through the weft of his existence. Perhaps the time had come to be the weaver, to assume control of the thread of his days. Duncan looked at the boy, weeping openly now, standing alone before the condemnation of kin and kith. He went and touched him on the shoulder. "Nae, laddie," he said loudly, so that all could hear. "Dinna fash yersel', for in a way, it *was* myself that kept ye from the door. T'was my own cries that ye kenned last night."

Only Kate saw the telltale tightening of Duncan's jaw and understood its source: pain, humiliation that he revealed to all what he had so desperately wished to hide.

" 'Tis the dreams," Duncan told them all, "fearsome dreams that come like the *bean sith* in the night. After those visions of banshees, I canna sleep, so I walk, prowl about like a *bean sith* myself in the night. Ye need not be shamed, boy, that ye were affrighted. At such times, I fear myself in all my bloody blackness. I say 'tis nae fault in ye, boy." Duncan encompassed everyone in his gaze, demanding forgiveness for the child's understandable error, but instead of the pity that he had dreaded, he saw something entirely unexpected, and it gave him the courage to continue.

" 'Tis nae only yerself, Tam, who ought ask for pardon. For too many years the lairds of Eilean Kirk have enriched themselves and let the clan suffer, left debts unpaid and taken much . . . but given naught." Duncan's look touched each one of those careworn faces, hardened by time and disappointment. " 'Tis my intent to make a start at setting matters aright. My father's debts will be paid, though at present I have nae the wherewithal to do it, but 'pon my oath as a MacLean, every crofter or tacksman will be recompensed for what was taken by force and trickery. Till then, there will be nae rent or share asked o' ye."

A ragged cheer went up. "The curse is nae mair. The curse is nae mair."

"Nay," Tam's voice boomed above the din, " 'tis nae passed yet. Recall ye what the Prince did say?

" 'Thus he spake, our Prince sae bold,
When MacLean places honor before his gold.
When the silent find words t' speak
and MacLean his vengeance willna seek.
Then this bane shall lifted be,
When the blind MacLean shall truly see.' "

The old man recited, like an ancient. "Seems to me that our new laird may have honor, but there is nae much gold," he added humorously.

Laughter erupted from the crowd.

"But he's willin' t'try," one hopeful voice piped up.

"Aye, so he is," Tam agreed warmly, putting a hand on Duncan's shoulder and drawing him into a hearty embrace. "The MacLean, I say, The MacLean!"

Duncan felt their eyes upon him, judging him. He wanted to tell them not to hope, that until now he had never truly considered their needs, his obligations to them. He was bound to disappoint their expectations, entirely unworthy of their trust. Yet, they thrust their faith upon him, shackling him with every touch of a hand, every tentative smile becoming another link in the chain that bound him. Slowly, the crowd took up the chant that Tam had begun, until the name that Duncan had hated rang in his ears. "MacLean! MacLean!" But for the first time in his life, there was no derision. It was defiance of the past, a wish for the future.

Never before had Kate seen a man so utterly dumbfounded. The people of Strathkirk crowded around Duncan, shaking his hand, hailing him with a warmth that melted his icy reserve. A bewildered smile lit every crag and corner of that powerful face as they enfolded him, welcoming their chieftain home at last. She had feared for him, she realized, but luckily that anxiety had been for naught. Certainly, he had no need of her now. She slipped off Fred's horse. But before she could make her way behind the crowd, Tam noticed her and quieted the din with a wave of his hand.

"Do ye forgive me, milady, for doubtin' ye?" he asked.

"As Duncan said, there is naught to forgive," Kate said guiltily. "In fact, it is I who should be asking pardon as well . . ." She knew that she ought to end the deception, to tell them all that she was not Duncan's lady. But as she looked around her, she saw joy, smiles on faces that had never before held a hint of happiness. This was not the time for such truth telling. "My daughter, too, had a nightmare last night. She was the one that your grandson feared as a she-ghoulie."

"There is nae a one among us who has nae cried out in the night, man nor child, milady, milord," Tam said, including them both in his consoling look. "And even had ye come, milady, t'was a seven-month babe and sickly, nae laing for the world. I would though that my daughter had the comfort of yer hand and yer healin'."

"She can have it still, if she wishes," Kate said.

"MacLean and his lady!" Other voices took up the cheer, and it echoed behind her as Kate hurried away to expiate her crime of fraud as best she could.

Time was running short. The doctors were shaking their heads even as they presented bills and false hopes. Vesey had allowed his wife the luxury of a small rally, not quite a recovery, but he hoped, long enough to locate his errant sister-by-marriage and her child. Once Chloe was dead, there would inevitably be questions, and it would be infinitely preferable to have matters settled.

At last, there was a definite clue to the whereabouts of his niece and sister-by-marriage. A carter near Dover had distinctly recalled two women and a child . . . a dark-haired child . . . had Kate dyed that glorious hair? The color of ripening wheat it was, fine and soft as silk . . . Vesey's fist clenched. He would not allow himself to think of it. Best to deal with that later and occupy his thoughts elsewhere. Prinny was hinting at another loan, and this time there would certainly be a barony when the debt was smiled away.

Clasping that thought to his bosom, Vesey moved on to the business at hand. His desk was piled high. All of the Steele family affairs had fallen to him, naturally, and as always, he was moving carefully, judiciously. On the face of it, no one could claim that Vesey was anything other than the diligent steward. However, he did not dare to hire a secretary to ease the burden of correspondence and administration. He had learned the hard lesson that the slightest indiscretion, the least bit of heedlessness, could lead to inadvertent discovery. It was a lucky thing, indeed, that Duncan MacLean had been fool enough to confront him directly. Otherwise, all his diligent planning would have been for naught.

Vesey scrutinized every bit of correspondence carefully, making notes, weaving his web of control over the Steele assets ever tighter. Still, he nearly tossed aside one letter as some mendicant's plea or tradesman's demand. The quality of the paper was poor and the seal less than impressive. However, it was addressed to Lord Steele. Vesey broke the wax, and the names Dewey, Cheetham, and Howe glared up at him. Solicitors?

Although he racked his brain, Vesey could recall no Edinburgh law firm with connections to his wife's late brother. Puzzled, he read on slowly, gleaning the gist of the man of law's somewhat chagrined narrative.

MacLean was alive. The paper crackled, nearly ripping as Vesey's hands closed convulsively. He breathed deeply, forcing himself to read on. The Scot was a lord now, it seemed, a bloody earl, and the solicitor was applying for the return of an odd bequest, a book of poetry and a ring.

It took two glasses of port to steady Vesey's shaking hand. Vesey knew himself a man to be reckoned with now, more influential, certainly, than he had been when MacLean had faced him with those accusations. It would be the Scot's slander against the word of one of the members of Prinny's most intimate circle. But the Scot was an earl now, and there was the possibility that MacLean did have the evidence that he had mentioned so long ago. Dimly, Vesey recalled the words of that conversation on the eve of the battle of Badajoz.

"I shall give you one chance only, Vesey, since I believe you to be only peripherally tangled in this affair," MacLean had told him. "However, any charges against you would cause a scandal and likely hurt Adam's career and name. Confess and resign your commission. You would get off fairly easily, in all likelihood, and avoid sullying your family."

"This is utter nonsense, MacLean." He had been bluffing.

"I have proof," the Scot had said, his expression hardening into granite. "Names, dates, places. Tomorrow, Vesey. Your resignation, confession, and an offer of restitution, or you may sing your songs of innocence all you will, for it will do you no good."

It had been a simple matter to arrange for MacLean's demise. There were more than a few senior officers who owed Vesey favors, men who feared being implicated. MacLean had been sent into the heart of the furnace, a section of the battlefield where he was sure to perish under fire, or so Vesey had thought. But now the Scot was back. However, if Duncan MacLean still had the evidence in hand, why had he not come forward yet? Vesey loosened the folds of his cravat, easing the points of his collar that were suddenly pressing against his throat.

From the recesses of Vesey's brain crept a deeply troubling thought. He read through the solicitor's missive once more, picking carefully through the tangled narrative. Blake's *Songs of Innocence* was the book that had been left to Adam. However, his brother-by-marriage had despised poetry as so much rhymed drivel and had oft condemned poets as posturing scribblers. Surely MacLean had known of Adam's tastes?

"You may sing your songs of innocence all you will."

Vesey recollected MacLean's ironic smile. Yes . . . it would suit the Scot's cursed humor to twit his enemy and dangle the hiding place for the evidence right before his nose. Vesey had searched MacLean's tent after the battle, of course, under the pretext of gathering his last effects after Badajoz. Vesey gnashed his teeth as he recalled the lavishly illustrated volume, remembered holding it in his hand and tossing it aside without consideration. He had falsely concluded that MacLean had kept the evidence on his person. No body had ever been confirmed as MacLean's, but there had been so many bodies that were charred beyond recognition.

Gradually, the hammering of Vesey's heart slowed. If the evidence was in that book of Blake, then MacLean did not have it. Obviously, the Scot still believed that Adam was among the living. Perhaps MacLean was still hoping to avoid embroiling his friend in a scandal, or was he just waiting for the return of the evidence that he needed? The book was the key. Vesey calculated rapidly, checking the dates mentioned in the solicitor's letter. The bequest would have gone to Kate, since Adam was already dead when the terms of the will had been executed. It was a month or two afterward that Vesey had moved himself and his wife into the Steele mansion and gradually set his plans into motion.

Kate had been pitifully easy to manipulate, believing him without question. It had been simple enough to convince her that he held the reins of power, for unlike Anne, she had seemed utterly without spirit, a pale, cowed version of that golden child. With difficulty, Vesey turned his thoughts once more toward the whereabouts of that book.

The volume was most likely lost, Vesey told himself, but somehow that possibility did not allay his fears. A vague picture formed on the periphery of his consciousness, of a picture of a tiger illuminated by moonlight. He cast deeper into the pool of recollection. The nursery . . . he had seen that book of poetry on one of his forays upstairs. One of Anne's books.

Vesey charged up the stairs, nearly knocking down the new chambermaid in his haste. He rushed to the bookcases, strewing the volumes in careless disregard as he searched for that one book. But it was not there.

The blond porcelain doll that he had given Anne sat perched upon her bed, staring at him with her green glass eyes. With a roar of rage he snatched up the doll and dashed it into the empty fireplace.

"There, that's the last in this bucket," Duncan said, daubing a trowel full of pitch on the sloped roof and surveying it with satisfaction. The sound of hammers echoed across the loch. Half the village of Strathkirk and nearly every MacLean crofter was up on the roofs, pounding and repairing the ravages of time and neglect. They had come at dawn, armed with brooms and mops, hammers and pitch. "I still think that I am dreaming."

Fred lowered the empty bucket to the ground and grinned. "Th' best dream yer 'ad in a long time, I'd say. Seen the innards o th' place yet? Daisy's got th' women in a lather, a'scrubbin an' a'polishin'. Scarce kin see, with all th' dust raised."

"They will have to be paid," Duncan said, calculating against the thinning contents of his purse. "Unfortunately, I can give them little beyond the butler's grace right now, my thanks and a few coins."

"They knows yer ain't flush with th' ready. Be right surprised, won't they, when they find out yer richer n' Golden Ball." Fred chuckled.

"Aye." Duncan allowed himself a smile as he squinted into the sunlight, almost expecting those busy figures to disappear. There was a curious tightness in his chest, a swelling of pride along with a stab of fear. He could not fail them as his family had so many times before. "Look at them. Every single one of these people is barely scrabbling by themselves, yet they are wasting their time on this old ruin. I can barely offer them a meal when they're done, but I shall make it up to them," he vowed.

"Not now, I 'ope," Fred said practically. "Ain't got much

left atwixt us, and milady ain't got more 'n two pennies t'rub together."

"Why do you keep addressing her as 'milady', Fred?" Duncan asked in an undertone, looking carefully about to make sure that there were no listeners. "You know it makes her feel ill at ease, especially now. She almost winces when one of the crofters uses it. Not that I blame her, mind. 'Tis more a pity than an honor to be known as MacLean's lady."

" 'Tis simple respect." Fred glowered. "Wager every pennypiece yer owes me from before and til' doomsday that th' title 'lady' is 'ers by right. Daisy makes use o' it, even when she's thinkin' th' two o' them are private like."

"Force of habit?" Duncan questioned.

"A long bred 'abit then," Freed reasoned. "In times o' need, 'tis *milady* that Daisy calls for. Been around long enough t'see what's what. If any o' it's a sham, 'tis this 'Katie' business, makes Daisy fair t' cringe yer kin see, t' call 'er by 'er Christian name. Slips sometime an' calls 'er 'Miss Katie,' Daisy does, but most times, 'tis 'milady,' that comes when she ain't watchin' 'er tongue."

"It would fit my suspicions," Duncan said, untying the length of rag wrapped round his forehead and wiping his brow.

"Seems t'me with what we knows betwixt us, we could find out 'oo she is," Fred suggested, dipping some water from a pail and offering it to Duncan. "Daisy won't spill nothin', stout lass what she is, but I 'eard enough bits and pieces t'put two t' two. Part o' the twenty-ninth regiment, was milady's father, and Daisy raised 'er when 'er ma died when Kate were but fourteen. Been in th' castle nigh on t' six months. But they're still scairt, sir, nervous as cats in th' kennel an' I'd as lief know the why o' it."

"So would I," Duncan agreed, looking down into the courtyard. Kate was below, drawing water from the pump. Though she was working harder than any, she was laughing and chattering easily with the other women. Dressed in a simple, nondescript round gown, she was attired no better than they, yet she was still as distinct as a peacock among the pigeons. The wariness that she habitually wore was temporarily cast aside. When Kate looked up at him and waved merrily, his heart could not help but skip a beat. Suddenly, he felt a smile stretching across his face.

"Got yersel' a bonny lady, milaird," Tam called, tugging on the line that held the bucket, "but mind the roofin', laddie. The pitch'll get caild afore ye will, I warrant."

A hearty gale of mirth came from below and above. Kate blushed till her cheeks nearly matched her fiery hair, but she gave no other sign of offended dignity and walked indoors unhurriedly, with all the pride of a queen. Luckily, his own embarrassment was more easily concealed, and he blessed the bushy thatch of beard that hid his own flush of vexation. Shamed that they had discerned his naked emotions so plainly, Duncan hauled up the bucket of hot tar, the laughter breaking in waves about him.

He had forgotten how ribald and familiar his people could be. With the close ties of blood and history, the MacLean clan of Eilean Kirk had always treated their chieftain more as a first among equals rather than an unreachable superior. Above all, Duncan found himself wishing that what his people believed were the reality, that Kate was his in truth. Of late, he had found himself thinking of her, wanting her, until it would seem that the price of honor might well be madness. Heeding Tam's advice, Duncan gave himself over to the rhythm of work, letting the steady pounding beat set his pace, filling his mind with nothing more than the warm fingers of sun stroking his back or the caress of the gentle breezes off the loch. Loch Maree glistened like a sapphire set amidst a jade field as he moved carefully across the slate.

There would be no rain tonight to test his roofing skill. The sky was a flawless blue, with nary a cloud to be seen except the perpetual coronet of white that hovered at the mountain peaks. He was nearly exhausted, but it was a form of fatigue that he had almost forgotten, the rewarding weariness that comes from work completed, a job done well. The straight rows of shingles brought their own peculiar contentment. Perched on the ridge, Duncan stretched like a panther, easing the soreness in his muscles, but feeling better than he had ever felt in his life.

It began as no more than a faint feeling, touching his

spine like cold steel. More than once that vague uneasiness had saved his hide on the battlefield.

"She's watching me, Fred," Duncan said quietly, between taps on the nail head. "Can you spot her?"

"The little mite again?" Fred asked. "Midst all these people? Thought that she an' that dog o' 'ers 'ad taken theirselfs off when th' folk started t'come."

"So did I," Duncan said, pulling a broken slate loose and tossing it to the pile below. "But she is watching me again, I can feel it. Has she been following you about at all?" Duncan asked.

The servant shook his head. "Not so's I know of it," he said. "No 'arm in it as I see, though I can't figger for the life o' me why she's been trailin' yer about."

" 'Tis deuced uncomfortable," Duncan complained, shading his eye against the afternoon sun as he surveyed the landscape, peering up toward the tower. There was a flutter of movement as a bird flew hastily from the ledge, but not before he had seen a glimpse of a face. "There now! Did you spy her up there?"

"Th' tower?" Fred clucked. "Yer seein' things, Major. T'was just a pigeon. Th' door up is locked tight. Tried it meself, other day. Daisy keeps 'er preserves in there."

"And you were thinking to help yourself? Well, why don't you check it again, Fred?" Duncan suggested, knowing full well that he was being foolish. Most likely it had been the bird that he had noticed, but if the child was climbing up in the towers, it would have to be stopped. Whether the deterioration was due to climate, careless workmanship, or Charlie's curse, none could say. But in this newer wing of the castle particularly, the rotting flooring was weak as cat's ice, unable to bear much more than the weight of a small animal. As Duncan recalled, Kate had warned him especially about that turret.

Fred climbed down the new ladder, grumbling as he went. Duncan went on working until his man returned.

"Bang on th' mark, yer was, sir," Fred called from the ground. "Must o' seen me comin' an' just run out afore I got there. T'weren't locked, th' door. Poor Daisy is beside 'erself, she is."

"I think Anne's mother and I are due for a talk," Duncan

said, checking the ground below for signs of the child, but she was nowhere in sight, though he heard the faint bark of a dog in the distance.

"Air ye lookin' for the wee one?" Tam asked, his eyes watering at the smoking pitch. "Saw her and the hound puttin' out toward the garden. Up to some devilment, yer lassie, from the look on her face and they way she were titterin'."

Duncan was about to tell him that the brat was no child of his, but for some reason he did not wish to disabuse Tam of his ill-founded notion.

"Perhaps the little lass needs a dose of her own medicine?" Duncan speculated, climbing down to stand beside Fred.

"Fair play, it is, ter turn th' game about," the Cockney agreed.

"Especially when it is a very dangerous game," Duncan said, rinsing off his hands under the pump. "I'll be back as soon as I can, Fred. This cannot wait."

"Go easy on 'er, Major," Fred advised, starting back up toward the roof.

" 'Going easy,' seems to be the problem," Duncan said, taking up his shirt. "The child has been pulling small pranks on a daily basis, yet those women dinna do a thing. She manipulates them like puppets."

"She's a clever one, she is," Fred said with a doting smile.

"You, too?" Duncan asked in disgust. "Did you account the eel in my boot clever? T'was you that had the cleaning of it, I recall."

"Cleaned worse things," Fred said, shrugging his skinny shoulders. "Almost worth it, it was, seein' you 'oppin about, fit to burst."

"You are dismissed, Fred. Pack your bags." Duncan slipped his shirt over his head only to find that his fingers were caught in the sleeve. "Damn!" he exploded.

"Need 'elp, Major?" Fred asked diffidently. "I'd be glad, but seein' as 'ow I ain't no longer in yer employ. A pity, t'would be, to ruin yer shirt, considerin' as 'ow yer ain't got many to spare."

"Fr-e-d . . ."

Although the drawn-out syllable was muffled by the linen, Fred knew that his erstwhile employer had reached the end of his tether. He helped his master untangle himself. "Aye, 'tis th' little one, al right," he said, eyeing the crude stitches used to sew the sleeve shut.

"You take care that the tower stays closed," Duncan commanded, his lips setting in a straight, tight line.

"You ain't 'ired me back yet, Major," Fred informed him. But the look that his master gave him was enough to send him scuttling back toward the roof. In the distance he could see the child, running through the heather and disappearing over the hill. She had stayed to watch her handiwork, the little minx.

Duncan moved swiftly, years of skill combining with boyhood knowledge to make his passage silent. The small marks of Anne's erratic course were as vivid as signposts to him. Prints of paws and tiny bare feet marched side by side, showing clearly where girl and dog had passed, stopped to look under a rock, pluck a wildflower. She was roaming far afield indeed, nearly the full mile length of the island. Abruptly, the trail veered, disturbed stones and foliage pointing their path up the steep hillside, and a smile played on Duncan's lips. So, Anne had discovered the fairy grotto.

Carefully, Duncan edged his way to the lip of the overhang, testing the wind's direction to make sure that the dog would not scent him, before peering out over the ledge, almost fearful to see if time had changed this special place.

But it had not changed. Silver water spilled into a misty pool while ferns waved their feathery tails in the breeze. This was the kingdom where his dreams had held reign, where dragons had kept watch with their fiery breath, searing strangers that would have dared disturb his peace. The dryads dwelt here in the trees, whispering to each other in the summer storms, telling secrets that no human could decipher. His mother had promised him that if he closed his eyes and believed with all his might, he could hear the fairies singing in this place.

"Tiger! Tiger! burning bright,
In the forests of the night
What himmortal hand or eye . . ."

The voice was high and reedy, the melody like none that Duncan had ever heard. Who had met Anne in the grotto?

"In what distant deeps an' skies
Burnt the fire of thine eyes?
On what wings dare he perspire?
What the hand dare seize the fire?"

Duncan smiled at the substitution of "perspire" for "aspire." From the pitch of the voice it was clear that Anne's companion was another child. The tune changed to one he recognized, a snatch of an old lullaby that his mother used to sing. But two verses later, the melody changed once again.

"When the stars frew down their spears,
And watered heaven with their tears . . ."

Somehow it did not fit to the tune of "Cherry Ripe," but the voice cut and sliced the words to fit, elongating syllables here, garbling words there, until the very end, soaring high to a rousing finish.

"Why himmortal hand or eye
Dare frame they fearful sinnet-treeeee!"

It was only as the last echo faded that the thought dawned. It could be no crofter's child who mangled Blake below, but the obvious answer was an impossible one.

The little girl who never uttered a word scrambled up onto a rock, followed by her dog. She picked up a stick and heaved it into the pool. "Bring it, Cur," she called. "Fetch it to me."

It was obviously a familiar game, for no sooner did it splash, than the dog was in the water, paddling toward the stick eagerly and then returning to the rock to shake himself off to Anne's delighted squeals. "You bad dog," she said, wagging a scolding finger with a voice that was a perfect mimicry of Mrs. Kent. "You've gotten me very wet, an' Mama will be mad if I come home soaking."

She was speaking. The silent child was not just talking,

but chattering, singing, words spewing from her mouth as if a dam had just burst. Duncan listened in puzzlement as she prattled to her canine audience, seemingly repeating everything she had heard that day. He was hard put not to laugh when he saw Fred, Mrs. Kent, and Kate herself through the mirror of a child's eyes. But it was Anne's impression of himself that hit him like a well-aimed blow. She threw her chest out, arranging her face in a sneering scowl. "I can't smile," she bellowed, pantomiming his struggles with his shirt. "It hurts when I smile. Anne can do funny things, but I won't laugh." Her voice dropped back to normal, but the words carried clear. "D'you think it was the Frenchies that hurt him like that, Cur?" she asked. "Or maybe The Mac-Lean is really a truly prince, under a spell."

The thought of himself as an enchanted prince brought a brief wry twist to Duncan's face.

"He's a lord, just like Papa was, an honest, truly lord," Anne explained earnestly. "Even though they call him 'The,' instead of 'Lord' MacLean. Mama said so."

Cur barked in canine concurrence.

So, Papa was a lord. But that confirmation of Fred's suspicions was the smallest of Duncan's concerns at present. He drew back, his thoughts in a jumble as he wondered what to do. If he challenged Anne, he might very well deprive her of the only place where she felt safe enough to use her voice. Confrontation might be the worst possible tactic.

"Did you see the castle, Cur? So many people." Her tone was disapproving. "But Mama was happy. She hasn't been happy in so long. 'Member how she used to laugh all the time before *He* came? Do you think He used to hurt her, too? He promised not to, if I . . ."

He waited for her to complete that sentence, but she swallowed and blinked rapidly, as if trying not to cry. There was something in her voice that capitalized that "He," making it the verbal equivalent of personified evil. What was that hurt that the child spoke of, that unspoken terror that kept her deliberately dumb?

"But He can't find us here, can he?"

A tremulous bravado in that small voice reverberated deep within himself. How often had he himself come to this place, staying in this hidden sanctuary as long as he dared sheltering from his father's rages or his mother's unhappiness?

"This place is magic, Cur, magic," she said with a vehemence that was based in fear.

Magic. Duncan recalled dozens of boyish spells, calling upon earth and air, wind and fire, but he had been rather a poor sorcerer. When he had emerged from his solitary conjurings, nothing had changed. His father was still the wicked Beelzebub MacLean. His mother had still wept in her misery. He only hoped that Anne's childish conjurings were better than his.

Duncan was about to creep away, ceding the place that had once been his haven to the child, when his foot hit a loose pile of rock, sending a shower of shale and pebble down the hillside. Cur began to bark furiously, and Anne cowered behind the collie, her only exit blocked by an unknown intruder.

" 'Tis just myself, Anne," Duncan said as he rose from hiding, trying to calm the terror that he had inadvertently caused. "I did not mean to startle you, nor spy upon you. Long ago this used to be my special place, too, but I ought not to have intruded. Please tell me that you forgive me." He climbed down the cliff wall and stood in the mist by the small waterfall, waiting for her answer.

The child regarded him, her eyes as wide and eloquent as her mother's. Duncan could almost read her thoughts. *How long were you there?* she was wondering. *Did you hear me?* "I know that you can talk, Anne," Duncan said softly, ending her uncertainty. "You sound just as your Mama must have when she was a girl. I hear her in your voice. She will be so happy, Anne, that you can speak again."

Anne shook her head in denial, patent terror in her expression.

Duncan knelt down, looking levelly into those horrified eyes. "Is it Him that you are afraid of?" he guessed. "Is that why you are silent, Anne?"

The child's breath came in shallow gasps, and Cur whined, nuzzling her hand in silent comfort. She looked about wildly, like a trapped animal, unwilling to affirm or deny anything.

"You do not have to tell me," Duncan soothed. "I just

want to help you Anne, to help your mother. But how can I protect you, if I do not know what I must shield you from?"

"I can't tell, I can't." She backed toward the edge of the pool.

"I won't let anyone hurt you, Anne, I swear."

"Not me," Anne said her little body shaking. "Mama, He will hurt Mama if I tell. He said so."

Duncan felt the rage rising in him, but knew that he had to control it. If he frightened her now, all was lost. Although an inferno smoldered within, he forced himself to speak calmly as he walked to stand beside her. "Do I really look so silly, Anne?" He puffed out his chest, exaggerating and deepening his voice as she had. "Do you really think that I am under a spell?"

The abrupt change of subject took the child by surprise, and she looked at Duncan with puzzled eyes.

"Perhaps I was under some wicked enchantment, Anne," he said, choosing his words carefully. "Something very terrible happened to me, something so awful that I thought that I would never smile ever again."

"The Frenchies?" she asked, her hands twisting nervously in the collie's fur. "Colin?"

"Aye," he said, laying his demons bare before her. "Though I don't know how much you heard of my nightmares. It was true, unfortunately, the Frenchies, Colin, and the ruin of my face."

"You can hardly see it now," Anne observed artlessly. "It's all bushy where the cut was."

His patent disbelief was obvious enough to irritate the child and make her forget some of her skittishness. "Silly," she said. "If you don't believe me, come an' look in the pool."

Slowly, he rose and walked to the still part of the water. A bronzed face stared back at him. The image's fingers lifted with incredulous hesitancy to touch the beard and sideburns that hugged chin and cheek. Beneath, barely visible, was the light shade of his scars. But there were worse scars to deal with, Duncan reminded himself as he saw Anne's wavering figure appear beside his reflection. "A rather scruffy-looking prince I make," Duncan said, "all rags and tatters with a castle as moldering as myself."

"But you are in disguise, you see," Anne told him earnestly. "In Mama's stories all the bestest princes are forever running about in disguise."

"As do princesses, if I recall," Duncan said gently, speaking to that childish image in the water. It seemed to put her at ease, her posture less guarded, her expression less fearful. "In *my* mother's stories they were always under terrible enchantments or captured by loathsome dragons until those wandering princes came to their rescue."

Anne nodded. "Yes, they always do."

"I want to rescue you, Anne," Duncan said earnestly to the face in the pool. "And your mother, but you will have to help me."

"No!" The word was ripped from her and she began to quiver like a leaf in the wind. "He'll kill her. He said so. He'll kill her if I tell. He'll kill her! He killed Papa! He said so! He said so! An' He'll kill Mama, too!" Her voice rose to a frantic shriek of terror and grief.

"I will not let him," Duncan said, turning back toward her, trying to calm the frenetic storm that he had unwittingly unleashed. "I swear, Anne. I will not let him harm either of you."

"You can't stop Him," she whimpered. "He's strong, stronger than Papa, an' Papa couldn't stop Him. My papa's dead an' He killed him."

"But your papa died in battle." Duncan tried to reason with her.

"That's what He wanted everyone to think, but He told me what really happened. He knows things; He's real smart about doing things so's nobody knows. It was a secret . . . secret . . . if He finds out that I've talked . . ." Her voice rose to a keening wail.

Duncan was utterly at a loss. The desperation in the girl's unfocused expression frightened him. Somehow, she had been convinced that her tormentor had killed her father. Those evil threats were entirely real to her, immediate, putting her beyond the reach of reason. He himself had stood at the brink, seen the abyss that yawned wide and ominous in those terrified green eyes, and so, he understood. This valiant child had kept herself silent out of love, out of fear. If she believed that she had placed her mother in jeopardy, there was no telling what Anne might do to protect Kate. Perhaps, Duncan shuddered inwardly, even choose that final silence that nothing could penetrate.

"He will not find out, Anne." Duncan got on his knees once more and reached out again to clasp the trembling child by the shoulders. "I will not tell, I promise you. I will not tell. I will not tell." He repeated those four words softly, over and over, until Anne's breathing slowed and recognition dawned.

"You won't tell?" she dubiously echoed, choking back a sob.

"No, cross my heart." Duncan released her from his grasp and went through the motion solemnly. "It does not go beyond this valley, unless you let it." He had thought that the child would move away from him once released, but instead she moved closer, laying her head trustingly on his shoulder, a butterfly that had suddenly chosen to light upon him. Tentatively, he raised his fingers and stroked her hair comfortingly. As she nestled her head in the hollow of his neck, he ached for her even as he burned with anger at the man who had burdened her with secrets.

"And Mama?" Anne asked in a hoarse whisper. "You mustn't tell Mama. If she knows, He'll see. Mama's no good at all about secrets. If you tell her, He'll know that I told and then . . ."

Duncan felt her shiver. She was so terribly fragile; the thread that kept her from plunging into hysteria was gossamer thin. Nonetheless, the thought of denying this news to Kate was almost beyond bearing. To let her continue to believe that Anne was doomed to silence was unconscionable. Yet, he knew that Anne was right. Even if he told Anne's secret in confidence, Kate could not help but betray herself to the child. The woman was far too transparent to conceal her joy.

There was no way of predicting how Anne would react if he refused to acquiesce to her terms. If he accepted this vow, Kate would have to remain ignorant of the truth. "No, Anne," he agreed, "I will not tell your mother, though I think it wrong."

The girl lifted her head, her eyes reaching deep into his,

that steady gaze disquieting in its wisdom. Apparently, Anne was satisfied by what she saw.

"No, you won't tell," she said, solemnly. "He'd hurt you too, you know. I wouldn't want that."

"I don't hurt easily," Duncan told her, touched by her concern, deciding not to press her any further. Perhaps with time, she might grow to trust him. "Do you know that there is a small cave behind the waterfall?"

"Really? Where?"

The child seemed almost as anxious to change the topic of conversation as Duncan was himself. Excitement quickly overwhelmed her anxiety.

"There are fish in the pond, Lord MacLean, but I can't catch any. Is it a treasure cave, Lord MacLean?"

"You had best call me Duncan," he said.

"Is it a treasure cave, Duncan? Do animals live there?"

"So many questions."

"Is it too much of a bother?" Anne asked wistfully. "I haven't had anyone else to ask, you see."

"Nae, you haven't, lass," Duncan said, trying to keep his sorrow for her from coloring his voice. "And 'tis no bother. You can talk to me, Anne, about anything you please. Remember, you can always talk to me."

Chapter Ten

"She was up in the tower," Daisy moaned softly. "Could have been killed. I thought I locked that door, milady. I swear I did, but then I heard the knockin' and the noise in the courtyard, and all these folks comin' round so unexpected-like, I must have forgot."

"There's no harm done, Daisy," Kate soothed, patting the older woman on the shoulder.

"None a'tall." Fred added his reassurance to Kate's. "Merry as a grig, she were, laughin' at 'er mischief. Major were fit t'be tied though. Fact is 'ee *were* tied, th' way she'd sewn up 'is sleeves." He showed them his master's shirt. "Look like th' mite ain't payin' much mind t' 'er stichery lessons, Daisy," he teased.

"Anne did this?" Kate asked, knowing even as she examined the childish seam that there could be no other explanation. "I am sorry. It is my fault. I was so glad to see her acting like a normal child that I turned a blind eye. However, it seems now that my daughter's escapades seem to be getting out of hand."

"Said as much ter me, 'ee did, th' major, afore 'ee went after 'er," Fred agreed.

"Duncan went after her?" The shirt slipped from Kate's fingers to the floor. Anne did not seem to fear the earl. In fact, Kate had taken those small tricks that the child had played upon Duncan as a sign of encouraging progress. However, a private confrontation with an angry man might very well destroy that precarious peace that Anne had achieved.

"Aye, 'ee did," the Cockney said, scooping up the linen

and eyeing the dirt upon it with a cluck of dismay. "Gonner 'ave ter wash it agin, now, I will."

"Stop your complainin' and tell her whereabouts the two of them went," Daisy demanded, reading the worry on her mistress's face with the ease of long acquaintance.

"Well now, I dunno." The little man scratched his head. "Seems ter me this is atwixt th' two o' them. Ain't a lot that yer've done about th' matter of 'er pranks till now. Cept maybe t' wag a finger an' say 'fer shame.' "

"Fred, please! There is a great deal about Anne that you and Duncan simply do not understand," Kate pleaded.

The urgency in her voice brought a reluctant answer. "Out past th' gardens," Fred told her. "Seen th' major goin' beyond th' stables, from up top o' th' roof. Dunno more'n that."

"Bless you, Fred," Kate said as she ran out the door.

"Biscuits for you, laddie," Daisy promised, giving him a kiss on his grizzled cheek, "and gravy."

"Might as well 'and me thirty pieces o' silver while yer about it," the little man grumbled. But he was whistling happily as he mounted the roof and watched until Kate disappeared from sight.

Kate had no difficulty following their direction since neither Anne nor Duncan had made any effort at concealment. The moist ground showed the clear imprints of small toes, boots, and paws jumbling all together. The mere thought of Anne confronting a belligerent Duncan made Kate's feet fly. But it was the first wild shriek that gave her wings. Then another scream followed close upon it.

It was Anne's yell punctuated by Cur's frenetic yips. Was she too late once again? What had Duncan said to Anne, done to her, that could evoke that awful noise? Though she knew it to be preposterous, loathsome memories slithered into her mind, the fears still fresh enough to set her heart pounding. Impossible though it might be that history was becoming the stuff of the present, the sound drew her down, pulling her into a dark vortex of fear.

As she ran those last yards, time slipped away and Kate was traveling down the long, dark, corridor of Steele House, treading the darkened stairs up to the nursery as a cry melded with the thunder's roar, a child's terror, her daughter's scream.

Kate burst into the clearing like a fury, her heart beating a wild tattoo as she raised her hand, ready to strike. How the knife had gotten into her grip, she did not recall, but the cold steel was there, solid and reassuring. She would not fail Anne, she vowed, not again. But the scene that confronted her was totally unlike the one that she had imagined.

"I would ask you, Anne, not to use my beard as reins, if you please, or else you may find that your mount will bolt," Duncan said, giving his broad shoulders a demonstrative shake. It was not nearly enough to dislodge the delighted young miss perched upon his shoulders, but it was sufficient to send her into another volley of transported squeals.

He whirled about, neighing and pawing the ground like a rambunctious steed, all the while keeping a careful hold on the fragile burden above him. Anne clutched him tightly, screaming loudly enough to make him wince, but the rain of giggles in his ears that followed was more than adequate balm for his pain.

Then, abruptly, that chortling sound ceased. Duncan looked up from his equine play and saw Kate, her eyes unnaturally wide, as if she had seen something unspeakable, her countenance contorted with fear and rage. "Kate?" All at once Duncan recalled where he had seen a similar expression. She had the glazed look of a soldier in the midst of a melee, that air of uncertainty when friend and foe were all as one. "Kate?" The blood drained from her face as she hastily lowered her hand into the pocket of her skirt, but not before he saw the flash of steel.

"We shall continue the ride later," he promised, gently setting Anne upon the ground. "Your mama seems to be somewhat upset. Shall we see what's troubling her?"

Anne ran to her mother, grasping her limp arm.

Kate tried to find a reserve of strength, but that rush of fear had utterly drained her. She gave the girl a weak smile, and to her surprise, Anne looked to Duncan.

"There's nae need to worry, lassie," Duncan said, reassuring the girl with a nod that pledged his promise would be kept. "T'was the noise that we were making that got your puir mother alarmed, I suspect. She must have been thinking all the ghoulies and ghosties from here to Glen Torridon were after her little Anne. Have I the right of it, Kate?"

"Indeed, ghoulies, ghosties, and beasties, too." Kate drew spirit from that steady supportive gaze and managed a pallid affirmation. She had to explain somehow, try to make him understand why she had come charging in literally with dagger drawn, but not with Anne present. "In truth, I came to speak with you, Anne, for I am most upset by your behavior. Why ever have you been playing such nasty tricks on Lord MacLean? It is the outside of enough, considering his kindness to us."

Anne looked at her toes with shamefaced fixation.

"Anne and I have already resolved that between us, have we not, Anne?" Duncan asked, wondering how much longer Kate could continue to hold up. As it was, she had been driving herself mercilessly toward the edge of exhaustion. Now she seemed about to step over that verge. "We are in accord, your daughter and I," he assured her.

Anne nodded, squeezing her mother's hand in anxious confirmation.

Kate gave an unsteady laugh, maintaining the fiction that nothing out of the ordinary had occurred, that she had not come rushing out like a madwoman, ready to strike. "Without bloodshed, I take it? Go home with you then, Anne, if you have made your apologies. I have little doubt that Daisy has a word or two for you, as well. You know that you are not allowed up in the tower."

Once more, Anne's eyes sought Duncan.

"I shall care for your mother, lassie, I promise." Duncan gave her a smile of encouragement. "And that's one thing you may be sure of, Anne, I keep my promises. Now go and tender your regrets to Daisy, for Fred told me that she was near to tears with blaming herself for your mischief." The girl's eyes darkened with guilt, but he could see that she was still hesitant to leave.

"Best to pay the piper earlier than later," Duncan told her gently. "Go on with you."

Anne gave her mother's hand a final press before starting back toward the castle, the collie trailing behind her. As soon as the child was out of sight, Duncan was beside Kate in a few strides. "Lean on me now, Kate, for I'd as soon not violate a sworn oath, but unless I miss my guess you are perilously near to fainting away."

Without a word Kate stepped into his arms, and he drew her close, supporting her trembling body. He whispered to her softly, murmuring the words of an ancient Gaelic lullaby that his mother had been used to sing, treating her much as he had the child. Yet, he was well aware that this was no child that he held, but a woman. It should have been easy to soothe her, but all of the old stratagems that he had used in the past seemed utterly useless. That fluent charm that had once been so simple to tap had seemingly run dry.

Never before had Duncan been so bereft of words. The diffident endearments, the casual promises that he had made so many times to so many women, would not come to his lips. With an awkwardness that he could not quite understand, he clasped her to him, wishing that he knew what to say, what to do to help her.

"It has been so long," Kate murmured, leaning her cheek against the hard plane of his chest, listening to the strong, steady beat of his heart. "I could not discern the difference between a shout of glee and a scream of fright, Duncan." She looked up at him, her eyes murky with sorrow and apprehension, wondering how she could begin to make him understand. "I was afraid . . ."

"That Anne would be hurt again," Duncan completed. "It does not take a man of great intellect to discern that something has happened to your daughter, Kate," he explained, forestalling the question in her startled look. "From what both you and Daisy have let slip, 'tis clear that the lassie was not always thus. Is that what you are running from, Kate?"

She was too tired to devise a credible lie, and even if she had been capable of one, he did not deserve it. Kate closed her eyes, recalling the scene that she had witnessed before her insane fear had destroyed the moment. Anne on Duncan's shoulders, laughing, screeching with all the joy and verve of a normal child. It was what Kate had hoped for, all that she had prayed for in these past few months, and somehow, this man had made her daughter trust again, made her laugh again. When Kate opened her eyes once again and saw Duncan's uncertainty, she knew that he would require no less than the truth. With a sigh, she stepped from the shelter of his arms, wondering if she would see that look of concern change into contempt once he learned of her cowardice.

"Yes, that is what we are hiding from," Kate said wearily, slumping to sit on the nearby trunk of a fallen fir. "Most of what you know is true. My husband did die in the battle of Ciudad Rodrigo, only I was not on the Peninsula with him. Anne and I were in England. Thinking me a rather flighty sort of female, I found that when he died, he left our affairs in the charge of his sister's husband. Perhaps I am a poor sort of creature, because I never deemed money to be very important. I was quite content to allow him to manage things, even to the point where I did not object to my brother-in-law and my husband's sister moving into my home. There were some problems . . . He swiftly took the reins of my household into his hands, ordering it to suit him, but so long as he left Anne in my charge, I did not make any complaints. But then, Anne began to change . . . ."

Duncan seated himself beside her, but he might as well have been leagues away. Her eyes had turned the color of clouded jade as she cast back to those disturbing memories.

"When I recollect how I ignored those small signs . . . but Daisy knew that something was amiss. She noticed far sooner than I that Anne had become withdrawn, sullen. My daughter had always been such a bright and candid child, but there were a number of easy explanations . . . her father's death . . . the alterations in her life . . . How could I have been such a fool?" she cried.

This time there was no question of oaths or promises. Duncan grasped her against him as she sobbed against his chest. His lips gently brushed against the sun-warmed silk of her hair. "We are all fools at one time or another, make errors in judgement," he said ruefully.

"But it was not I who paid the price for that mistake," Kate protested, her words vibrating with shame. "It was Anne. Anne who suffered because of my blindness. When I think how long it must have gone on; how I only found out by chance . . ."

Her fingers gripped his arms much too tightly with all the force of her bitterness and guilt, those faraway eyes peering inward toward the past. But Duncan bore that small, nipping pain in silence, content to be her anchor in the midst of the maelstrom of self-blame.

"I had been about to go to a small gathering," Kate said in a distant voice. "A musical evening, 'entirely suitable for a woman in the latter part of her mourning,' he told me. He encouraged me to go, damn him, and by then, I was glad enough to get away, even for a short time. Those eyes of his were always devouring me, stripping me naked with secret glances. His salacious hints had long passed the pale of the acceptable. That was why I had insisted Daisy sleep in my dressing room, you see, instead of the nursery where she had been accustomed to sleep. I was afraid that one night the door would open and I would have to fight him off . . . If I had only left Anne in Daisy's charge . . . if only . . ." she choked.

It was almost as if he were watching a mail coach taking a turn too fast. Duncan found himself praying that his conclusions were wrong, but the direction of Kate's tale, the facts that Anne had unknowingly placed in Duncan's possession were all pointing toward inevitable disaster. The bare anguish in Kate's eyes dashed all hopes for a happy outcome.

"Just before my husband's sister departed, a storm broke. It was one of those autumn tempests, all thunder and lightning as if the heavens themselves were threatening to break apart. I decided to cry off and spend the evening in the nursery with Anne, watching the storm from the windows. We both used to love seeing the jagged bolts streak across the sky. Even the footman was unaware that I had returned home, and I wished to keep it so. My brother-in-law was to spend the evening at his club, so I though, that I might be sure of being left alone."

The thought of her skulking about, sneaking in to her own home to avoid molestation was almost too much to bear. A killing outrage for her, for Anne, was threatening to consume him. Kate's fingers were icy, loosening and clenching in spasms as she continued her story.

"There were so many buttons to that dress," she recalled. "And it took me some time to free myself, for I did not even wish to call for Daisy to help me because it might have alerted him that I was home. Then I went upstairs . . . It was so dark as I came up, not even a light in the passageway. . . . I wondered why the nursery maid had extinguished all the candles."

There was a quaver in her voice, a portent. He wanted to deny what he saw in her expression, to somehow forestall the truth that he knew was coming. Kate could have stopped then and there, and Duncan could have told the end of her story, but he did not stop her. Somehow he knew that she had to say it, even though he did not wish to hear.

"When I heard the screaming," Kate said, "I wasn't even sure what it was. The sound of the thunder was so loud, and the rain on the roof, like the beating of a thousand drums. Then I saw a shadow slipping out the door. It was my brother-in-law and I wondered what he was doing up there in the nursery? He had shown Anne only the mildest of interest, previously. Fool! Fool! Fool!" She shouted the word in self-condemnation. "I suppose that it was fear for myself that kept me from questioning him then and there, fear of what might happen were he to find me defenseless in the dark. So, coward that I was, I kept quiet, waiting until he went down the front stairs."

"And what would he have done if you had confronted him, Kate?" Duncan asked softly, but she would not hear him. She got up from her seat, and he followed her to the edge of the loch.

"I found Anne, huddled in the corner of her bed, unmoving, still as a stone. Were it not for her breathing, I would have believed that she was dead. Her eyes were wide open, but she did not see me, I swear. I put my arms around her . . . but it was like grasping a piece of statuary," Kate said, remembering the clammy feel of Anne's skin, the utter lack of response. "Still, I did not understand . . . did not suspect . . . until I smelled a strange odor . . ." Her nose wrinkled in recollection. "It wasn't one of the usual nursery smells, milk or jam, child or chalk, but a man's smells—snuff, brandy, and the musky scent of . . ." She could not say it, shaking her head helplessly as she relived that moment of horror. "He had not even feared discovery sufficiently to clean it away. I suspect now that the nursery maid must have been in collusion or too frightened to speak up. He had dismissed the girl that I had hired . . . but she *must* have known, what with the blood and the . . ." Kate's voice trailed off into sobs.

Once more, Duncan pulled her close, keeping his own anger at bay in the face of Kate's need.

"I do not know how many times it happened," she whispered. "How many times Anne had screamed unheeded into the night. That was why when I heard her yell today . . ."

"There is no need to explain," he told her, cupping her chin in his hands. "I understand."

"How can you?" Kate asked sadly. "How can you bear the sight of me, knowing that I did nothing to help my own daughter?"

"It is not your fault, Kate," Duncan said, smoothing away a tear that was drifting down her cheek. "It is only reprobates like myself who suspect evil in all they see."

"But I stood by and allowed him to go free," she protested.

"And what could you have done?" he asked. "Confronted him that night? Think upon the result of that? Rape, perhaps? He had obviously planned his campaign thoroughly, replaced your nursery maid, made certain that you would be out of the way, that no one would discover his dirty secret."

"I should have stayed and fought him. He has stolen more than Anne's innocence. He has taken her birthright," Kate said.

"And what proof would you have had?" Duncan asked. "A bloody, soiled sheet? A silent, intimidated little girl? Would they have believed you, Kate, any more than you believed it yourself? 'Tis unthinkable that a man could force himself upon a child, his own niece. They would have branded you a liar, or worse still, insane; and where would that have left the lassie, I ask you?"

She thought about that, considered the consequences of an outright accusation. John would have used all the power at his disposal to crush her without so much as a qualm. "Anne would have been left at his mercy," she said at last.

"Aye," Duncan agreed, "with none to protect her. You did the best thing you could have, the only thing. As for her birthright, Kate, I swear that I will help you regain what is rightfully hers. I shall get justice for you both, Kate, if you will but give me his name."

She looked at him, this man who had just vowed to become her champion, and knew that this was no idle promise. There was determination in the chiseled set of his jaw; his defiant stance was as hard and uncompromising as the mountains that stood at his back. All that was needed was armor to cover the broad, bronzed expanse of his chest, and he would easily be one of those knights of old, ready to right wrongs and slay dragons. Duncan was an avenging demon, a warrior who had placed the full measure of his power at her command. It was a gift beyond comparison, beyond price, but even as she pictured John kneeling at sword's point, begging for mercy, Kate knew that she could not make Duncan her weapon.

"Duncan, were it pistols or swords or even bare fists, I would want for no better ally," she said with a fragile smile. "But he would never meet you on Primrose Hill before breakfast, my friend. The Inns of Court are more to his style than the fields of honor. He would use writs as his choice of weapon and have a bevy of barristers to second him. The man would strangle you with suits, bury you with briefs, and failing that, I would not put a knife in the back past him. No, Duncan, but I thank you." She brought her hands up to rest on his shoulders. "He is a very powerful man, with a great deal of wealth and influence. I appreciate your offer, but I could not let you put yourself at risk."

She was attempting to protect him. However, it was difficult for Duncan to decide whether he felt flattered or insulted. Nonetheless, as present matters stood, Kate was correct; he did not have the ability to confront a man such as the one she was describing. There had been no word from Dewey, and more oddly, not so much as a line from Adam. With neither evidence nor funds, he could not fight his own battles, much less hers. Silently, he resolved to send Fred to Edinburgh to determine if any progress had been made on reclaiming the MacLean legacy.

In the meantime, there was Kate and the gentle touch of her hands on his shoulder. "My friend," she had called him. Females had given the "Mad MacLean" numerous titles: lover, protector, a hundred meaningless endearments moaned in passion's heat, and often as not, lying bastard, but no woman had ever before named him "friend." A simple word it was, but its echoes reached the dark hollows of his soul, summoning a part of him that he had thought long dead. That candid assertion of friendship bound him inexorably to her, pledged him to a level of honor that had hitherto applied only to other men. At that moment, he accepted the burden of her pain and swore to ease it. Both justice and vengeance were a part of the silent vow; the enemy of his friend was now his eternal foe.

"Please, Duncan," she implored, somehow reading the meaning in the glare in his eye as the grey shifted from a warm shade of dove to a narrowed steel. "Do not try to go after him; promise me."

There was a decided trembling to those fingers that sat so lightly on his bare shoulders, and those verdant eyes were still shadowed with fear. And part of that worry was for him ... for Duncan MacLean. "There's no need to fash yourself for me, Kate," he soothed. "I canna very well seek him out, not when you do not deign to trust me with his name."

" 'Tis not a matter of trust, Duncan," she explained, distressed by the hurt in his voice. "We have already lost so much because of one man's evil. I would not put you at risk. I do not want to lose you."

Once again, Duncan found himself bereft of words, not quite daring to believe that Kate actually cared for him. *As a friend*, he reminded himself, as his hand rose to touch the pulse at the base of her throat. *Nothing more*. Her breathing was shallow, touching him with warmth as his fingers traced their way to her lips. *Beast that you are*. He was drowning, going down in a pool of green as her eyes widened. *To take advantage of her when she is vulnerable*. Her hair was fire in his palm. *Mad you are MacLean, mad as they have named you*. He felt her grip on his shoulders grow tighter, sending waves of heat down his spine to the core of him, kindling an conflagration within. *If you would toss friendship away for a touch*. The need, that aching need consumed him.

"Duncan?"

Through the roar of the inferno, he heard her anxiety, saw the uncertainty in her expression.

"I do trust you, Duncan," Kate said, softly, trying to shroud the intensity of her feelings by looking away. When had the comfort of his closeness been transformed into this agonizing yearning for more? Was she truly a wanton, to thrust herself upon him as she had, using her overset state as an excuse to cling like the worse kind of tease? His body was as taut as a drawn bowstring, and Kate was mortified, knowing that she was the cause. Adam had told her often enough that all cats were much the same in the dark, and that tension signified nothing more than a reaction to female proximity. Reluctantly, she pulled away from the safe haven of Duncan's touch, feeling bereft, vulnerable once more. "Never doubt that I trust you, Duncan MacLean." Unfortunately, she could not say the same for herself.

It shamed him, that simple assertion coupled as it was with withdrawal. Obviously, she had not failed to feel the raw hunger in his touch, to discern the depths of his naked desire. Yet, absurdly, she still believed in his honor. He longed to run, to hide himself from that undeserved faith. Another moment and there would have been no holding back before the searing blaze.

But more hellish yet was the fear that Kate felt nothing more than the simple friendship that she had professed, that the flare of emotion had left her wholly untouched. Oath or no oath, he longed to pull her into his arms, to find those embers and nurse them into flame, but it was a risk that he refused to take. Kate's friendship and her innocent belief in him was more than he had ever dared to hope for. Yet, how much credence would she place in that questionable integrity once she found out that her daughter could speak and that Duncan had concealed it from her?

"Shall we go back to the castle?" he asked, breaking the awkward silence.

Kate shook her head, staring mutely into the loch as a nebulous realization began to solidify, like a vision in the mist. The swirling storm of emotion within her took shape and significance, until the meaning was beyond any denial. She could not look at him for fear that she would be unable to conceal the truth, that he would see the feelings that Kate herself had only begun to acknowledge.

It was unconscionably foolish to fancy herself in love with Duncan MacLean, she told herself. There were as many reasons to avoid the entanglement as the smooth spheres on

Daisy's rosary. First and foremost, he did not love her. She enumerated those other rationales, one by one, letting those beads of bitter truth tell through her mind, reminding herself of the cruel hoax of Adam's wager, the pain of wondering if love had ever existed, the futility of believing in happiness, the lunacy of handing her heart to a gazetted rake. To offer Duncan the full measure of her feelings, knowing that he did not love her in return, to risk the forfeiture of his respect for an illusion was outside consideration. But though Kate knew it was beyond sense, beyond sanity, she was aware that her heart was a lost battlefield. She could only pray that Duncan would remain ignorant of his victory. "I shall be along later," Kate murmured. "I need to think."

"Think upon your sins?" Duncan asked his voice deep with dismay. The posture of her body, the defeated slump of her shoulders spoke volumes. "Don't do this to yourself, Kate. Are you going to let the past destroy you? Will you allow the fear and guilt to gnaw away at you until you have lost all hope for the future?"

She stared silently into the rippling water. How could she dare to put faith in tomorrow when yesterday would pursue her always? "Hope?" she asked, putting her bitterness into words. "What license have I to reach for expectations beyond today? I am responsible for what happened to Anne. Due to my carelessness, she has been injured beyond repair. So spare me the platitudes, if you please, milord. Surely you know that there is always a penance to be paid?" *And you are part of that retribution*, she added silently. *To be near you, to want you, to be bound to you forever though I must leave this place. You shall be my perpetual purgatory, Duncan MacLean, and the hell of what might have been, my living damnation.* "I have no future," she declared.

"Aye, you fancy yourself a martyr, do you?" Duncan asked, his tone crisp as a slap on the cheek. He understood only too well that feeling of helplessness, the almost unbearable burden of responsibility. "What do you accomplish, Kate, with your eternal guilt. Do you think that it helps Anne to know that you have mounted the cross for her? Does it bring her attacker any closer to justice?"

How dare he? What right had he to judge? To tell her what she ought to do? To feel? "You are a great one to talk, *Laird* of the MacLeans," Kate retorted. "You with all your ranting about destiny and doom. You hold Charlie's curse to your bosom and bemoan your fate. But it seems no more than a bloody excuse to me, a pretext for neglecting your obligations, your people. And were that not sufficient to absolve you from harsh reality, you nurse your wounds in the darkness, as if a marred face somehow makes you less of a man. You have the audacity to chide me, as if I do not thirst for justice."

Drawing a choked breath, she turned to look at him, her nails digging deep into her palms as she fought to control her rage. "But can any man know what it is to be powerless, to know that your life turns upon another's whim? I burn for justice, sir, want it so much that sometimes I feel as if that desire will consume me, but vengeance is a luxury whose cost I cannot presently afford. And I will allow no one to pay that price for me, Duncan. It is my obligation, my burden, but I doubt that you can understand that."

"Aye," Duncan said with quiet vehemence. "I can, Kate. I know that thirst, for I, too, have a blood debt to settle. My men, all but Fred, were murdered, deliberately manipulated by a greedy man in the hopes of destroying the only man who had evidence against him—myself." He paced in agitation.

"Those who were lucky were slaughtered on the field, but those of us who survived received the worst of the bargain. It was then I lost my eye, but I have since found that to be the least of my injuries." He paused, struggling to articulate something that was only barely comprehensible to himself.

"Those are the visible wounds, but I begin to think that there may be worse injuries that are beyond sight. I would hear my men's voices, Kate. Their hants rose even in the light of day to point fingers and accuse me. And they would scream in the night, demanding retribution. Sometimes, I thought that I was going mad." He forced himself to continue although, for once, he could not read her reaction. "Though you condemn yourself for what happened to Anne, the fault was not yours. Unlike you, I was the architect of my own downfall."

Kate shook her head. "I do not understand."

"My men and I were deliberately sent into the arms of the

enemy in the expectation that I would die. The reinforcements and artillery support that I was told to expect never came." He shook his head at her confused expression. "Inadvertently, I had stumbled upon a scheme, you see. At first, it seemed a simple whiff of fraud, happens all the time in the army. But as I investigated further, the stench of corruption was undeniable. A swindle of massive proportions was occurring; thousand of pounds worth of material and supplies were being diverted." Duncan looked toward the loch, shamed at his own stupidity.

"My nose led me to one man, and t'was with him that I made my error. I thought him to be a mere dupe, a basically decent man who had become innocently befouled. He was the kin of a dear friend. Since I feared that the scandal would taint my comrade by association, I gave the man the chance to redeem himself, to avoid besmirching the family name, arrogant ass that I was. Naysay though you will, it was the MacLean conceit implicit in Charlie's bane caused good men to die." His lip twisted wryly, no smile in his gaze. "There are times when men, too, can be as powerless as babes in swaddling."

Guiltily, Kate recalled that Duncan had been more of a prisoner than she had ever been. More than anyone else, he truly could understand what it was to be without hope, without choice. But the accusations that he had made set her mind awhirl. A chill fear invaded, creeping with questions, suspicions, as she frantically tried to recall the little that she knew about the circumstances of MacLean's "death." She knew that Adam had been Duncan's equal in rank, but little beyond that. Adam had always discouraged her queries about army life, deriding them as evidence of her unorthodox upbringing. Although there were above a dozen question hovering in her head, she could not inquire for fear of accidentally revealing too much. Yet there was one that she could ask.

"Who was the man that did this to you and your men?"

Duncan shook his head. "You would never have heard of him. He was the merest of ciphers, a sharpener of quills and a pusher of paper. I discounted him as a threat. And his worst crime is, in a sense, the result of my stupidity. It is as you say; he is my obligation, my burden."

He stood beside her at the water's edge, staring into his distorted image, his shoulders tensed, waiting. What that admission had cost him, Kate could only guess. There was but one reason that she could discern for Duncan to swallow his pride, to admit failure. He had spoken for her sake, giving her the only comfort that he could. Now he seemed very much in need of solace himself. Slowly, her fingers reached out to twine with his. In the wavering loch, two reflections embraced, sharing a silent understanding that was beyond passion, beyond tears.

"The world is filled with wickedness, Duncan," she said at last. "Sometimes it cannot be fought."

"Aye, there's evil aplenty to be found," he agreed softly, turning to her, then cupping her chin in his palm. "And it is true that you have to chose your weapons wisely, to understand the enemy. That was my mistake. I underestimated him. I believed that my foe had some shred of honor, some spark of decency left within him. I'll not make that error when next we meet."

"You intend to go after this man then?" But there was no need to ask the question. Once more his aspect had changed, and the gentle concern had been replaced by a fierce determination.

"I shall." With that simple resolution Duncan felt a sudden lightness, as if a tremendous weight had suddenly shifted. He, himself, would go to Edinburgh to see if Dewey had received any reply, then on to London, and if need be to Portugal. If the volume of Blake were to be found, then Duncan would have the satisfaction of seeing Vesey face the king's justice. If not, there were other ways to exact retribution. Duncan himself would be witness, judge, jury, and . . . if need be, executioner. It was difficult to decide which possibility was more pleasing. "I swore it that day on the battlefield, when I realized that my men and I had been deliberately led to slaughter. But 'tis waiting, I have been, to make my charge of treason. Unfortunately, while I rotted in prison, my adversary has become more formidable than before. I begin to wonder if it is wise to bide any longer."

The skepticism in his voice was plain. "Yet you think it hopeless?" Kate asked.

"I doubt anyone will believe me," Duncan said. "Then again, they dinna call me the 'Mad MacLean' for naught."

A brief smile lit his face, transforming it, and Kate knew why women had nearly swooned at the mere mention of his name. But the grin was quickly gone, replaced by a thoughtful expression. His palm caressed her cheek, smoothing her hair back with a languorous touch.

"It used to be that I would hear those voices calling me . . . my men asking 'why?'" He inhaled the scent of her, feeling the warmth of that silken skin beneath his fingers, as if that reality could banish the chimeras that plagued him. "Sleeping . . . waking . . . till sometimes the din was so loud that all I wanted was silence. The shame, the guilt, t'was the center of my existence. I wondered why they had died, all of them men with much to live for, wives, children, sweethearts . . ." His lip turned up slightly in a lopsided smile. "Yet, now I realize that I have hardly heard them of late, those voices in my head. They have become faint . . . distant . . . and I have been waiting for the right time. Or so I told myself."

"There is nothing ignoble in acknowledging that your enemy's strength is superior," Kate said, giving voice to a growing dread. There was a withdrawal in his tone, as if a chasm were suddenly yawning between them. "As you yourself just said, only a fool would confront sure defeat. Perhaps it is better to defer?"

"It has been many months now, since I saw their blood mingling with the tide," Duncan said hoarsely, letting the memory stir the crucible within. "in your case, a retreat was both prudent and honorable. You were attempting to shield your daughter. However, unlike you, I have no one to protect, save myself," Duncan said. "Ah, Kate. It would be so easy to let those voices echo into oblivion, to convince myself that vengeance will be a fruitless pursuit." Her eyes glistened, and he felt a curious wonder. Could those tears possibly be for him? "But now, I begin to think upon what you have told me, and I realize that evil cannot be ignored. I cannot stay forever, hiding like a wounded beast."

"I did not mean . . ." Kate flushed, stepping back in mortification.

"Never apologize for the truth," Duncan said, putting a

restraining hand on her shoulder. "It seems to me that I have been running for as long as I can remember. Fleeing from my father, escaping my grandfather's house by bolting to the army, and now it appears that I have come full circle, back to Eilean Kirk." He shook his head, his hands falling to his sides. " 'Tis as you say, I am my own hant, with chains of my own making. I am going to Edinburgh."

"Why?" Kate whispered, aghast at what she had unwittingly caused.

"You," Duncan said. "and Anne. You have reminded me that corruption thrives in the dark, festers and grows. I may not have the evidence that I once possessed, and if I speak out, I will likely be called a liar. But I am thinking that there are a few who might listen. At least there will be a brief light shining in those shadows, and perhaps people will examine more closely where they did not bother to look before."

"A single candle may be easily snuffed," Kate said.

"Or it can be the spark that ignites a legion of rockets," Duncan reminded her. "I have to try, Kate. Surely you, of all people, can comprehend that. And once that oath is fulfilled, I intend to seek redress for Anne."

"No," Kate protested. "I have told you—"

"What if there are other little girls?" Duncan asked. "I doubt your daughter was the first, or the only. Nor, unless something is done, will she be the last. Will you leave him to prey on other innocents? Allow him to be forever a threat to you?"

"And what if your efforts lead him back here?" Kate demanded, trying to ignore the pricks of her conscience. She knew that he spoke the truth. "Do you not realize that he could drag Anne back to hell, with all the force of the law on his side?"

"So that is your true fear." Duncan turned away, cut to the core with pain and disappointment. All those fine phrases of concern for his welfare were no more than dissembling talk. "I would never allow Anne to come to harm. You know that."

"*Allow?* Are you like the King of Denmark, Canute was his name if I recall, who tried to command the tide? *You would never allow!* How could you stop him? If you believe that you have conquered your trait of arrogance, Duncan MacLean, you are sorely misguided."

"You lack faith," he murmured.

"I had faith once." Kate lamented that loss, the time when she had seen the world through the lens of innocence. "I believed that my husband loved me. I believed in virtue, accepted as undeniable that devotion and honor would always be victorious. But no longer. I have since found that virtue is more often than not a mere appearance, that even in marriage, devotion is not worth a ha'penny without respect. Moreover, when honor is unaccompanied by strength, evil does triumph."

"Only if we allow it," Duncan said, starting back toward the castle. He could not very well fault her for a credo that so closely coincided with his own. But then he had never before made the fatal error of believing in anything or anyone. "I intend to fight, even though I may well be doomed to failure."

"Then wage your own wars, not mine!" Kate called after him.

He did not look back.

"Damn you, Duncan MacLean!" Kate called. "Damn you."

He turned to face her, his gaze desolate.

"There's no need to curse me, Kate. It's been done already, by a man who wove his maledictions far more eloquently. But if you wish, you are welcome to add your damnation to the heap already upon my head. It's no more than I deserve."

"You could not hope to win," Kate said, trying desperately to explain. She knew that she had wounded his pride, but Anne's safety was paramount. "He is like a spider hiding in the corner of an enormous web. The slightest tremor, even the most discreet touch would bring him scurrying forth. Do you not see that I would have to take Anne and leave here, rather than risk him finding us?"

"So now we arrive at the truth. Very well, Kate. I shall take no initiatives. You need not flee," he told her, keeping his voice steady. "But you might wish to consider this. If he is as powerful and determined as you believe him to be, he may well find you, sooner or later. Sometimes, a surprise offense is the only way to defeat a superior enemy. That is the tactic that I intend to employ. John Vesey still thinks that I am a dead man. I suspect that my sudden resurrection will come as something of a shock."

Kate willed herself to stay upright, commanding her legs to remain rigid until Duncan was out of sight. Then slowly, she wilted to her knees, sobbing in gasping breaths.

Chapter Eleven

There was feasting by the light of the full moon. Makeshift tables groaned with scones and bannocks, fresh salmon, savory stews, and even hot steaming haggis. In the space of an afternoon, Daisy and the village women had turned simple fare into a banquet.

Despite his disappointment in Kate, Duncan felt his spirits lifting. Smoothing the fold of fabric beneath the brooch that held his tartan, he rose from his place. Silence fell upon the courtyard.

"I am not a man who puts much credence in miracles," he said, surveying those work-worn faces. "In my life I've found that it is mostly self-interest that drives people. 'Tis the way of things, I suppose, to believe that others are just like ourselves."

Kate felt his eye upon her, heard the note of disillusionment. If he noticed the redness at the corners of her eyes, he made no sign. His look tore right through her, and for a moment she feared that the shards of her hard-won composure would be shattered. John Vesey . . . his enemy was hers. All the Steele money, the patronage, the power would be arrayed against Duncan. By comparison, David's stand against Goliath appeared a well-balanced match. Hastily, she directed her attention to her plate.

"But try though I have," Duncan continued, his look touching each and every one of them, "I can see no selfishness in what you have done here today. You who owe me naught but scorn have opened your hands to me, given me the fealty that my father and father's father had deservedly forfeited. You've wrought wonders here, and I humbly thank you, along with my lady."

The subtle emphasis on those last words cut like a lash, but she rose, as was expected of her. She would have to leave, take Anne and Daisy. If Duncan bearded Vesey in his lair, it would only be a matter of time before her enemy was drawn to the scent. Did Duncan have any inkling of what he faced? Would he believe her if she warned him, or would he think that she was only trying to protect her own interests? And if she told him that Vesey was the man who had assaulted Anne, would that not be as bait to the bear?

"Wrongs *can* be righted," Duncan said, as much to Kate as to the crowd. "Let us drink to that together. But I cannot, in all honor, toast a new beginning properly with Adam's ale, especially since I have better to offer you. Fred?"

The clink of glass penetrated Kate's confused thoughts. She watched in shock as the little man came forward, cradling a basket of bottles like a newborn. There was an astonished murmur from the crowd as the dusty vessels were passed around and uncorked.

"Eilean Kirk *uisgebeatha*," Duncan confirmed, pouring a liberal portion of the golden liquid into Kate's cup. "Savor it, for as far as I know, this is the last of the MacLean's Gold ever brewed."

"And there is nae mair, ye ken?" Tam asked, his bushy brows wrinkling.

"Nary a dram," Duncan confirmed. "Unfortunately, these are the only bottles in my cellars, and never will its like be brewed again, but I would be honored if you will all share it with me." He filled his cup and raised it high.

"Do ye ken that?" Tam's face broke into a smile. " 'Tis honor he puts before the MacLean Gold."

As the import of Tam's words penetrated, the inhabitants of Kirkstrath rose to their feet, lifting their cups in pledge.

" 'Wrongs righted.' " Tam raised the bottle and put it to his lips.

"Wrongs righted," came the echo.

Tam took a long pull, before addressing himself to Duncan once again. "Milaird, I ne'er thought I would be sayin' this to ye, but it was muh father's last wish. T'was his ain hand that brewed this before Culloden, and as ye ken, any made after, didna taste quite the same. Muh da, canny man that he was, couldna outright refuse to brew the gold for his laird, but he changed the malt. Yer grandfather thought it to be the curse, and in a way"—his look was sheepish—"it was. But I could make this for ye', milord. Muh father showed me th' right way o' it, should the curse ere be comin' undone."

"The curse is not yet broken, Tam," Duncan said. "But a revived distillery might help to rebuild Strathkirk. I leave for Edinburgh tomorrow. If you will tell me what equipment and provisions you will need, we can start minting the MacLean Gold again."

"It may well be verra dear," Tam warned. "The distillation machine was o' muh da's own design. All these years laing gone, there's nae mair left o' th' auld t'be saved."

"You shall have whatever you need," Duncan promised, pouring again.

"Save the bottles, laddies," Tam called merrily. "No use in wastin' good glass or a fine evening." He scooped up a sack from beside him and pulled out his pipes, inflating the bellows with a discordant whine.

"Where will you get the money?" Kate whispered under cover of the noise.

"The funds will be found, Kate. I keep my promises," Duncan told her. "They trust me to do as I say, even though they have no reason to."

Do you trust me? The words were as clear as if spoken aloud, but Kate could find no answers within herself, only endless choices, every one of them bad.

A flute was pulled from an apron pocket. A fiddle yowled as it was tuned relentlessly. Restless fingers tapped, seeking a beat upon a taut leather drumhead. Then suddenly the instruments joined in unison, and the night was filled with wild music.

All at once, Kate knew that she had never heard a true reel. This was a pounding wave of sound, an electric force beguiling her feet into motion. But it was Mrs. Kirby who was the first to be charmed from her chair. The older matron began to dance, her pattens pounding the stone, adding a peculiar music of their own. Although she had seemed utterly exhausted just moments before, the woman whirled, clicking her toes to the ground, before leaping with an agility that belied her years. With a smile she beckoned to Duncan, and the crowd sighed as he gave her a courtly bow. He raised his arms above his head, the folds of plaid draping with a ripple. Slowly, he began to move to the music, the brooch on his plaid flashing as the jewels caught the torchlight.

The tempo increased, until Kate could barely follow the intricate pattern of steps, and his trews became a dizzy riot of color. Mrs. Kirby stepped from the circle, and Duncan beckoned toward the shadows. "Will you dance with me, little lassie?" he asked, crouching at the knees.

Kate gasped as Anne stepped into the torchlight, like some shy woodland creature under a spell. Duncan rose, but bent over to take the child's hands. The flute trilled gently, and the pipes hushed as she skipped to his simple steps and tried to mimic what she had seen. The people watched, charmed, as he caught her up and whirled her round until she whooped, then held her until she was steady on her feet. With a bow and a dainty curtsey it ended, and Anne wreathed in smiles, ran to her mother.

Kate buried her face in her daughter's hair to hide her tears. It would be hard on the child, to take her from the only place where she had found a measure of happiness, a sense of security. But, as always, the decision had been wrenched from Kate's hands. As she watched Duncan dancing amidst his people, she told herself that he truly did not need her any longer. The spell of solitude had been broken. Although it would take far more than a few superficial repairs to restore the rotten floors and the other results of years of neglect, the castle was fast becoming a home. Some of the younger women had been eager to offer their services, claiming that it "was nae richt for milady to be workin' like a drudge." It would be a relief to end the deception, to get away from the disturbing Lord MacLean, she told herself. But just then, the rich mellow sound of his laughter mingled with the pipes, and she caught a glimpse of his rare smile. A pity that she had never been good at lying, not even to herself.

Duncan could feel her gaze, almost like the touch of a fingertip, but he refused to allow himself to be drawn. Once again, the pain flooded him. He had been a fool to believe that Kate had come to care for him, to trust him. "A friend," she had called him, but any lackwit knew that there were degrees of friendship. His feet pounded the floor, slapping against the stone with all the force of his frustration and bitterness. Thought was willingly suspended, and Duncan gave himself to the pulse of the dance.

He hardly noticed when the music stopped and the floor emptied. Duncan stood alone, waiting, drawing heavy breaths in anticipation. The drum began a solo staccato cadence, like rifle shots at first, hard and sudden, slowing as the pipes swelled to a martial keen. The flute riffled, with the flutter of a banner in the wind. Duncan looked at Tam, and the old man dipped his hoary head in acknowledgment. It was "Eachainn's March," otherwise known as "The Laird's Dance" that the old piper played, banned by the guilty MacLean lords since that fateful day at Culloden.

Tam himself had taught Duncan the forbidden steps long ago, and the younger man prayed that his feet had not forgotten. But as the first notes echoed defiantly against the stone, Duncan forgot the watchers. A fierce joy possessed him, and the music sang in his blood. His brogues seemed to barely touch ground while his body moved with a lithe warrior's grace. There was battle implicit in those steps, advance, retreat, a lunging, leaping mimicry of combat with an unseen enemy in a dance that was as old as warfare itself. The song ended abruptly, leaving Duncan standing at the center, his head thrown back, a sheen of sweat beading his brow. A pledge had been made, a broken bond forged anew. He was their laird.

"MacLean! MacLean!" The cheer began as a whisper and rose to a shout as Duncan walked purposefully toward Kate, his hand extended in an unmistakable gesture of demand.

"Will you dance with me, milady?" he asked when the clamor faded. "That is if the wee lassie can spare you?"

Before Kate could stop her, Anne nodded and slid from her mother's lap. The crowd's gaze was upon MacLean's lady. Other than the insult of outright refusal, there was little choice. "I fear that I am not the best of dancers. I could never quite learn the steps," Kate said, her eyes pleading, hoping that he would allow her to cry off. But the hand was not withdrawn.

"I hope you do not expect much of me," she murmured, putting her fingers on his palm.

"No more than you are willing to give," Duncan said,

capturing her fingers between his hands. They were chilled, fluttering with nervous appeal. "Trust me, Kate, and let the music in."

The pipes sighed once more as he led her to the center of the courtyard. As she stood, he began to dance around her, his spine ramrod straight as he turned to regard her with burning fixation. Swiftly, she became a prisoner of that smoldering glance, holding him in the corners of her eyes as the violin hummed passionately, countering the gentle caress of the flute. Kate could feel his body, the undulation of air as he flew round her, moving with a sinuous style that stole her breath. With each beat, he drew nearer, until the heat of his exhalation warmed the back of her neck. Yet, even as she braced herself for his touch, he would move away, tantalizing her, wooing her without words.

The world narrowed to a small spinning space with Duncan at its center. Somehow, all unaware, Kate's feet had begun to move, seduced by the music and the man. All the rigid steps and patterns that she had thought of as dance were forgotten as the elemental rhythm took hold of her. The drum became a second heartbeat. Her hair flew loose from its moorings, to mingle molten with firelight against Duncan's dark mane. Round and round they whirled, linked in the passion of the pipes until the sound waned into silence. Then, suddenly, motion ceased. Time stopped. Kate looked up at Duncan, waiting for the inevitable.

He saw himself in the green shadows of her eyes. His deepest secrets, his worst fears were plainly writ in his face for her to see. He loved her. Heaven or hell help him, he loved this woman, and he did not even know her real name. She did not fully trust him or believe in him, but as his thumb traced the outline of her lips, nothing else seemed to matter except the feel of her, the sensuous whisper of silken strands against his shoulder, the scent of heather and smoke. He felt her hands stealing across the nape of his neck, the gentle tug as her fingers twined in his hair. He took all the sweetness that she offered, pulling her close, as if she could somehow fill the gaping void inside him.

All at once, Duncan knew that what he had said at the outset of the dance was true. He would accept whatever she was willing to give, content himself with any bone that she would deign to throw him, if she would only stay. The thought of losing her made him wild with fear. Yet, he understood that if he tried to confine her, she would fly from his grasp.

Kate savored every sensation, painting each detail of this moment indelibly upon memory. The scents of torch fumes, wool and sweat became a part of that mental image. The tang of *uisgebeatha* on his tongue and the flavor of his lips were linked forever with Duncan MacLean. The bristled roughness of his beard, the callused touch of his hands as they traveled down her back to pull her against the taut surface of his body were fixed in her mind as was the sound of his heartbeat and all the shades of grey in the depths of his eye.

Then, abruptly, the kiss was ended with a laughing wheeze of the bagpipes and the good-natured cheers of the crowd. Before she could say a word, Kate found herself whisked away in the arms of one of Tam's gawky grandsons while courtesy demanded that Duncan dance with an ancient crone. But though the melody had slowed, their thoughts continued at a feverish pace, blaming the music, blaming the whiskey, blaming the night, blaming everything but themselves.

The lanterns bobbed along the causeway like will-o'-the-wisps as the last of the villagers started back home. Duncan felt more alive at this moment than he had in a lifetime, even though his back was fair to aching with a good-natured thumpings, his hand sore from shaking, and his legs weak from dancing. But his exhilaration faded when he chanced to look at Kate. She stood beside him, her hand raised in a final farewell. However, as she turned to face him, her piquant smile disappeared.

"You are still determined to do this thing?" she asked.

Though the question came without any prelude, Duncan knew what Kate meant.

"Aye, I mean to go to Edinburgh," he said, stiffly. " 'Tis far too long that I've waited. Do you still fear that I will betray my word? Is that is what troubles you?"

Kate shook her head. Even in the moonlight he could not fail to see the misery on her face. He knew that it was unfair to expect too much of her, to hope for more than she could in justice give. But he suddenly realized that he could not continue with half measures. He wanted everything, her name, her history, to spend a lifetime discovering the details of her life. However, unless she freely offered him the key to her past, it was worthless. "Do you think to run forever, Kate?" he asked softly. "Is that fair to Anne . . . or yourself?"

"As if I had a choice," Kate said bitterly. "Choice is an illusion, Duncan."

"Is that what you truly believe?" He could not help asking the question even though he knew it to be a foolish one. "Or is that what you tell yourself? It is an excellent excuse, to fancy one's self the captive of a malevolent fate. In fact, I have used that rationale for most of my life."

"And your view has changed?" Kate asked, avoiding an answer. His evaluation came too dangerously close to the mark.

"Aye, I've been doing some thinking of late," Duncan said, "about destiny and curses, the making of decisions, responsibility . . . you."

Once again that pewter gaze held her hostage.

"I am not Pygmalion, Kate," he said, "I would not have you be anything other than who you are. You have a right to make your own choices, for both your child and yourself. But I wouldna be the friend you named me if I left my fears unspoken. Unless you make the decisions, my dear, you may find that destiny will choose for you, will you, nil you. But if you do go, I ask only that you let me help you, for Anne, if not for you. If it's money you're needing, or a strong arm to protect you, let me be your man."

A breeze from the loch caught her hair, lifting the tendrils to momentarily obscure her face. He lifted a hand with the intent to brush them away, then let his fingers fall back to his side. If he touched her right now, he was bound to forget all his resolutions.

Let me be your man, no stipulations, no reservations. For as long as Kate could remember, those that she had loved had tried to mold her to their expectations. Her father had tried to make her into a son. Her mother had attempted to

turn her from a hellion to a lady, and both had failed. But at
least they had acted from sincere affection.

It was clear to her now, however, that Adam had viewed
her from the start as so much raw clay. Painful though it was
to acknowledge, she had been the partner in her own muti-
lation. Because she had loved him, she had willingly given
her husband the stuff of her soul to twist and mold to his
own conception of who she ought to be. Bit by bit Adam had
pounded away at her until she had been reduced to a spine-
less lump. But the supreme irony was that Kate had succumbed because she had believed that Adam had loved her.
She had considered her true self unworthy of his regard.

Let me be your man. Without terms or conditions, Duncan
accepted her, even knowing that she had lied to him, that she
was unwilling to trust him. It was far more than she deserved. She pushed the curtain of hair aside, wiping away
tears with an impatient sweep of her hand. The time had
come to seize control of her own destiny. If that meant for-
feiting Duncan's respect, then so be it. He had to be advised
of the danger that he faced, and, if possible, convinced that
confrontation was futile.

"You said earlier that this man, John Vesey, was a mere
paper shuffler?" she began tentatively.

"Supplies," Duncan said, puzzled at the sudden change of
subject, but willing to follow where she led. "There were
huge amounts of supplies being ordered, paid for, but diverted or never sent at all."

"Are you certain that his relative had no part in it?"

Duncan laughed. "No, I would swear that it was entirely
Vesey's game. Adam was the soul of honor, besides being
possessed of a fortune that would make Croesus himself
look like a pauper. I confess myself surprised that he ever
purchased a commission in the first place. He was an only
son after all, and the pickings in London were always far
better than the assortment of camp followers that he con-
sorted with. Most of us thought that he was trying to get
away from his wife; had her tucked away in the country
somewhere. 'The worst mistake of his life' he used to call
her. But I suppose London's loss is Wellington's gain. Adam
is a damned good soldier, a brilliant tactician."

"*Was*," Kate said, turning away as she fought against the waves of pain and humiliation.

The quiet emphasis in her voice startled him. "*What did you say?*"

"Was," she repeated, her tones flat as she forced herself to face him once again. "Adam, Lord Steele, is dead, and if his marriage was his worst error, milord, then it was his own fault. The girl made no effort to deceive him, to be anything other than what she was—Colonel Braxton's brat." The fury boiled up within her. "That 'soul of honor,' as you call him, wed an innocent on a whim simply for the sake of a foolish wager, then proceeded to destroy every shred of her confidence, every iota of her self-worth. How dare he fix the blame anywhere but himself? That bastard! That selfish, bloody bastard!"

The feeling of disbelief was impossible to conceal. Adam's wife . . . he had not mentioned her often, never in Duncan's memory had he even referred to her by her Christian name. "The Steele Trap," Adam had called her. Duncan silently blessed whatever benevolent being had kept that sobriquet from his tongue on this night. How many times had Duncan listened to the story of her first sortie into Almack's and laughed? Although he had long respected Lord Steele as a soldier and a friend, his regard for the man waned. How could Adam have looked at another female with this woman waiting for him, loving him so desperately? Pangs of pity intermingled with jabs of jealousy.

She could see from his openmouthed astonishment that he had pieced it all together. "Galetea, milord, at your service." She swept a sardonic curtsey.

"And John Vesey—"

She cut him off before he could complete the question. "—is the man who was left to control my fate and that of my daughter. I never quite fit Adam's mold of the perfect society wife, and he doubted my competence. John Vesey is now on the verge of becoming a baron by virtue of judicious loans to Prinny. All the Steele fortune, all the Steele power are his to command. That is why we are trembling in this ramshackle castle at the edge of the world, hoping that he never finds the hole to which we have bolted. That is why I cannot dare to touch a penny of my jointure, for fear that he will trace me through his connections in the bourse. It is no impotent pusher of papers that you will face, but a man of considerable influence."

"Vesey raped Anne!" The words escaped in a raging roar. "I will kill him, I swear; I will kill him with my own bare hands. But before I do, I vow, I will make him suffer for every indignity, every outrage that he perpetrated on you and your daughter. He will cry for mercy, and there will be none. He had none for you, nor for the men who died for his greed."

"And what will that profit me, that vengeance?" Kate questioned. "To see you hang for the sake of justice? I could not bear it, Duncan." Tentatively, she stepped forward, reaching up to brush her hand against the roughness of his cheek. "I could not bear it."

He caught her hand and held it there until he felt the warmth returning to her fingers. Moonlight accentuated the pallor of her face, turning her into a tormented ghost. "I am sorry, love," he whispered as the implications of what she had told him became clear. There was agony at the core of those jade eyes. "I was fond of Adam, I will not deny. He was a good man to have at your back in a fight, a man who played his cards straight and fair, who held his liquor like a gentleman. I do not say that those qualities make for an ideal husband, but he was a fair friend."

"He was self-centered and vain."

"Aye, he was," Duncan admitted. "And I was much the same as he. "

"No, Duncan, do not malign yourself," Kate said. "You are the most unselfish man that I have ever chanced to meet. You have sheltered me and mine, knowing nothing but that I deceived you. You did not shame me before your people; allowed me to act the part of your lady, even though I do not deserve the title. You care deeply—about your men, about the people of Strathkirk."

"Dinna try to make me into a hero, Kate," Duncan said uncomfortably. "I am nothing of the sort. The hants of Eilean Kirk are probably laughing at such foolish talk."

"Then let them laugh. 'Tis a powerful healing thing, laughter, and it would even do a ghost some good to have a chuckle or two," Kate said. "You made Anne smile, Duncan, you helped her to laugh again and heal, I think. No truly selfish man would have bothered with a small sad girl."

"I'm a scoundrel, a philanderer, and a wastrel."

"You forget reprobate, gambler, and reputed madman," Kate chided him mockingly. "My husband was quite liberal with his descriptions of the attributes he so envied. If you are cataloging your sins, let us not omit those from the list."

"Aye," Duncan said with a snort, his hands slipping round to hold her at the waist. "All those and more, Kate. Och, you dinna ken what manner of man I am."

"I have come to know something about who you are, Duncan MacLean," Kate retorted. "Sometimes I almost believe that I know you better than you know yourself. For all your fits and starts you are a relatively straightforward individual. That is why I fear for you if you go after Vesey. He has more to answer for than those deaths in France and on the battlefield. There is a fortune in his control—Anne's inheritance. Vesey is a viper, a powerful and deadly viper."

He could feel the shudder pass through her body, and now that he knew the assailant's identity, he truly understood the depth of Kate's fear. Vesey had ripped apart the fabric of her life and nearly destroyed Anne. Kate spoke no less than the truth. Vesey had already proved himself capable of murder for a far lesser gain. "I would not entangle you. There is no need for Vesey to know anything of your whereabouts," he assured her.

"I realize that you would do what you could to protect us," she said miserably. "But if he finds us . . ."

"Marry me," Duncan said, the idea bursting upon him like a rocket. "Then you and Anne would be legally under my protection."

Yes hovered on her tongue, but she held the word behind her teeth and shook her head with bittersweet sadness. "Why, Adam must be turning revolutions in his grave," she said, trying to make light of the moment though she was weeping inside. "He would tell me that you were far too clever to ever get yourself shackled in the parson's mousetrap. Surely, you could not think to forgo your riotous way of living for anything as mundane as marriage."

"I no longer have the face for the riotous life, Kate," he said, his fingers going automatically to touch the scar.

"Are we back to that again?" Kate asked taking his wrist and firmly pulling the hand away. "Do you think that you consist entirely of a face, Duncan MacLean? You are a decent human being, kind and entirely too honorable for your good. And as for your countenance. . ."

His heart began to hammer at her hesitation.

"I noticed many a woman looking hungrily your way tonight, milord, for all that they thought you were mine," she said softly, marveling at her own daring as her fingers slipped up to lightly trace the scar beneath his whiskers. "The beard suits you, Duncan. I suspect that some women find that unshorn appearance attractive."

And you Kate? he asked silently. *Do you hunger as I do?* "Shall I tell Fred, then, to forget about purchasing a new razor?" he joked. "If you prefer me to look like a wooly savage, then I would gladly oblige, so long as you marry me."

"And you dare to call yourself a rogue, Duncan MacLean? For shame! I vow I do not know what the world is coming to when rakes pledge to go about righting wrongs and selflessly offering marriage to damsels in distress."

Duncan wanted to tell her that there was nothing selfless about the gesture, that he wanted her with every selfish breath in his body, to hold and to cherish according to every maudlin sentiment and romantic sensibility in his Celtic soul. That if she would have him despite his marred face, he would move his castle to London stone by stone if it would make her happy. But Kate's next words caused him to halt at the brink.

"I married once with love on but one side, Duncan," she said, her fingers straightening the displaced folds of his tartan. "Never again will I make that error, least of all with a man whom I count as my friend. If I have learned anything from my errors, it is the difference between love and passion."

"And that is?" Duncan asked, hoping that his tones were as airy as hers.

"You will laugh," she said.

Her pixie half smile set his heart to aching. "If I am lucky. I could use the practice."

"Love is like a good peat fire and passion is a bonfire," Kate said. "A pile of wood may burn hot and bright, but passion is quickly consumed. A peat fire, however, may not be nearly as spectacular; at times it even appears to have died, but stir it and you always find live embers at the heart. How is that for homespun philosophy?"

"Charming."

"Trite."

"A bit of both perhaps?" Duncan allowed.

"Thus quoth the rake." She twitched the last fold into place, fastened the brooch, and stepped back to view the results. "Elegant."

"Absurd, a grown man in a skirt."

"A bit of both perhaps?" Kate retorted.

Duncan's laughter echoed across the loch, carrying all the weight of his bitterness, all the strain of his frustration in a long bellowing peal. Kate did not love him. He told himself that he was not surprised. How could she after all; a ill-reputed reprobate with neither face nor, seemingly, fortune to recommend him? But she had trusted him; he clutched that small comfort to his bosom even though it seemed like an exercise in self-deceit. Even a false hope was superior to no hope whatsoever.

"It is not that funny," Kate said, perplexed.

"No," Duncan gasped. "Ironic is what it is, most definitely ironic."

And though she badgered him all the way back to the castle, he would explain no further.

Chapter Twelve

The day dawned in a mizzle, the sun shrouded in a grey haze as Duncan strapped Selkie's saddlebags.

"Now we've got a need for every single one o' these things," Daisy warned, handing Fred a piece of paper.

"Gonna be needin' a dray an' oxen, sir, t'get this lot 'ome," Fred commented, his mouth rising into a brownie grin. "Th' woman's writ down a list long as me arm. Wheat'cher got 'ere, Daisy?"

"Wheat flour, for one thing," Daisy said saucily, "but I might be forgettin' what to do with it, if a certain little man don't stop his yappin'."

"No mercy." Fred wagged his head. "An' t'think I gave 'er me 'eart for a biscuit."

" 'Tis me who got the worst o' the bargain," Daisy sniffed, "considerin' the quality o' my biscuits. Now inside with you, little man, I've got some food packed for your journey."

Duncan watched with a touch of envy as they went inside. Their faces mirrored their feelings, and beneath the bickering was an undertone of undeniable affection. Poor Fred— if Kate chose to leave, Duncan had no doubt that the steadfast woman would go with her mistress. It would break the little man's heart. *And yours, Duncan MacLean*, he silently acknowledged. *How can you leave, not knowing if she will be here when you return?*

The nagging thought came that Kate might be right, that he would risk losing her because of a fool's errand. He had slept little the previous night, contemplating what she had said to him. Without the evidence contained in the book of Blake, no court in the world would convict Vesey. Now, with the news of Adam's demise, his last shred of hope had disappeared like dew in the morning. After so much time, the chances of recovering the book were not worth a Cockney's curse. Like as not, it was mingled among the thousands of volumes in the famous Steele library or perhaps Adam had simply given the colorfully illustrated volume away to one of his trollops. Duncan had come to discover that there had been precious little poetry in Lord Steele's soul.

His reverie was interrupted by a tug at his elbow. Anne stared up at him solemnly, her thumb firmly ensconced in her mouth. At least she had come to bid him farewell.

"Is there anything you'd like from Edinburgh, lass?" Duncan asked. "A ribbon for your hair? A doll, perhaps?"

Anne shook her head and gestured toward the saddlebags.

"She wants you to stay," Kate said.

Duncan looked up to see Kate standing in the doorway. There were shadows beneath her eyes. It would seem that there had not been much sleep for her either.

"I have told her that you will return as soon as you may, but I do not think that she quite believes me. Her father never came back, you see."

"I am not going to the battlefield, Anne," he told the child. "Just off to Edinburgh." But when Kate's eyes met his, he knew that it was a half truth he told. Likely he would be facing the biggest battle of his life, and the most futile. "The question is," Duncan addressed Kate, "will you be waiting for me when I return?"

"I do not think that I will have much choice but to wait for you, Duncan," Kate said wryly. "Not after I give you this." She held out a small, worn reticule. "I want you to take it, and I will brook no protests."

"Black velvet? Has Brummel dictated that reticules are de rigueur with breeches during my confinement?" Duncan asked, masking his relief with humor. She would stay. "Will it be appropriate with evening wear, do you think? It does match my eye patch rather well."

"Silly wretch . . ." Kate faltered, not wishing to wound his pride. "I know that you are not a rich man, Duncan, and your undertaking will require some funds." She pulled the drawstring open and drew out an exquisite brooch. "This was my grandmother's. Accept nothing less than a hundred pounds for it. It is worth far more." She tugged his hand open and tucked the brooch between his fingers. "And there are ten guineas in here as well."

He understood now what Kate had meant when she had commented that she would have no choice but to remain. This was the sum of her worldly possessions, all of her resources should she be required to flee. Yet, she was giving it to him in the mistaken belief that he had nothing. Touched beyond words, he searched for something to say, but before he could tell her just how much he loved her, she spoke again.

"This belongs to you," she said, fishing around in the bag. Her fist opened to reveal the glint of ruby and gold. At first Duncan thought that the light was playing tricks, but it was the MacLean ring. The heir's stone had been in the family as long as there had been MacLeans on Eilean Kirk. It was the only bit of the MacLean heritage that his mother had brought with her, more for its proof of his birthright than its value, Duncan suspected.

"I know that it is an heirloom, but I suspect you could get a fair amount for it. Certainly enough to hire the services of a canny man at law," Kate continued, unaware of his shock.

"Wh . . . where? . . . Where did you . . . ?" was all that Duncan could stutter out.

" . . . get it? From your Mr. Dewey, of course," Kate said. "It was your legacy to Adam. Were I you, Duncan, I would retain myself another lawyer. It took better than a year after your supposed death for him to send it on to Adam, by way of Spain, I might add. Of course, by then, Adam was already long gone. I suppose that I ought to be grateful that the man was both incompetent and indiscreet. If I had not received his letter asking if I knew of any buyers for a 'deserted Scot castle in a gothic state of disrepair,' as he put it, I would never have thought of hiding here. I really should have returned the ring to you sooner, knowing how your finances stand, but I could not without revealing my identity."

"Was there not another part to the legacy?" Duncan asked.

"Nothing of monetary value," Kate said, surprised at the intensity of the question. He was totally disregarding the ring. "There was also a book of poetry that you left to Adam, but I did not think that you would be wanting to carry it along with you on your journey. I was going to give it to you when you returned."

"You have the book?" He croaked out the words.

"It is one of my favorites, actually," Kate said. "I have always enjoyed Blake and Anne adored the pictures. She would beg me to read from it in the evenings. In fact, she once had many of the poems by heart."

Tyger, tyger burning bright . . . his eye turned to Anne in a silent query. "Do you by any chance know where it is?" he asked, his voice raw with emotion.

"It was one of the few things that we brought along," Kate said. "It was familiar and . . . a memento of happier times. I had thought though, that you might appreciate the ring more. Would you like the book back now as well?"

Duncan nodded, unable to trust his speech.

Without being bidden, Anne ran inside.

"Duncan?" Kate tried and failed to interpret his odd expression. "I understand if you do not want to sell the ring. I do have some personal funds, but I have not dared to touch them for fear that John would be able to trace us." She took a deep breath and made her decision. Sometimes the final card must be turned. "I am beginning to believe that you are right. We cannot hide from evil and hope that it will not find us. Perhaps with that money at your disposal you might find the help that you need?"

"You would risk that for me, Kate?" Duncan asked, startled from staring at the kitchen door.

"If we combined forces, between the two of us, we might manage to hold him at bay," Kate suggested.

At that moment Duncan forgot the book, forgot Vesey, forgot everything but the woman standing before him. What she offered was no less than her all, for he knew full well that the contents of that tiny bag were the entire sum of her reserves. That she had even suggested chancing access to her accounts was a gesture that bespoke complete trust.

He looked at that open hand, and his heart filled with an uncanny wonder. It was true that he had known himself to be in love with her before, but this emotion unfolding within him was entirely new, infinitely deeper. With this gesture she had claimed the last shadowy places of his heart. She had granted everything and asked for nothing in return.

Slowly, he took her hand in his and closed her slender fingers around the ring. " 'Tis yours, Kate."

"But you need . . ." she protested.

He shook his head. "There is but one thing that I need, and that is—"

Just then, Anne appeared in the doorway, a familiar volume in her hand. Duncan held his breath, not daring to believe until she actually placed it in his grasp. With a whoop of joy he grasped Kate around the waist and whirled her in a spinning dance that was both an expression of elation and love. "Forgive me . . . Kate . . . forgot the . . . oath," he said winded as he set her down at last. "But with this"—he waved the book like a banner—"we need not be content with keeping him at bay. He's gallows-meat."

" 'Tis th' *book* then, sir?" Fred asked, his smile stretching the full length of his face as he came into the courtyard.

"Aye, *the* book," Duncan said, "the one I feared lost forever."

"I do not understand," Kate said.

"Did you never notice the markings?" Duncan asked. "Underlined parts of passages, numbers in the margins?"

"Yes, but?"

"Here, look." He opened to a page at random. "See, this marked passage? W-a-l-t-e-r-s and these numbers? They reflect a specific date, September 18, 1803. Walters received a shipment of guns on that date, yet they were never distributed, vanished without a trace. And there is enough here to damn Vesey and his friends for eternity."

At the mention of Vesey's name, Anne shook her head and tugged at Duncan, her fears as plain as if she had spoken them aloud.

"Dinna trouble yourself, lassie," Duncan told her, squatting down to meet her eyes. "Thanks to you and your mother, no one need fear John Vesey ever again. The men at Whitehall cannot ignore this, sweetheart, and it is on my way to London, I am, to wave it in Wellington's long nose. There is no way that he can fail to smell the stench of it now."

"Not Edinburgh, then?" Fred asked.

"No, Fred," Duncan declared with a slap on the man's shoulders. "We are bound for Town, my friend. But first, I still mean to stop in the village and get the list of parts that Tam needs for his distilling apparatus. I'm certain that I can get whatever he requires in London." He opened his saddle-bag and wrapped the precious volume carefully in oilcloth. "The book of vengeance, Kate," he said as he tucked it in securely, calculating how many days it would take before he would see Vesey before the dock, the crowds pelting him with offal as he stood at the gibbet. "He will suffer, but not enough for my taste. I would wring his neck with my own hands if I could. Vengeance is my right."

Kate shook her head uneasily. Her yearning for Vesey's downfall was no less than his, but the wild light in his eye was disturbing, touching her with a cold chill. "Vengeance is ultimately not ours, Duncan," she said, "but is meted out by a higher justice than any at Whitehall or Windsor."

"Do you not want to see him suffer, Kate?" Duncan asked, swinging himself onto his horse. "To make him pay for what he has done?"

"I just wish to be certain that John Vesey will never hurt anyone, ever again," Kate told him. "That would suffice for me. As for suffering and ultimate payment, leave that in Divine hands."

"Needs must," Duncan said, "when the Devil drives. And Vesey is the Devil."

There was a harsh promise in those clipped words and no trace of mercy in an eye that was as hard as slate. For a moment she almost pitied John Vesey.

It would be far easier than he had anticipated. John Vesey watched as MacLean and his man rode across the causeway, noting their saddlebags with satisfaction. Excellent. He would have more than ample time to arrange matters satisfactorily. By the time MacLean returned, the trap would be set.

That babbling fool Dewey had been wonderfully easy to manipulate. A drink or two and the confidences were as free as water. It had taken less than a half of an hour and a quarter bottle to determine MacLean's location. MacLean and his man were supposedly living in the isolated ruin by themselves. Nothing could have been better. There was no need to take the risk of hiring help. No witnesses.

But to find Katherine here . . . his tongue darted out to lick his lips in anticipation. That was luck beyond his wildest dreams. It could not have worked out better had he planned it so. His two nemeses were under one roof. All that was required was a minute change in plan, and Anne would be back in his charge.

The child had long gone when Kate finally left her spot on the hill, but that was no matter. Anne would be easily dealt with. Vesey stole in to the kitchen. The old besom of a maid did not even hear him as he came up behind her and hit her with the butt of his pistol. He had avoided a fatal blow. She might yet have some value as a tool. His sister-by-marriage was foolishly fond of the servant and that affection could be used. With quick, economical movements, the woman was bound and gagged. Unfortunately, Vesey was forced to drag the weighty body from view himself. He had no assistance. He had determined that there would be no witnesses.

"Daisy?" Kate set her basket on the table and began to unload the produce. "The cucumbers are thriving again. We may yet have enough to pickle."

"I have always despised cucumbers," came a voice from the shadows.

Kate whirled, knocking the basket to the floor as Vesey stepped into view.

"I would not flee, Katherine," he said, leveling his pistol. "It would be tragic for Anne to lose her mother, would it not?"

Kate fought a rising sense of panic. "What have you done with Daisy?" she forced herself to ask with a semblance of calm.

"Nothing . . . presently," Vesey said. "However, she is somewhat . . . er . . . tied up." He tittered. "So, I would not count on her help. It is just the two of us, my dear. And of course, little Anne. Where is my charming niece? Why has she not come to greet her dear Uncle John? But then with you as a teacher, 'tis no wonder that she is rag-mannered as well as dull-witted."

Kate was silent.

"Call her, Katherine," he commanded, waving his gun

menacingly. "If you do not bring her, I vow the sound of a gunshot might."

Kate inclined her head in the cowed manner she had long ago learned. Slowly, with a show of reluctance, she went to the window. "Anne! Uncle John is here! Hide, run!" was all that she could say before he hauled her aside roughly and slapped her across the face.

"Stupid bitch!" he said. "What do you think that you have gained by that? She'll come, I vow, when she hears her mother screaming." ·

"I will not let her suffer at your hands again, John," Kate said.

He scrutinized her coldly. "So, you know."

"Yes," she said, drawing herself upright in defiance. "I know what manner of worm you are. You will not use my daughter; I will die first."

"No," he said, grabbing a handful of her hair and pulling her head back sharply. "You will die *last*, Katherine. Last and in suffering, watching them all go before you, your beloved Daisy, your Scots lover. And I will be left with dear little Anne. It will be such a tragic tale; a lover's quarrel, ending in gunshots, the servants dead, and poor little Anne out of her mind with grief. I can just picture Prinny weeping as he laps up the gory details. There is nothing that the royal fat fool adores more than a lurid melodrama."

"Well, you can leave Lord MacLean from your fiction. He is gone," Kate said. "I am certain you saw him go. We quarreled, and I doubt that he will return any time soon."

Vesey laughed softly. "You always were a poor liar, Katherine. Those eyes betray you every time. He will be back, and we will be waiting. But while we wait, I have a few questions to ask. Where is Anne's book of poetry?"

So, Vesey knew about the book. "Which book?" she asked vaguely. She had to stall for time, keep him talking. There was no certainty that Anne had heard her warning. And if she had? What could the child do?

"Be certain that the pipes be copper," Tam admonished Duncan. "A cheaper metal willna do near as well."

"I will remember, Tam," Duncan said, impatient to be off. Duncan had sent the Cockney with his slower horse on ahead, hoping to save time. By now, Fred was likely wondering what had become of him. Tam had already spent well over an hour, describing every detail of the distilling mechanism down to the last bloody bolt. The sudden commotion outside was a welcome interruption. Perhaps Duncan could say his farewells at last. A crowd was gathering, and a familiar bark drew him to the center of the disturbance.

"Anne!" Duncan scooped the child up, ignoring Cur's frenetic yips and the gathering crowd. She was gasping for breath, and her dusty feet were bloody. "What happened, child?"

"Uncle John . . . the castle . . ."

She fought to get the words out, but the terror in her face filled in sufficient detail for Duncan.

"And the dumb shall speak," Tam murmured in wonder.

"To hell with your talk of the bloody curse," Duncan roared. "My lady's in danger. Start for the castle with some men, Tam." He tried to hand Anne over to one of the women, but she would not release him.

"I shall get to her faster by myself, lassie," he said quietly. Reluctantly, she let go. "He'll hurt her," she whispered.

"I won't allow it," Duncan promised as he mounted Selkie. Try though he might, he could not keep the name "Canute" from his mind.

"Call her, Kate!" Vesey demanded.

Kate rested her cheek against the cold metal of the pump, flexing her wrists unobtrusively. The bonds that held her to the impromptu whipping post were not to tight. Given time, she could slip the ropes loose, but time was a commodity that seemed to be limited.

"Call your daughter!"

She pulled a deep breath, exhaling as she heard the whip whistling down toward her back. The trick of taking a flogging, an old sergeant had told her long ago, was to stay flexible, to avoid the tendency to go rigid. Unfortunately, although she moved as much as possible with the impact, the pain could not be totally avoided. She bit her lip, keeping the scream sealed in her throat.

"Call her!"

"You know, they would do something quite similar to this

in India, when tigers would prey on their flocks," Kate said when she caught her breath. "The natives would stake out a goat and make it bleat in the hopes of luring the tiger into their trap. I will not bleat for you, John."

"Where is she, damn you?"

"Do you think that I would tell you, even if I knew?" Kate asked, her voice rising. "My daughter knows every inch of this island and the shores of the loch. She could hide from you forever, and I pray that she does. You might as well finish me now, John."

His laugh made her skin crawl. "You would like that, wouldn't you, Katherine? An easy end? But the game is not over yet. I doubt that she will be able to ignore her mother's cries. And I will have you screaming, my dear. One way or another, you will bleat for me. Call your daughter."

She shook her head, loosened her wrists a bit more, and waited for the inevitable.

Duncan cursed silently as he assessed the situation. Once, when his sight had been whole, he might have tried to down Vesey with a shot, but it was far too much of a risk for a one-eyed marksman.

"If you are watching, Anne, you had best come help your mama. 'Tis most wicked of you to allow her to suffer so."

Duncan could hear the frustration in Vesey's voice and steeled himself as the whip came down again.

"I do not want to hurt her, Anne," Vesey called, pulling the pistol from his belt and holding it to Kate's head. "I shall count to ten, and if you do not appear by then, you will force me to shoot her. One . . . two . . ."

Duncan was almost certain that Vesey was bluffing. He would not be foolish enough to destroy the only hold that he had on the child. Or would he?

"Four . . . five . . . six . . ."

Not a fool perhaps, but a madman?

"Seven . . ."

"Vesey!" Duncan called from his hiding place. "Your game is over."

"MacLean? Back so soon?" Vesey laughed raucously. "I have not yet reached ten. Would you like to see what will happen at the magic number if you do not come out and show yourself? Eight?"

"Release her, Vesey."

"You jest, MacLean. You always have underestimated me, you know. That was your fatal error. Nine. Are you willing to chance ten?"

Duncan stepped into plain sight, and Kate moaned softly as Vesey's pistol trained on him.

"The girl, MacLean, where is she?" Vesey asked. "She's mine."

"I doubt that you want her, Vesey, not now," Duncan said. "She talks, quite articulately. In fact it was Anne who told me that you had dared to come here. I suspect that the child would be most interesting in a witness box. Perhaps she might not be believed, but there might be some uncomfortable questions raised." Duncan could see that he had hit the mark, but that would not get Kate out of Vesey's clutches.

Desperately, Duncan scrambled for some semblance of a plan. Then the wisp of a thought materialized along with the howls and protests of his dead comrades. He could not repudiate that blood debt, but he could not allow Kate to suffer anymore at Vesey's hands. "But I have something that you want, something far more valuable than a wee girl who might say some embarrassing things about you, John," Duncan said. "What I have is a book, a book of names and dates and happenings involving one John Vesey and a number of other fine fellows. 'Tis worthwhile reading, all those wicked doings, and unless I make certain arrangements, it will be on its way to the gentlemen at Whitehall."

"No, Duncan," Kate whispered hoarsely. "No."

Vesey blanched. "You are bluffing, MacLean."

"Are you willing to chance it?" Duncan asked pointedly. "With the information in that book, I can cut you off at the knees. Without it, I can do nothing."

Once again the pistol went to Kate's skull. "The book, MacLean, or I kill her."

"Do you think that I would be fool enough to keep it on my person?" Duncan asked. "Or that I would be sufficiently stupid to hand it over to you without some assurance of safety for Kate, the child, and myself? If you want the book, you'll have it on my terms, Vesey. Kate and Anne are to be free of you, in writing. I will supply the materials and the text."

"You must think me insane," Vesey retorted.

Duncan smiled. "Consider your position, Vesey. Should you harm Kate, a hempen rope would be the least of your troubles, for I would tear you apart with my bare hands. Refuse my offer, and Wellington will have the evidence within a sennight. Those are your choices."

Vesey thought for a moment. "I could kill you right now."

Duncan debated the wisdom of drawing Vesey's fire, but quickly rejected the idea. "Aye, you might get lucky at this distance, but I dinna recollect you being the best of shots. Would you risk missing me, Vesey? Besides, if something were to happen to me, I've left specific instructions regarding the disposition of the book. Your sins will be the talk of Carlton House."

"And the girl?"

"Would not stand witness against you, unless you were fool enough to force her back to your house. I would not put a child through that pain unless absolutely necessary." Duncan shrugged in a show of nonchalance. "I will meet you at the causeway in an hour to make the exchange. The book in return for Kate and a signed statement."

"That is all you offer?"

"That and the opportunity to leave here in one piece," Duncan said.

Vesey laughed. "You must be as mad as they say, to think that I would agree to so poor a bargain."

Kate saw her opportunity. With Vesey distracted, she worked loose the last of her bonds. Her fingers slipped to her knife, and she brought up the blade with a quick slashing motion. She barely scratched him, but the second of surprise was all the opportunity she needed. Kate dashed toward the castle as Vesey's gun fell and discharged harmlessly.

Vesey snatched up the gun and made a fumbling attempt to reload, before following his fleeing captive. The look of murder on MacLean's countenance had made the decision a simple one. Katherine was his only chance. Without her as a shield, the Scot would like as not tear him to pieces for the sheer pleasure of it. Vesey hurried inside just in time to see Kate fleeing into the servant's hall.

Kate struggled with the iron key, opening the heavy door just as Vesey came into the room. There would not be time to lock it behind her as she had hoped. She ran up the stairs, the plan forming in her mind. She could hear the door swing shut, the protest of the rusty tumblers as the key locked them in together and the sinister sound of laughter as Vesey started slowly up the stair. Praying as she went, Kate boosted herself out the small window, reaching for handholds, hoping that Vesey would not even pause to think.

"Katherine, you might as well stop this nonsense."

She could hear his voice.

"You are trapped, little fool. Trapped."

He was perilously close to the window. Kate held her breath, not even hazarding to inhale. A peculiar sound came from below, and she uttered a silent blessing. It sounded as if Duncan was pounding at the door. Vesey was momentarily distracted.

"Do not force me to come up after you, you stupid bitch."

Vesey's anxious voice echoed as he called up to the tower room. Her fingers protested with pain as her tenuous hold began to slip, but she did not dare to try for better, not yet. She strained to hear his footfall as he mounted the stair, imagined him climbing to search the dark reaches of the windowless room.

"Katherine!" The angry roar was muffled as it reverberated through the tower. "Kath-h-h-h-h—" The cry cut off abruptly as the groan of wood became a roar. Rotting timber protested as ancient beams splintered beneath his weight and were pulled downward by the irresistible forces of gravity and momentum. A hail of debris flew through the window, showering her with bits of wood and plaster dust. Then there was silence.

Kate tried to haul herself up, but there was no strength left in her. She felt herself sliding until firm hands gripped her wrists and hauled her in.

"Duncan," she whispered as he grasped her close.

"Och, Kate, did you expect me to catch you from below again?" He tried to smile, but the effort was beyond his ability. "I damn near lost you, Kate. When you needed me, I couldna protect you. You were right."

"No less than you," Kate said, coughing and catching her breath. "It was foolish to hide my head and believe that evil would never find us again."

"He won't," Duncan told her, nodding toward the gaping hole in the floor. He lifted her into his arms and carried her down the stairs but try as he might, he could not avoid the sight of John's unseeing eyes staring into emptiness. "You need not fear John Vesey anymore, Kate."

"You, sir, are breaking your oath," Kate protested weakly.

"And did you not swear to me that you would keep yourself off my roofs?" he asked.

"That was different," she said, laying her head in the hollow of his shoulder.

"As is this," Duncan said softly. "If lightning is going to strike for the sins of untruth, then we're both of us fried like herring."

"I see no clouds. Not a one who would believe that . . . Daisy!" she exclaimed. "The poor dear is tied up in the pantry."

"You sit," Duncan said, easing her gently onto a bench in the sunshine. "I shall see to Daisy."

Kate breathed deeply, trying to calm the panic that still ruled her. Vesey was dead. It was all over.

Duncan seated himself beside her. "Daisy is unhurt, a bit numb from being trussed up like a Christmas goose, but she sent me back to you posthaste. She said that she would be brewing some tea once the pins-and-needles feeling stopped."

Kate shook her head. "Trust Daisy to know the proper remedy. It is a strange feeling, Duncan. I can scarcely believe that it all happened. I killed him . . ."

"You gave him a kinder end than he deserved," Duncan said. "If anything, he killed himself."

"The running, the lies . . ."

"Are done with," Duncan said. "You are a free woman now, Kate. You can go and do whatever you please. Do you go home to London?"

"Home to London." Kate gave a wistful smile. "An oxymoron if ever there was one. London could never be home to me, Duncan; it never was, in fact."

"You need not fear spending your wealth," Duncan pointed out, knowing he was a fool for doing so. "You do not have to choose London. Home could be wherever you wish to make it, Kate."

A ruined Scot's castle in a gothic state of disrepair. "Let me help you, Duncan," Kate suggested. "As you just pointed out, I am free to use my money. We could restore Eilean Kirk Castle and build a distillery that would outdo Tam's wildest dreams. Let it be my gift to the people here who have been so kind to me. My gift to you."

"Och, Kate, you had best be watching that pretty head of yours, for I am certain what I'm about to be saying will make the sky fall in," Duncan said. "I cannot take your money." He covered his head with his arms and peered up expectantly. "Did you hear that, Charlie, the Sassenach woman is offering The MacLean gold, and I am not taking it."

Kate could not help but laugh. "Be reasonable, Duncan. Call it a loan."

"I have no need, Kate," he said, his expression abruptly earnest. " 'Tis deceiving you, I've been. I am actually a very rich man, or I will be once that incompetent Dewey retrieves my inheritance."

"If that is true," she asked, encompassing the castle with a doubtful wave of her hand, "why did you choose to live like this?"

A hundred flippant remarks came to mind, witty comments that would turn the subject to safer ground. Instead, he choose to tell the truth. "For a long time, Kate, I didna care much how I died," he said. "So when I found out that I was bound for the living, I didna care how I lived either. A crumbling ruin was much to the taste of a man who half fancied himself a living ghost. And then, when I found you here . . ." He looked away from her. "When I found you, I was afraid because you did not believe. You did not think me the monster I knew myself to be; you trusted me. Och, Kate, that was a heavy burden, a terrible trial to a man like me. You spun your fantasies about my kindness, my goodness, and vain coxcomb that I am, I couldna disabuse you of your notions. Though I did try, you must admit that, Kate. I did try."

"Not hard enough," Kate said gently.

"Aye, that was the worst of it." He ran his hands through his hair like a nervous schoolboy. "You see, I wanted you to stay. And I knew that all you said, you truly believed, not because of my face for certain and not because of my wealth because I was keeping it from you. I wanted you to remain here in my ruin with me, groom my horse, darn my socks, and tell me your lies about my kindness and charity and honor."

"So you lived in poverty, though there was no need? It lacks logic."

"Logic has nothing to do with what I feel for you," Duncan said, raising her hand and stroking it gently. "There is so much I dinna understand myself. When I came here, the only thing that kept me going were the ghosts. Yet, when Vesey had you, I could hear them screaming in my ears, telling me that the book was their right, their monument. But then I saw you there, and I knew that it is the living who need the comfort of vengeance, Kate. My first obligation was to you."

"You would truly have given Vesey the book?"

"What do you think, Kate?" he asked, letting her plumb the depths of his soul with a searching look.

"Aye," she said at last in an awed whisper. "I believe you would have."

Duncan smiled. "I had hoped I would have found some way to retrieve it, mind. So dinna be thinking too well of me, woman."

"I will think what I please, milaird, and if I think you the most marvelous man on earth, would you dare call me a liar?"

"Foolish, deluded, but never a liar, Kate," he said softly.

"And if I were to be foolish enough to delude myself into believing that I love you?" she asked, looking away. She felt his hands upon her cheeks and heard his whisper.

"I would think you had been hanging too long by your thumbnails, or feverish from the effects of a whipping, or some idiotish man has been keeping you talking too long in the afternoon sun." He put his palm on her forehead and a finger at her throat. "How is it that you're not even warm? But och, that pulse of yours is pounding."

"And if I claimed to be perfectly lucid?" she asked, searching his face for answers.

"I would ask you why you would choose a beast, a man with an accursed name and a worse reputation. A woman like you . . ."

She put a finger to his lips. "Colonel Braxton's brat? The woman who informed Lady Jersey that the cake at Almack's was stale and the orgeat insipid? That pillar of propriety who bet a member of the Four-in-Hand Club that she could tool a phaeton far more expertly than himself."

"And did she win?" Duncan asked.

"The race and an indefinite stay on her husband's country estates," Kate said with a laugh. "I do not want a man who will manage me, Duncan MacLean."

"I would not dare try," Duncan said, his hopes rising. Her eyes were clear and guileless as green glass. No woman had ever looked upon him with love before, but this shining gaze that wrapped him in tangible joy could be nothing but that mystical wonder. "There are ghosts enough already on Eilean Kirk."

"I know," Kate said. "I have met one of your MacLean hants. He visits me in the darkness and fills my dreams, this bearded ghost."

"Och, most unfashionable." His hand stole around her neck.

"Yes, and it tickles this phantom's bristle, but I've come to like it quite well." She reached up and stroked the curling strands.

"Have you now?" Duncan asked in fascination. "What else about this ghost pleases you?"

"He looks quite dashing in a plaid, and exquisite without one, at least from the limited amount that I have seen."

"Shameless spirit," he said, caressing her cheek. "And what else have you learned about this ghastly ghoulie."

"His kisses are unearthly, both heaven and hell. Heaven when I am in his arms, hell when he leaves me."

"Heaven." He touched his lips to hers, gently at first in a pledge of newfound faith, but she pulled him closer. He could feel the strength of her need, the full measure of her longing. Tenderly, he began to fill the void within her, and to his surprise, the yawning emptiness within him was gone.

Kate was in that hollow place, and somehow he knew that she would always be there.

"You will be the death of me yet, Kate. You have no idea how difficult it is to stop here," he said, tracing the gentle slope of cheek and chin. "The death of me and the life of me, love, even though you were blinded to my true nature. Even now 'tis hard to believe that you love me."

"It is far more difficult to credit that you care for me," Kate told him. "I fully understand that I am not the type of woman that a man like you would fall in love with."

"What kind of woman would that be?" Duncan asked, an idle finger reaching for the nape of her neck.

"Beautiful?"

"You're the most beautiful woman that I have ever set eye upon," Duncan said.

"Sophisticated?"

"Worldly, you mean?"

She nodded.

"Och, Kate, I've had entirely too much of the world, with its polite lies and sophisticated conduct, where women and men change lovers and credos more often than they change their smallclothes. I would much rather have your world, your honesty."

"Intelligent?" Kate smiled.

"Now you are fishing for compliments, my love, for intelligence was never one of the hallmarks of one of the Mad MacLean's females. Any woman with wit would avoid me like the Devil."

"So, you are saying that I lack wits, Duncan MacLean?" Kate asked.

"Aye, if you love me, it follows you must."

"Well then, by that logic, I am quite brainless."

"And I, poor Kate, am just enough of a blackguard to take advantage of your witless state," he said, raising her hand to his lips and kissing it gently. "I love you, Kate, and I hope you remain in a state of loving foolishness to the end of your days."

"Do you?" she asked, feeling his touch with every fiber of her being.

"Aye, I do. And if you ever show any signs of intelligence, I will have to take desperate measures."

"Such as?" Kate smiled.

"This."

His lips came down upon hers, claiming her, plumbing the farthest reaches of her emotions. His tongue probed and taunted until she was plunged into a world of pure sensation with Duncan at its heart, at her heart.

"What are you thinking?" The teasing words whispered in her ear.

"Mmmph," she murmured. "Can't think, but wait, I feel a fragment of a thought." As she had hoped, Duncan moved quickly to banish that wisp of threatening intelligence.

With a blaring skirl of pipes, a mass of humanity erupted into the courtyard. The crofters of Strathkirk, armed with clubs, hayforks, and dirks, stormed the castle and came to an abrupt halt before the laird. The two of them broken hastily apart.

"See, told yer th' major would set all t'rights," Fred said proudly.

"Mama! Mama!" came a shout, and the crowd parted to let Anne through. The girl launched herself toward Kate, babbling a mile a minute. "They wouldn't let me come at first but I cried and cried and so Tam said that I could come but only if I stayed toward the rear and Fred's horse cast a shoe . . ."

"Anne," Kate whispered, her eyes widening with disbelief. She sank to her knees and gathered her daughter into her arms. "She can talk—what you told Vesey was the truth then? Not a bluff?"

"Vesey had threatened you," Duncan explained. "Anne thought that she could keep you safe with her silence. I had to keep it from you, Kate, and I'm sorry for it, but I had no choice."

Anne nodded solemnly. "I was scared what Uncle John would do. He told me he would kill you if I told. So don't be mad at Duncan. I made him promise, Mama. And you know about promises."

Kate looked at the two of them, child and man, their expressions an identical plea for understanding. She could not be angry, not with so many blessings showering down upon her. "Yes," she agreed. "I know how promises can be."

"Where's my Daisy?" Fred asked, peering anxiously past Duncan. "If Vesey 'as 'armed an 'air on 'er 'ead . . . I'll—"

"What would you do, little man?" Daisy asked.

"Daisy!" The Cockney threw his arms around her, and to everyone's surprise, Daisy burst into tears.

"Oh, Fred," she wailed, "I was so frightened."

" 'Ush, dumpling, yer Fred's 'ere now. Just come in th' kitchen and 'll pour yer a cuppa," he said as he led her indoors.

"Daisy loves Fred," Anne declared smugly. "And Fred thinks you should marry Duncan, Mama, and Mr. Tam thinks that you're very bonny. What's bonny?"

"Anne!" Kate blushed.

"Is it a bad word?" Anne asked. "People say lots of things when they think you ain't gonna talk about it."

"Bonny means 'pretty,' lassie," Duncan said, noting Tam's raised eyebrows. "And what you have heard ought not always be repeated. It is called eavesdropping. Now run along and get Cur a bone; he deserves one."

"Nae married?" Tam asked. "Did I hear aright?"

"A minor misunderstanding," Duncan said hastily. "Soon to be corrected."

Tam laughed heartily. "Och, a misunderstanding, indeed. Yer married all right, laddie, at least if I ken the laws of Scotland proper." He clutched his chest and howled.

"Are you daft, man?" Duncan asked in irritation.

"Why do ye think those fool Sassenach ride over the border to Gretna when they wish to marry quick, mon?" He whooped. "One witness and a declaration is all it takes. Half the village has heard th' one or t'other or both of ye callin' 'wife' or 'husband,' 'milord' or 'milady.' By my way of thinkin' ye *are* wed."

"I want it done right," Duncan said doggedly. "There will be nothing havey-cavey about this marriage."

" 'Tis the law," Tam said skeptically. "Nae need t'be wed if ye are wed already, I say."

"The nearest curate is well past Loch Ewe," Kate added. "It will take several days to get there."

"Aye," Tam agreed, a twinkle in his eyes, "and he'll be wantin' a goodly sum from The MacLean, verra expensive, it'll be."

"And with the crops coming ripe soon," Kate added, "I do not know if I can leave just now."

"Och, Kate, I surrender," Duncan said, taking her hands and drawing her up to his side. He raised his voice so that all could hear. "Do you agree to be my wife, Kate? I love you more than life itself and will be the best husband I can, for all that I am a wicked MacLean."

"I want to be your lady, Duncan MacLean, and I will marry you, though you be the Devil himself. I take you for my husband, crumbling castle, curse, and all," she said. "And I fully expect never to have another intelligent thought for the rest of my days."

"The curse is broken, milady," Tam said. "The blind man has begun to see."

"Indeed, he has," Duncan said, hoisting his wife into his arms. "Indeed, he has." And he proceeded with the pleasant process of kissing Kate senseless.